Good Girl

Susan Wright

107th Ave Press

ISBN-13: 978-0692255735

ISBN-10: 0692255737

Trade paperback printing July, 2014

Acknowledgements

Thank you to Kelly Beaton, my Beta reader extraordinaire!

Cover art by Emily Lam

Chapter 1

Kali

I was lost in a daydream, staring at the skyscrapers of downtown Manhattan through the floor-to-ceiling window, imagining it was the view from my living room. I'd love to wake up to *that* every day… I could still hardly believe I was living in the city, but this incredible view at work was a constant reminder of how far I had come.

The door opened behind me. I was supposed to be switching the covers on the proposals by the two finalists, and if my boss caught me sitting here looking at the view, I would be in big trouble.

I looked around guiltily, but it was only the receptionist, Lindy. Her eyes were wide as she said, "One of the artists is here!"

"Which one?" I asked.

"Hunter Munro. Why didn't you warn me? He's so hot! I would have worn my cleavage shirt." Lindy pulled her sweater smoother, and checked her lipstick in the chrome plate behind the door handle. "Wish me luck!"

With that, she headed back out to the lobby. Lindy wasn't the most picky girl, so I took her enthusiasm with a grain of salt, but still...

Flipping open the cover of the proposal, I looked at the black and white headshot of Hunter Munro. Handsome, moody and mysterious with half of his face covered by shadow. My boss didn't do "moody." Selina thought Hunter's headshot was arty and pretentious. But his was one of the two proposals that had received the most votes in our online contest, so Selina had no choice but to offer up both to the executive committee of SunTech. After all, the competition had been her idea.

Actually it had been my idea, but Selina took credit for it because she was the head of the PR department. Through the windows, far down below, I could see the old stone fountain that practically filled the plaza. It looked so solid and permanent that I wondered if that fountain would outlast me in the end.

Selina had ruined everything for me. My move to New York City, after getting my dream job for SunTech, was hanging in the balance. I lived every hour in dread of making a mistake because Selina would fire me in a shot. Then what would I do? I had only gotten the job because of a letter from a journalism professor at Jefferson College who had once hailed Ryan as a visionary. My mom was an administrator at the college and had finagled the recommendation out of him.

I didn't want to think about how she had pulled that off. She amounted to little more than a glorified secretary in that place, but somehow she had done it.

If I lost this job, there was no way I could pull off that kind of nepotistic feat on my own. I would be lucky to be a waitress at the TGI Friday in Midtown Manhattan. I'd rather do anything than go back home to Jefferson, but convincing my mom of that would be much harder.

For six glorious months so far, I had balanced on top of the world. From the fourteenth floor conference room, the brown tenement buildings of the Lower East Side spread out before me punctuated by a dozen other modern glass towers poking above the rooftops. The towers were built right before the financial bust, but SunTech was the only one with its own wind-powered generator and water recycling system. Far to the left, the Williamsburg Bridge spanned the East River, pointing to the Brooklyn neighborhood where I now lived.

I wasn't going to let this city beat me. I had to do well on the plaza redesign project. If anything went wrong, Selina would be sure to pin it on me so I would get the blame instead of her.

From personal experience, I knew it wouldn't be easy. My father was an artist. He did whatever he wanted, whenever he wanted, and it didn't matter who else it affected. My poor mom had been struggling to deal with him my whole life.

I knew from personal experience that you can't trust an artist. But my tender new-budding career was going to be in the hands of one of these two sculptors. No matter how professionally they had put their pitch together, I knew that deep down they were psycho-divas who would inevitably act out.

There was no way I could control that. But Selina would expect me to. And my job was at stake if I couldn't make it work.

I decided to go out to reception to get a good look at Hunter Munro.

...

Sidling up to a frosted glass partition, I peeked through the narrow clear strip below the sunburst SunTech logo.

There he was. Dark hair, tanned skin and nice broad shoulders. I could hear Hunter's laugh through the glass, and he seemed relaxed sitting in the chair closest to Lindy's reception desk. Lindy was giggling self-consciously, touching her hair too much, chatting about a restaurant she had been to the night before.

Suddenly Hunter turned and looked at me, meeting my eyes through the glass.

I drew in my breath. Blue eyes. He had bright, piercing blue eyes framed by long black lashes and dark brows. I had expected his eyes to be dark, like a Latino. But even from a distance, I was struck by the vivid blue color.

He stared at me, while Lindy kept chattering as if she hadn't noticed anything.

Then I blinked and the spell was broken.

I ducked down. I was being stupid, of course. He had seen me! And now he could see the shadow where I hunched behind the frosted glass.

3

But nothing could make me look through the narrow chink in the glass again. Bent over, I turned and hurried down the hall to the conference room. I felt like a real idiot. But I couldn't help it. The way he had looked at me… almost as if he was reading my mind. And knew the fear inside of me.

I was so flustered that I didn't tell my boss that Hunter Munro was waiting in reception. I tried to put it out of my mind. He had only seen my eyes—the rest of me had been hidden behind the frosted glass. He wouldn't recognize me if I kept my cool.

The senior executives eventually arrived at the conference room, including Robert Ryan who was now pushing sixty and had a passion for renewable energy that inspired everyone in his company.

Before Selina called in the two artists, the proposals were discussed by the executives. I didn't say a word. I took notes for Selina who led the discussion and was in charge of the project. Selina pushed Tami Han's concept of wide bamboo planters with benches as being better suited to our building over Hunter Munro's modernistic sundial design.

"Bamboo is renewable," Selina said, holding up the red folder. "And it will cast some shade on the plaza, which really needs it since we're facing south."

"That's why the sundial would work." Ryan lifted the blue folder with Hunter's proposal. "But I'd like to hear from the artists themselves."

Lindy showed in Tami Han and she looked just like her photo—a pretty Asian-American woman with an easy smile. Tami had plenty to say for herself and her "green design" and what she didn't say, Selina said for her. I had to admit that the idea of islands of lacy bamboo forests sounded appealing. I could sit there and eat my lunch.

The bulk of the questions came from the CFO in regards to re-piping the plaza to water the bamboo in the giant planters. The dozen or so participants who were gathered around the table seemed to like the idea of bamboo. I didn't see any reason why Mrs. Chapel, the

4

Director of Human Relations, was involved in making this decision, but Robert Ryan always made a big deal about how he liked to work from consensus. This project was tailor-made to bring his entire company together in one giant PR stunt, and everyone seemed to like Tami Han.

"I can work with her," Selina said, after Tami left the room. "She's got an international appeal that we can parlay into overseas coverage."

Nods went around the oval table. For myself, I thought Selina was overly-pushy and domineering, but then again, my boss had been fighting her way through the corporate world for nearly twenty years so she knew what she was doing.

"Hunter Munro," Lindy announced as she opened the door.

He was suddenly there, his eyes sweeping the room. I thought he hesitated a moment when he saw me.

Selina went forward to greet him. "Welcome, Mr. Munro. We have a seat for you here."

But Hunter just smiled and nodded to her as he went straight to the man at the head of the table. "Mr. Ryan, it's a pleasure to meet you. I wanted to tell you how impressed I am with your work. I'm very proud to be a finalist for this project."

I watched along with the others as Hunter Munro shook hands with our founder. The sculptor knew a fair bit about SunTech and Robert Ryan, which he displayed as they chatted quietly for a few moments. I wanted to be cynical; I had seen enough of Selina's maneuvers to know a practiced charmer when I saw one. But Hunter was so relaxed, wearing black jeans and a navy blazer, his curling hair in need of a cut. He didn't fit the image of a slick self-salesman or a huckster trying to steal a buck. There was a distinct whiff of bad-boy about him, and I was sure he had at least one tattoo covered over by his business-casual clothes.

Hunter worked his way around the table, shaking everyone's hand. They were pleased, and showed it.

When he got to me, my hand was in his before I knew it. It felt square and hard, a little rough like he worked with them a lot. And then I was looking into those remarkable blue eyes again.

He recognized me.

How could he not? The nerves in my hand seemed electrified, like a spark ran from his body into mine. His smile deepened at my reaction.

"This is our copywriter, Kali Jones," Selina was saying behind me.

"We've already met," Hunter said. His voice was low and confidential, as it had been with everyone.

"You know each other?" Selina demanded. "How?"

"We met in reception," Hunter said.

My boss dismissed that as irrelevant, and directed him to the empty seat at our end of the table. I sat down quickly, suddenly wishing the table was square so I could hide behind Selina. I knew I was red in the face because the pressure was unbearable.

I tried to act like nothing had happened as I opened the blue folder and stared blankly down at Hunter's graceful rendition of a sundial in geometric shapes—a triangular base, long spear for the dial, and round balls grouped in a semi-circle marking each number of the clock.

Hunter noticed that we were all looking at the image in the folder. "That's an old drawing. I brought a newer one for you to see."

He unzipped the black portfolio he was carrying. Selina protested, "I told you not to bring new materials. We have to consider each project on the same basis."

Hunter paused, the large painting half out of the portfolio. Looking down at Robert Ryan, he grinned. "Then it's a good thing I didn't bring the clay model of the sundial. I was afraid it wouldn't fit in the cab."

In the midst of general laughter, Hunter pulled out a striking watercolor of the blue-glass SunTech building. The concave front of the tower seemed to catch the light of the afternoon sun. In the front of the semi-circular plaza stood the dramatic slash of the sundial. Hunter had given the painting a low perspective, showing the dark purple shadow of the sundial crossing the bench that was labeled IV.

I drew in my breath as did several others around the table. I always liked the idea of a sundial.

"I love it," Mrs. Chapel said immediately. She was leaning forward eagerly, looking younger somehow despite her plump forty-something frame. "The antiquity of a sundial is unexpected. It's exactly what the architect intended when he put a 100-year-old fountain in front of our modern building."

There were murmurs of agreement from the rest of the women. Even Mr. Ryan was nodding, though not as enthusiastically. Were they looking at the painting or Hunter Munro?

Hunter's eyes met mine again for a moment, and I quickly glanced down at the proposal. I tried to tell myself that it wasn't my fault; the others seemed just as mesmerized by him. Including Larry, Mr. Ryan's assistant.

"Get Hunter an easel," Selina ordered.

I went to pull out the easel from a narrow closet in the wall paneling. Hunter had certainly gotten around Selina easily enough. She wasn't protesting his use of unauthorized materials anymore.

On my way back, I checked the thermostat. It felt too warm in the conference room. But it was reading 78 degrees, as usual, and Mr. Ryan wouldn't allow us to lower it any more than that.

I set up the easel next to Hunter's chair and took the watercolor from his hands without directly looking at him. I wasn't going to turn into a giggly girl like Lindy. I was a professional and planned on making something of myself in this company. I wouldn't let him get to me.

As Hunter turned back, he knocked his pen off the table. It landed on the floor between his chair and the easel. He started to reach for it, but I was already bent over picking it up. Our heads came very close, so close that I was enveloped in his musky scent.

"*Good girl*," he murmured under his breath.

I looked sharply him. *He didn't just say that!*

Selina was busy looking at the specs in the blue folder as if she hadn't really considered them before. She didn't hear him say it.

Hunter took the pen from me slowly, so slowly that I had to look at him again. He was smiling at me, seeing my embarrassment. But there was approval in his eyes.

He did!

I pulled back, feeling flustered.

How dare he say that to me! Like I'm a trained collie or something.

I felt even worse as I went and sat down. My hips shifted in the seat, and now I was definitely red in the face.

Maybe he meant it as a joke, but it wasn't funny. It was completely inappropriate.

Only one thought managed to rise through the emotions he had shaken and stirred with hardly any effort—I wouldn't let him see that he had gotten to me.

Chapter 2

Hunter

I smiled to myself. *She picked up the pen.* I knew she would. I could always tell.

Ms. Kali Jones was looking straight at me, her expression hard. Before that, she had been avoiding my eyes, embarrassed by what happened out in reception. But now she was apparently so affronted by my praise that she refused to back down, even if it was a silent war that was happening right in front of her coworkers.

It was just the sort of fun that I enjoyed the most, the contest of wills. But right now I had more important things to deal with. I needed this job. Badly. I couldn't let myself be distracted by a fine ass and a fiery disposition.

But she did have a fine ass. Her skirt hugged her curves just right, and her heels were high enough to give a nice sway to her hips. I thought when I had glimpsed her peering through the glass, that she would be pretty, and I wasn't disappointed. With her up-turned nose and sweetly curling lips, she was more cute than beautiful, but I liked that elfin look. Innocence could be a wonderful thing to play with, and she had that in spades. She may have been as young as her early twenties, but she would probably look youthful well into middle-age.

Now is not the time... I dragged myself back to the priority at hand.

"As you can see from this painting, your eye is drawn from the street up to the concave curve of your facade," I explained. "But the fountain is too big, like a pyramid squatting on your front doorstep. It blocks the portico that runs along the first floor of the plaza, echoing that enticing inward curve. With a sundial, the art will work *with* the building in harmony instead of concealing it."

I was glad to see that Selina Stern, the head of the PR

department, was nodding along. Selina was the one who had called to let me know I was one of the finalists in the competition. She had told me that I beat out hundreds of other proposals.

I wasn't sure if Selina was on my side or not, but right now she was returning my easy smile. Selina was a stylish woman, packaged and polished, as if every detail had been considered carefully. People in publicity were always hard to read. They were experts at the smoke-and-mirrors game.

But from her demeanor, I was sure I had passed the background check that they put the finalists through. I had always been careful, but you never could tell these days with how connected everything was. One slip was all it would take for them to know everything about me.

But the proof of my success was in the fact that I was seated here, talking to a roomful of corporate-types.

"That is something to consider," Selina told the rest of the table. "The bamboo planters would hide the front of the building at the street level."

"Even more than the fountain does now," Mrs. Chapel agreed. I could tell Mrs. Chapel was on my side. I always did well with maternal, older women. She even looked a bit like my mom with her plump cheeks and tired eyes.

"The question is: do we want a forest maze or an open plaza in front of our building?" Robert Ryan asked from the top of the table.

I had seen the proposal that Tami Han had submitted, just as I had carefully examined all of the plans entered by my competition during the online contest. I had heard of Tami before we became finalists—she was part of the post-postmodern school in urban planning, using an organic and sincere approach, seeing that as a comment on the destructive tendencies of postmodernism. I had scrabbled my way up as outsider artist, and if anything, admired the meta-modernist architects who defied tradition and relied on the tension of transformation, finding the hidden beauty in something awkward or even ugly.

I had tried to get Tami to talk while we were waiting together out in reception, but she was tight-lipped. She focused on large-scale corporate work, and made things that filled space in a harmonious way, rather than art that made you think. Bamboo was exactly what she would propose—a soothing green mass to balance the hard glass of the building, literally symbolizing Robert Ryan's green roots. She was probably dying for a job right now, too, and she had a much bigger nut to meet than I did.

"Your company is all about natural energy," I reminded Robert Ryan. "Your building faces south and should embrace the sun, not the shadows."

The others around the table were nodding. The CFO brought up the biggest line item of the budget—the cost for the raw bronze for the sundial and benches. But I knew my stuff and could answer every question, from the comparative exchange rate if the casting was done in Canada vs. an American-made product. American-made won the day, as I had expected. It was quick work to clear up the last few questions of cost, including the fact that the plumbing for the fountain could be left under the plaza so we wouldn't have to rip up the flagstones that were already laid down. We would only have to replace the flagstones under the fountain and remove the ones under the base of the individual benches to install the anchors.

Ryan's assistant Larry was now frankly appraising me from the other end of the table, silently letting I know that I had his vote! The women were also in the palm of my hand, except for Kali Jones. I shouldn't have allowed myself to murmur those little words of praise when she picked up the pen. Who knew what kind of pull she had as a member of the PR team?

But I couldn't help myself. I really wanted to tell Kali that she was a *bad* girl. She spied on me through the glass door of the reception room, and then ran away when I noticed it.

Kali met my gaze firmly. "I'm not sure about those round balls for benches. They look like they might be uncomfortable to sit on."

Bad girl, was on the tip of my tongue. I knew Kali said it because I had gotten to her.

Selina Stern turned to that page of the proposal, tilting her head at the benches formed by three balls grouped together. "They look like bronze exercise balls. I've never seen seating like this before."

"You said no flat surfaces or people would try to sleep on them," I reminded her. "And I don't like those tacky benches with arms or with ridges built into the seat." Tami had put ridges on her benches. "The balls contrast with the linear thrust of the sundial. They echo the semi-circle of the plaza itself."

"But are they comfortable to sit on?" Robert Ryan asked.

"I've already made the pattern and it's very comfortable. It's at my studio in Bushwick. I couldn't bring it with me because it definitely wouldn't fit in the cab!"

Everyone laughed again, as I intended.

Ryan said, "You certainly went the extra mile on this proposal, Hunter."

"I want to work with your company, Mr. Ryan. It would be a real honor to design the plaza for this ground-breaking building." I hesitated, but now was the time to ask. "I am curious, though, how a man like you ended up with a fountain in the first place?"

Ryan let out an exasperated "humph!" The others looked uncomfortable. "Truth be told, in the original plans it was supposed to be part of the cooling system for this building. But that's outdated technology. SunTech developed a breakthrough in our HVAC system that regenerates the heat to supplement the power of the pumps. We should have scrapped the fountain when we went with the new technology, but there were too many other details we were dealing with."

I smiled. "Well, I'm glad. Or you wouldn't be getting my sundial now."

Ryan was nodding slowly, tapping a pen on the proposal in front of him, looking down the length of the table at the large painting that I had worked on for weeks. Nobody else dared to speak. Ryan was known to run his company like it was a team, but everything I had read about the guy proved that he had the final word on anything important. Seeing that useless fountain every day must really piss him off.

"I like it," Ryan finally said. "I liked the idea of a sundial from the beginning. But I want to be sure you can sit on these benches. Selina, why don't you go to Mr. Munro's studio and give the bench a test run? I want a report back by Monday."

Selina looked anything but happy at the surprise task, but she said, "Absolutely, Robert. I'll send everyone a memo on Monday morning." Turning to Hunter, she said, "We'll work out the details before you go."

This was my cue to pack up, which I did, shaking hands with each person who stopped by on their way out of the conference room. Larry, Ryan's assistant, hung back as if to speak to me, but was called out by Ryan as he left.

Only Selina and the perky but still piqued Kali were left in the end. I made sure Selina had my address to come by my studio tonight, even though it was a Friday.

I would have agreed to anything if it would land me this job. Even if it meant I had to sanitize my place and carry all the contraband to Jeremy's loft down the hall.

This could change my life.

"I have a red-eye to catch tonight to Los Angeles, but I can make it if I come by around six," Selina told me.

When I said good-bye to Selina, she turned to her assistant, "Show Hunter the way to the elevators, Kali."

I stuck out my hand to Kali, knowing she couldn't refuse to shake it while her boss was standing right there. "Thank you for your help, Kali. I'm told you put together our proposals. I liked the blue cover."

Kali slowly shook my hand. "Selina picked out the blue one for you."

I pulled her hand slightly towards me, unbalancing her a bit and bringing her onto her toes. "Thank you, anyway."

Kali took a tiny step forward to regain her balance, unclasping my hand. I had to let go of her, though I wasn't ready to, yet. I usually didn't care much about whether women liked me, maybe because so many did. But I wanted to give Kali a spanking for questioning my round benches, even if it was a metaphorical spanking.

I followed her through the hall and back out to the reception area where the flirty receptionist leaped up to say good-bye to me. But I wasn't thinking about her. I was watching Kali disappear behind the frosted glass again. I was sure she would glance back at me.

But she didn't.

That was different. Usually girls who flirted with me took another last look.

As I took the elevator down, I began to wonder. Maybe Kali wasn't flirting with me. Maybe she really was upset, and not turned on by my teasing.

That wouldn't be good for me. I could have just stomped all over a good thing.

But my instincts told me that she loved it. I was never wrong about that.

I decided I would know if Kali Jones was interested in a little game play if she came to my studio tonight with her boss. There was no mention of her coming, but if she was curious, she would make sure to come. There was no doubt about that.

I could still feel her hand in mine, soft but firm. I had a feeling her whole body was soft but firm, just like her hand. A fresh, ripe girl ready for the picking...

But if she did show up, I would have to focus on the job at hand.

This means too much to me to fuck it up.

Chapter 3

Kali

I was hardly through the door of the communal PR office before Debby, the graphic designer, said, "I heard one of the artists is really yummy."

"He's hot as hell," I tossed off. "He'll photograph well if we choose his design."

Even if Selina hadn't been busy at her corner desk, I wouldn't have gone into what had happened with Hunter. Debby and I were friendly, but I kept my private life strictly separate from work. Debby had no problem airing her personal stuff to me and anyone else within earshot, including Selina. Selina loved to gossip, so she encouraged it. But I wasn't playing that game anymore. I had found out quickly that anything I exposed to Selina would be used against me.

"I wish I'd seen him," Debby said. "Lindy says he's super-cute! Are you going to pick him, Selina? It would be nice to have a new guy around here."

Selina rolled her eyes in exasperation. "I wish it was that easy! Instead I have to go sit on a stupid ball. All my careful planning, covering all the bases... I didn't expect to have to take a side trip to Brooklyn before my flight."

Debby gave me a puzzled look. I tried to clear up the confusion. "You remember the benches for the sundial? Mr. Ryan is afraid they'll be uncomfortable. So Selina is going over to check them out."

"Call for a cab to be here at 5:30, Kali," Selina ordered. "A half hour to get over the bridge should be enough time. I tell you, those balls better work or I'll break some balls of my own."

I felt a little bad that I might have ruined Hunter's chances by pointing out the unusual benches. But someone had to. It was one of Selina's biggest criticisms when we first sorted through the proposals.

Besides, he shouldn't have been rude. He shouldn't have called me *good girl*.

I didn't even like thinking about it.

For the rest of the afternoon, I worked with Selina on plotting our potential PR strategy if Mr. Ryan decided to choose Hunter Munro. Selina had already developed a plan for Tami based on her international appeal, but for Hunter's hook she focused on his small-town Pennsylvania roots and the local foundry that would cast the sundial. I could tell that Selina was now questioning her earlier preference for Tami, even though she would never admit it. The meeting this evening at Hunter's studio would decide his fate.

I couldn't help but feel satisfied knowing both Hunter and Selina were being put out because of me. It was totally passive-aggressive, and I shouldn't have felt that way, but there it was. I also wished I could point out Selina's wavering loyalty from Tami to Hunter. But Selina didn't like being teased or tested, not in any way. She had no sense of humor about herself.

I knew the type well. All I could do was tiptoe carefully around her and hope I wasn't in the cross-hairs when she went off.

When it came time to pack up to go, I was brought up short when Selina grabbed her rolling suitcase and said, "Come on, Kali. The car's waiting."

"I'm going with you?"

"Don't be so stupid! I told you when you ordered the car." Selina gave me a disgusted look. "What's wrong with you, Kali. Are you sick?"

Yes, I wanted to say. *I'm sick and tired of* you.

Now I had to go to Hunter Munro's studio and act like nothing was wrong. "I'm a little under the weather," I managed to say.

"Suck it up!" Selina ordered. "I'm not going to Bushwick alone."

16

"How am I going to get home?" I asked.

"Grab a cab."

I didn't want to try to explain to an uptown girl like Selina that Brooklyn was not like Manhattan when it came to finding cabs on every corner. Even in my short time in New York City, I had learned that confirmed Manhattanites knew very little about the outer boroughs where I lived.

Selina rushed us both down to the street past the ugly fountain that squatted like a fat, beige troll at the base of our glass building. I could almost see the sundial in its place. The bamboo was a little harder to imagine.

As we were whisked over the Williamsburg Bridge in the cool limo-car, I was cross about having to go to Hunter's studio. Selina didn't need me. It was a stupid waste of my time, another jab to show me my place.

I was tired and ready to go home. But Selina... she looked perfect. She must have been gone for nearly twenty minutes before she had reappeared to drag me away with her. Her frosty blond hair was freshly cut, curving gently at her shoulders and around her cheekbones. She was in her mid-thirties, and was toned and hard from her daily workout. Men responded to her because of her presence and confidence, but I could see the tiny signs of strain in her face. The lines around her eyes, and even worse the wrinkles in her neck. Selina dated a lot, almost constantly, and often told me and Debby stories about her dates that were sometimes very funny, and sometimes very cruel. She wasn't kind to the men who didn't meet her exacting standards, and to hear her say it, she told them their faults straight to their face.

I let out a sigh. Selina was angling for Hunter.

This whole thing was such a mess. If I thought an artist was going to be tough to work with, it was going to be a million times worse if Selina was putting him through her wringer. I wondered if Hunter would bite on Selina's hook in order to clinch the job.

If that's what Selina wants, then she shouldn't have brought me along.

Then again, maybe Selina had brought me as protection, to keep things from going too far, too fast.

The car took an abrupt left turn, and we drove through a badly pot-holed street, making us bounce into each other on the seat. The sidewalks were lined by squat industrial buildings with loading docks and vents dotting the long brick walls. A lone straggly tree rose up here and there from the sidewalks.

As we pulled up, Selina sounded doubtful. "Are you sure this is right?" she asked the driver.

He pointed to the number on the side. "Three, two, zero. Like you asked for, Miss."

It was an old red brick hulk, two floors with broad factory windows dotting the second floor. The small panes were crisscrossed with wire and some were levered open for ventilation. Several bikes were chained to the wrought iron grate in front, protecting an empty square of dirt. Faint lines of graffiti still showed where the paint had been water-blasted off the bricks.

Selina told the driver to wait and she left her suitcase in the car.

The black steel door had several swirls of fresh spray paint across it. Selina pressed #3 that was marked with H. Munro, and a buzzer sounded to open the door.

A sign on the door to the ground floor space was for a sheet metal fabricator. We had to walk up a battered set of steps to the second floor. Everything was out of scale, with super-high ceilings and wide passageways. It felt so strange that I was a bit uneasy. But Selina marched up like she couldn't care less.

Whatever happened, I prepared myself to not react, no matter what Selina or Hunter might do. I had gotten back at Hunter for irritating me at the meeting. Now that Selina was trolling for him, I would have to stay far away.

Hunter had his door open waiting for us to emerge from the dim stairwell. "Welcome to my studio. Come on in."

The space was a raw rectangle with exposed ductwork high

above our heads and a wood plank floor with scars and discolorations where the factory equipment had once stood. Behind a folding screen was a small fridge and microwave. The only walls in the room were a sheet-rock cube that enclosed the bathroom in one corner, with a ladder leaning against it to the open platform on top.

The studio was filled with art. Splatters of color and odd shapes jutted from every surface. People seemed to be emerging from walls or in the process of sinking in. A giant quarter lay on the floor in one corner, forming a platform for a small table and two chairs. Wood racks held paintings and several were covered over, with stacks of canvases leaning against the far wall.

It was a real artist's studio, and it reminded me of my dad's workroom in our backyard at home. But instead of fine art, my dad's shop was filled with wood-working equipment, table saws for making scenery, and shelves of electronic equipment for sound systems and instruments.

Hunter was gesturing to the bench that was sitting in the middle of the empty floor. The three balls were joined at their bulging middles, forming a gentle curve.

"This is the bench," Hunter said. "It's the model that I'll use to create the pattern for the mold. When I get the job."

His grin was infectious, but I didn't respond. All of my defenses were on high alert in this artist's lair. Besides, this was the Selina-show. I was supposed to disappear.

"It's lovely," Selina said, stroking the bench. Her manicure was perfect, with dramatic red and black square tips. "Will it be translucent like this?"

"That's the resin covering it. The finished surface will be polished bronze."

I liked the amber-like quality of the resin as the slanting sun caught the edge of the ball. I thought it was too bad the finished piece couldn't be the same.

"Have a seat," Hunter offered Selina.

Selina made a little show of stepping forward and taking his hand as she sat down. As if she needed help.

Selina's face lit up. "Wow! I'm surprised. It's really comfortable." She wiggled around on it. "You wouldn't think a rounded seat would be this comfortable."

Hunter sat down on the ball at the other end. "I had to find the perfect size for the human butt. And you can sit in different directions, so it's not a one-way experience."

Selina slowly moved her feet, shifting around to face the other way. "That's a nice touch. We could make renderings that show people sitting in whichever direction will face you away from the sun. That was a concern of ours with a southern-facing plaza."

"My design works *with* the sun not against it. I spent days hanging out in your plaza while I was coming up with my design. Listening to that god-awful fountain!" His grin included us both. "The sun is the main feature of your plaza. I don't want to hide it with bamboo—I want it to be front and center, twisted in a way that makes people look at the light and interact with the sundial—reading the time, sitting on the benches, looking down on it from the offices above. It will be different from every perspective, so you'll always connect with it in different ways."

I was convinced. If passion alone could get us through this intact, then Hunter had that in spades. Selina looked like she wanted to say yes, too. My boss was nodding at him, as if she really liked what she saw. I couldn't blame her—*what's not to like?* He was articulate and engaging. He also looked as delicious as a man could, with his strong hands gesturing as he spoke and his T-shirt hugging the muscles of his chest. There was something so sexy about him, like he wasn't even trying but all I wanted to do was touch him.

Stop thinking that, I ordered myself.

Selina stood up, looking thoughtfully down at Hunter, as if wheels were turning over in her head. As if she was judging him on various different points.

"You like it, don't you?" Hunter asked her, looking up at Selina from his own seat on the bench.

Selina smiled at him, really smiled. Not her professional smile that put up a wall between her and other people. My eyes opened wide in surprise.

"I do," Selina said softly.

They were looking at each other so long that I shifted uncomfortably. If this was going to be *that* kind of meeting, they could have left me out of it!

Then Hunter stood up, breaking the spell. Selina's smile was now kind of smug, and she told me, "You try it, Kali. See what you think."

I went over to the center ball, on the opposite side from where they had sat down. As I turned, I caught Hunter's eye. He mouthed the word, "*Sit*."

My butt hit the ball as my mouth fell open. *What!?*

Did he just order me to sit?

His eyes were laughing down at me. He had just ordered me to sit!

I popped back up again, my lips tightening in outrage. Selina hadn't seen anything; she was absorbed in looking around the room at the various pieces of art. From the poses she was striking, she was letting Hunter get a good look at her assets.

I didn't say a word. But I did glare at Hunter so he would know I didn't appreciate his jokes.

He laughed. Actually laughed! Which made me even madder.

Should I say something? Would it sound awful if I did?

Yes, it would.

Selina turned and saw me standing there. "Kali, sit down! I want to know what you think."

Reluctantly I sat back down, irritated when Hunter looked amused. I was squirming on the bench. "I don't know…"

Hunter grimaced as Selina looked up from the watercolors. "What?" she asked sharply. "What's wrong with it?"

My heart was beating faster, and my palms were sweating. Why was I so flustered by one joking word? He was just teasing me. The way teenagers teased each other. So why did it bother me so much? I felt like I was overreacting, and that made me feel even worse.

"Kali, I asked you, what's wrong with it?" Selina insisted.

Hunter's blue eyes were pleading with me now. He was half-turned away from Selina, so she couldn't see him, but I could. From his expression, Hunter knew I was upset, and he felt bad about it. With his obvious remorse and those full, anxious lips, how could I hurt him?

"It feels good," I said. "I like it because it's different."

Hunter gave me a grateful look. "I designed it so your hips tilt forward. It's a very comfortable position."

Satisfied, Selina wandered on and soon called Hunter over to the model of the sundial that was placed in the center of the table. I stayed sitting on the ball, feeling flushed.

This was going to be trouble.

Chapter 4

Hunter

I felt bad about ordering Kali to sit. It served me right that she almost blew it for me by complaining about the bench. I had never asked her if she wanted to play, which was the first cardinal rule of kink. I had put her on the spot, but she'd gotten her own back, that's for sure.

I was so stupid. Why was I messing with her like this? Self-destructive didn't begin to describe what I was doing. I was going to ruin the best thing that had come along in a very long time. What if Kali told her boss what I'd done? If she told anyone, she sure as heck wouldn't say that it turned her on. It was exactly the kind of thing that got bigger and uglier with the telling of it. They would think I was a sexist pig and they wouldn't hire me.

So here I was doing damage control. That meant pleasing the boss. Selina Stern was the kind of woman who needed to be stroked and admired. I was willing to do it because I knew my design would win on its merits, all else being equal.

I wasn't sure what type Kali was. At first I thought she was the "new-to-NYC and on the man-hunt for a good husband" type, but she hadn't made any special effort to spruce up for our meeting. She wasn't wearing lipstick anymore, as if it had rubbed off during the day and she hadn't bothered to fix it. And with the sinking sun streaming through the giant window, her hair looked more red than brown, a deep true auburn. I could swear that sparkling fall of many shades didn't come from a bottle.

The fact that Kali could put up with such a tyrant for a boss showed she had some inclination for submission inside of her. But then again, there had been no spark of recognition each time I had said those words to her. Only outrage and arousal. The best combination in the world, as far as I was concerned.

Only, I really should have asked her to play first. I refused to go down the road that Selina took—getting my sadistic kicks out of ordering people around who couldn't say no. Those were the kind of people who ended up being rude to wait staff at restaurants. Or worse, ignoring a girl's safeword.

It was only a few minutes later that Selina announced, "I have to run or I'll miss my flight. Thank you for showing me your work, Hunter."

"It's been my pleasure." My glance slid from Selina to Kali to include her in my compliment.

Kali wasn't looking my way. She hadn't said a word since she gave her opinion on the bench.

I walked them downstairs. Most of the live-in artists in the building were very young, and I didn't want some rude kid leaving a lasting impression on them that would hurt my chances. But luckily no one was hanging out on the stairwell or in front of the building.

I gave Selina's hand a final shake, which she managed to make last a few seconds longer than usual, before she stepped into the limo car. Her last words for Kali were, "Write this up for me so I can send out the memo on Monday."

We both watched the car drive away. I had the feeling that Kali could hardly look at me. I felt a pang again at the way I had played with her without asking first.

"Which way is it to the subway?" Kali asked.

I glanced at her high heels. "It's five blocks. I think I should call you a car. It'll only take a few minutes to get here."

She was looking down the block. "You think so?"

He felt for my phone but he'd left it upstairs. "I've got the number in my phone. I'll be right back."

Kali protested, "Really, don't bother."

I smiled at the perfect submissive response. "Why don't you come up, so you won't have to wait down here alone?"

"That's okay. It's a pretty evening." She looked up at the sky visible through the low buildings.

I was surprised. I couldn't remember the last time I had asked a girl up to my place and she refused. Not that this was a date. But it felt sort of like it because I had played with her, even if she didn't know it.

I couldn't do that again. I had to keep it professional. So I went upstairs to get my phone. I called the car company on the way back down and gave them my address, all the while wondering how I could make it up to her without ruining my chance at winning the competition for the plaza.

When I got outside, Kali was gone.

It was like a punch in the gut. I had expected her to be there, had been thinking of what to say to her, how to apologize for what I'd done without making things worse.

I ran up to the corner, but I couldn't see her in either direction. *"Crap!"*

It was like my vision narrowed. I had to find her. What if she went in the wrong direction and crossed into the barrio? It was only a few streets away. The women I dated could handle themselves in my neighborhood, but I wasn't sure about Kali. There was a fresh-off-the-barn feel about her that worried me.

"Crap...," I muttered through gritted teeth.

I ran, first up the street and then crossing over several streets. There were people getting home from work, some walking and even more riding bikes. I ran all the way to the subway. At the entrance, I didn't see her. I felt like a tool, breathing heavily, but then I saw a bunch of guys loitering outside the stairwell. So I kept on moving.

I ran down inside the subway and leaned over the turnstile. Kali wasn't on the platform. I didn't see how she could have beaten me there, but I had to check.

Back outside, the homeboys were looking me over, nudging each other and pointing me out.

What if Kali had gone in the other direction, into the barrio towards the next subway station? It was about five blocks away from my studio, but in the other direction.

I set off towards Flushing Ave at a fast clip. It was my fault that she had gone off alone. I made her feel uncomfortable, messing with her at her job. I deserved to lose this gig. But most of all, I didn't want Kali to get hurt or scared because I was an asshole.

I had to find her.

I was running across a street, when out of the corner of my eye, I saw Kali. She was almost to the corner, and couldn't help seeing me. I skidded to a stop. In a few steps I returned to her side.

"There you are." I tried to say it lightly but was too out of breath to pull it off. But I couldn't stop smiling, it was such a relief.

Kali was surprised. "Did you run after me? Seriously? You thought I couldn't walk to the subway by myself?"

"I called a car for you."

"I only live a few stops away. In Williamsburg." She stepped forward. "And the entrance is right there."

I could see the homeboys still hanging out in front of the subway. "Let's go." I made sure I was walking on the inside, between her and the guys.

She noticed the group of young men at the same time. Or maybe it was the sudden serious tone in my voice. She stopped protesting and warily went along with me.

I tried to take it easy, but the guys had just seen me run up in some kind of desperate funk looking for someone. And now here I was walking with a pretty girl who was obviously keeping her distance from me.

Several of them started hooting at us. "Yo, you have a fight, man?" "I'll take her off your hands." "Yeah, you know *that*…"

I could feel myself swelling up in the chest, ready to bash heads if any of them took a step towards Kali. I glared at them and flexed my muscles a bit, letting the warning in my eyes speak for me.

It was like throwing gas on the flames.

The comments got louder as we pushed past them at the

entrance. Kali moved closer to me as we went down the steps.

The homeboys followed us down inside the station, but they paused on the steps just out of sight of the bored MTA employee sitting in the bullet-proof glass booth reading the *NY Post*.

I hesitated only a moment, then swiped my card through the slot so Kali could go through the turnstile. I swiped again and followed after her, but stopped her from going further up the platform. We could still see the MTA booth from where we stood.

The gang didn't follow us through the turnstile. They didn't want to pay another two bucks each to get closer when they could taunt me from the stairs. They also couldn't come down into the narrow lobby or the MTA employee would order them to leave.

Under the eyes of the homeboys who continued to make comments, Kali turned away to look out at the platform.

I felt like I'd won. They were stymied and I was standing on the platform with Kali. "That takes care of that."

"Thank you for finding me." Her eyes met mine frankly for the first time since I had ordered her to sit down. "I didn't realize it wasn't safe."

I kept watch on the gang on the stairs. She had her back to them, trusting me to look out for her.

"They're just assholes with nothing better to do," I said.

The gang may not have caught the words, but my attitude was clear. Their jeering picked up. Even the MTA employee looked up from his *Post* for a second.

Kali moved even closer to me. "There's a train coming."

Her hair was blowing in the incoming breeze as a subway rushed down the tunnel towards us. "Good, it's almost over."

"You can't go back out there." She put her hand on my arm, looking up at me. "You don't know what they'll do."

I stared at the gang openly now, as if judging them. "They're all bark, no bite."

"Don't be like that," she insisted. "Come with me, even if it's only to the next station."

I thought I had seen a couple of the guys around before. This was my neighborhood, my subway station. I wasn't going to be run off by a pack of goons. Now I had to defend my right to be here, and that's not what I wanted. There was always a cost to not fitting in. I never did. I learned from always being the new guy, moving around with my family. I knew how to watch what was going on around me and react the right way, so I wasn't noticed.

So how did this situation get so out of hand? There was Kali, her eyes fastened on me. My deep down spinal reflex was to jump those mother fuckers and see how many I could take down, scaring off the others while doing it.

I wiped my hand across my face. *What is wrong with me?*

With a squeal of brakes, the subway train pulled in. I was already walking forward with Kali, still watching them so I knew it almost before they did. Several of them leaped forward, going for the turnstiles.

"They're jumping," I told Kali, hustling her inside the subway car and down to the end.

The conductor tried to close the doors when he saw several guys come flying over the turnstiles, but the doors had to open all the way to close again, and three of them managed to wiggle into our car.

"Oh, no…" Kali breathed.

I put my arm around her and could feel she was trembling. With a lurch, the car started. "It's okay," I said. "Come on."

The guys were laughing at their success at the back end, while Kali and I passed through the front door onto the rocking platform outside the car. Kali looked through the window behind us. "They're coming after us."

"Let's get to the conductor car."

The subway going into the city was fairly empty this time of evening, while trains passing the other direction were packed full. We passed through two more cars until we reached the conductor's box blocking the doorway at the end. There wasn't a window on the inside, but I knew I could rap on the metal door to alert the conductor if things got really crazy.

I took up position in front of the door. Kali looked scared, and I took a moment to assure her, "It'll be fine now. They won't do anything with the conductor right here." I was stroking her arm. "Now get behind me. If anything happens, bang on that door until he comes out."

I shifted her so she was standing behind me, her hands trembling on my back. I was ready to do whatever it took to keep them from getting to her.

The scattered people in the car knew that something was wrong even before the homeboys arrived. My adrenaline was pumping. I would have backed away from any guy as hopped up as I was right now.

It was a bad moment when the homeboys came into the car. I lifted my fist to pound on the door if they made another move. They knew conductors, and this conductor had just seen three guys jump the train.

They stayed at the back end of the car, talking and cursing loudly, making arm motions to punctuate their words. Everyone was watching them intently, with a few of those closest getting up and moving away. At the next station, almost everyone poured off, and I could see the passengers getting back onto cars on either side of us. Someone called out a warning to the conductor, "You better watch out in there!" But nothing happened. A couple of the men stayed seated, obviously eager to see a fight.

I half-turned towards Kali, more to try to defuse the situation than anything else. She looked up at me imploringly. "Why are they doing this, Hunter?"

I felt a deep pang. It was my own fault. But I couldn't admit it. She would have been fine if she had walked to the subway on her own. Oh, they probably would have made comments about the "fine little mama" as she passed by, but that was par for the course out there. I was the one who had caught their attention with all of my running back and forth, frantically searching for her.

Then I had gotten all defensive over her. I knew better than to come back at a gang like that. But from the first second, I was ready to fight them for her.

I never felt this way before.

I let out my breath with a long sigh, realizing this wasn't going to stop until I let it go. I was reacting like a caveman protecting my woman. And I didn't even know the girl!

I forced myself to calm down, to take deep breaths and slow my pulse rate. I no longer wanted to look back at the homeboys, and they jeered louder, feeling like they'd cowed me enough to claim victory.

"My station is next," Kali said. "What if they follow us off?"

"Just do what I say."

As the subway car began to slow down, I told her, "Don't move," as she started to shift. "I'll tell you when."

She stayed perfectly still as the car squealed to a halt. The doors opened. I waited a couple seconds to time our exit just before the doors closed, then grabbed her hand. "Come on."

As soon as we hit the platform, I turned to finally look back at the guys who had chased us down. Then pointedly I looked at the conductor's window. Right beside me, the conductor was in the window watching the stragglers board the train. I hoped that if the conductor saw a fight start, he would keep the train in the station and call the cops.

The guys almost jumped off, but when I made no move to talk to the conductor, they contented themselves with yelling curses at me, pointing their fingers at me as if they were weapons.

The doors of the subway pinged closed, and Kali let out a relieved breath. I waited until the train pulled away, watching their moving mouths through the window.

"Oh, my god," Kali murmured.

I almost admitted it was my fault. But she was finally looking at me with breathless admiration, the way I wanted her to look at me. It almost made the whole sick thing worthwhile.

I took her arm and walked out of the subway with her. It wasn't until she reached the top of the stairs that she realized what I was doing. "You don't have to walk me home, Hunter."

"After *that?* Do you think any red-blooded man could let you walk home alone right now?"

She didn't protest, and I felt like I'd said too much. I could still feel her hand in mine as we waited on the platform, staring down the gang. I had felt invincible because I had to be, for her.

We walked in silence the two blocks to her apartment building. She didn't chatter nervously about what had just happened, and I was glad about that. I needed time to get hold of myself.

Kali lived in an old tenement building with three floors, the kind with two railroad apartments on each floor. This neighborhood was mixed industrial and apartment buildings, so it wasn't as bleak as my own neighborhood. Plus the main drag of Williamsburg where the subway station let out was always crowded with people. Her apartment was probably half the size and cost more than my studio. But she had restaurants and boutique shopping right around the corner, just like Manhattan used to be before it got too expensive for anything but chain stores and luxury brands.

Kali took a step up her stoop. "This is me."

She had separated herself from me, so I didn't have a chance to touch her again. After all I had done, she still couldn't trust me because I had messed with her.

"I'm sorry," I said. "I should have asked first."

She tilted her head, not understanding.

"Before I got kinky with you. I shouldn't have said those things to you without asking first."

Now she got it, and she flushed so hard she had to look away. She took two more steps up. "That's all right." Even though it wasn't.

"I didn't mean to drive you away," I said honestly. "I feel bad. I don't know why I did it. I know better than that."

She hesitated, looking back down at me. She didn't understand;

it was true, she really hadn't played any power games. But she could tell I was sincere about my apology.

"That's okay," she said, this time meaning it.

I suddenly felt better, like a weight had been lifted. My pseudo-fight with the homeboys seemed stupid now. I should have just made it up with Kali the second we were alone. None of this would have happened.

"Put it down to the stupendous stress I'm under," I admitted, running a hand through my hair.

She smiled, like the sun coming out. "I understand completely. This project is a big thing."

"It is for me."

"Me, too. It has to go well." Kali nodded at me. "Thanks for walking me home, Hunter."

I waited until she was inside the heavy front door, protected by iron over the glass. "I'll ask next time," I murmured under my breath.

For some reason, I waited until she was through the inner door with a wave of her hand, before I turned away and left.

Chapter 5

Kali

In a daze, I went up the two flights of stairs to my apartment. I wandered around my place for a while until I realized I was sitting on my bed with my hands clasped together to keep them from shaking. They had been trembling as I rested them against his back, as Hunter faced off with those men on the subway. As he stood between me and them.

It made me weak in the knees to think about it. I knew he would protect me, whatever it took.

He had been perfectly calm the whole time, assuring me in low, even tones and never once making me feel like he couldn't handle it. Even though things were so out of control! I kept thinking about when got off the subway, when he told me to do what he said. We were standing there exposed on the platform with those angry men just steps away, with only his hand to hold me there...

I had trusted him. Even though I had no reason to trust him. I stayed there with him when every part of me wanted to run away.

I would never forget the way Hunter had looked at me as he insisted on walking me home. Like he wasn't going to put down his sword until he knew I was safe.

I had never met a more manly man in my life.

I wondered what would happen when he got back to his station? Would that gang be waiting for him? What if they hurt him?

I felt so guilty for walking off alone to the subway. None of this would have happened if I had just been sensible and waited for the car to come. But he never said a word of blame.

Instead, he had apologized for saying those things to me. Now I felt embarrassed about making such a big deal about it. It was just teasing.

Finally, I couldn't stand it anymore; I was thrumming with nerves and too much adrenaline coursing through my body. I went downstairs and walked. New York was made for walking, and the night was really fine with a nice breeze off the river ruffling my hair. Everywhere I looked there was something new and interesting to see.

But I couldn't stop thinking about Hunter, the way his broad back blocked my view as my palms rested on him, and the way his hand enveloped mine, firm yet careful not to squeeze too hard.

I tried to tell myself to stop. He was off-limits for a lot of reasons. I was sure Selina would try, at some point, to cash the check he was writing. I couldn't let her know that I had the hots for him. Selina would have no qualms telling Hunter that I was mooning around after him. Then she would smile as she watched me squirm.

That was *not* that going to happen. *No way.*

No matter how much I kept thinking about his tanned arms, and the way his muscles strained the T-shirt over his shoulders. No matter how much I thought about his blue eyes looking into mine, I knew nothing would come of it.

Getting my emotions involved would just make my job harder.

•••

On Monday, I was at my desk listening as Selina called Hunter to congratulate him on winning the contest. I emailed him the contract to sign. Hunter replied that he would drop it off at the office tomorrow so we could open the escrow account to pay for the materials and subcontractors. He would be managing the entire project, reporting directly to Selina and the Chief Operating Officer.

On Tuesday, I wore a skirt and heels as I usually did when a meeting was scheduled. But I did pick my best hip-hugging skirt and a button-up shirt that could go down an extra button for a nice sexy effect. As sexy as a suit could look, but I wanted to try.

When Lindy buzzed that Hunter had arrived, Selina told Lindy, "Give us five minutes, then take him to the conference room." To me, she ordered, "Let Harold know that Hunter is here."

Harold was our Chief Financial Officer and he had papers for the checking account that he needed Hunter to sign. I had coordinated the paperwork with his assistant to be sure we had everything set.

Selina took those five minutes to examine her face in a mirror, applying makeup and slicking down her fly-away blond hairs.

"Look at you! You act like you're going on a date," Debby said from her computer. "I'm going to have to get a look at this guy, if he's all *that*."

Selina didn't like being poked, and Debby knew it. But she had been at SunTech longer than both of us, and was enough of a fixture to get away with things that I never would have tried with our boss.

"If this guy knows what's good for him, he'll fall right in line," Selina bragged.

I didn't know what to expect from Hunter after what happened in the subway. But the moment he saw me, his eyes lit up and his voice lowered slightly as he shook my hand. As if he felt it, too.

I focused on my iPad, checking off the items as Selina and Harold went through them with Hunter. It was a complex job, and I hoped Hunter was up to it. Any overruns would come out of his commission, so he would be motivated to make sure the project came in on budget.

While we were meeting, a steady flow of office staff filed by the glass walls of the conference room. It was funny, especially when Debby and a few others sashayed by a couple times before they got their fill. Harold didn't notice with his back to the glass and his figures in front of him, but Selina did, and she didn't like it. I was fairly certain Hunter also noticed the unusually heavy traffic in the hallway.

When we were done, Harold packed up everything, including Hunter's signed copy of the contract, and congratulated our new coworker before he left the conference room.

Selina thoughtfully tapped her pen on the folder in front of her. "We need to get some publicity stills first thing for our announcement. I'm thinking we can use that model you made of the sundial. And the model of the bench. The light through your window was quite nice and it should make for some interesting shots. No more black and white portraits." She leaned forward. "It doesn't do justice to your beautiful eyes."

I had to look away. Selina couldn't be serious, not with me listening! She was trying to get an advantage on him, as she always did with the people she worked with. But her cougar-like approach was not a flattering look.

Hunter didn't smile back. "Whatever you say, Boss."

Selina hesitated. He had just barely emphasized the word "Boss." He was pointing out the fact that he worked for her.

Selina sat back. "I'll come by tomorrow with our photographer."

Now Hunter did smile. "I'm busy tomorrow. But I could do it tonight."

"I'm busy tonight. And I don't think the photographer would be free on such short notice."

I decided to help Hunter out, if he was going to fight back. "I'll text Fran to find out."

Selina and Hunter kept staring at each other, and I was reminded of the way he had squared off with those guys in the subway. The tension was not as deadly, but it did fill the room.

After only a few seconds our freelance photographer responded by text. "He's free this evening. He asks how about 5:30?"

"Fine by me," Hunter said easily.

"I'll send him your address," I said.

Selina was smiling tightly. "Good, I'm glad that worked out. I'll handle the interviews and give the media a couple of nice quotes from you. I'll pass them by you tomorrow." She stood up abruptly, holding out her hand. "Welcome to SunTech, Hunter. I'm sure you know your way out by now."

I was still gathering up my stuff as Selina opened the door. "Come on, Kali. We have a lot of work to do."

When Selina's back was turned, Hunter gave me a grin and a

thumbs up. He looked so boyish suddenly, like we were kids conspiring behind our mom's back.

It wasn't funny. I shouldn't have gotten involved in his power struggle with Selina. I had too many of my own problems with her.

The last thing we heard was Hunter whistling as he came out of the conference room behind us. Selina picked up her steps, as he walked the other direction toward reception.

"Arrogant asshole," Selina muttered. "They're all like that. So sweet at first, until they get what they want. Then you see their true colors."

I was afraid to say anything and have Selina's anger backlash on me. After all, I had just helped Hunter get the better of her. But Selina was so focused on the fact that he had dropped her in a deep freeze the second the contract was signed, that she couldn't see anything else right now.

"At least Fran knows what I need. You'll have to be my eyes and ears, Kali. Make sure he gets a shot through the sundial with Hunter's face behind it. You know like the Vessey Davis kind of angle? And try to position the bench so the light shines through it. I know the real ones won't look like that, but it will be sharp in the photos if you can get it right."

"I'm going?" I asked.

"Yes, what is wrong with you, Kali? I'm counting on you to make sure I get the shots I need. I'm not breaking my date tonight. And I'm not trekking all the way out there to no-where's-ville just for work."

Selina didn't bother to ask if I had plans. But I didn't have much of a life outside of work. It was tough to make new friends in the city. I had considered getting a roommate, but I had never lived with anyone before. I stayed at home while I got my degree.

I felt lucky that I had managed to befriend the two women who lived on the ground floor of my building. Pam and Karen were a really sweet couple, in their early thirties. They asked me to go for drinks every now and again at some of the local bars. They were fun to hang out with, but usually I went for my morning pancakes alone or read in the used book store on Saturday afternoons. I met a lot of guys in Williamsburg, and had gone on a surprising number of dates. But none of them had clicked with me. Too young, too old, too weird, too pushy... it got to the point where I could tell an unemployed actor from an unemployed musician at a single glance. After a couple of dates and my refusals to have casual sex, they usually stopped calling.

Now I would have to go back to Hunter's studio. The scene of the crime, so to speak. At least I would have Fran there for protection.

But the more I thought about it, the more I wondered if it would be necessary. I didn't think Hunter would make a move on me. He was a coworker now, and he had very neatly put Selina in her place when she tried to flirt with him. But then again, that could be his latest tactic in their dance. It had certainly made Selina sit up and take notice, and she might even treat him with more respect now that he had proven he wasn't her lap dog.

There was no reason to think Hunter was really interested in Selina. But when I ran into the Human Rights Director in the bathroom, I blurted out, "What's the company policy on dating coworkers?"

Mrs. Chapel didn't seem surprised by the question. "As long as he or she isn't in your direct chain of command, it's fine. So if you want to date Selina, she's off limits. As is Ted, and of course, Mr. Ryan. You're not thinking about dating Mr. Ryan, are you, Kali?"

"No!" I hadn't considered that Mrs. Chapel would think I was asking for myself. But I was relieved to find out that Selina couldn't date Hunter under the terms of her contract with SunTech.

"Now if you and Debby wanted to date, you could since you're coworkers. It's not anyone's business. In fact, it's better if you can keep your behavior private during business hours. The less talk the better for everyone involved."

I laughed at the idea of dating Debby. "I won't need the info, but thank you."

"It's always good to know what you're getting into before you take a big leap."

As I returned to my desk, I thought that was the kind of advice my own mom would give me. Too bad I couldn't tell my mom what had happened in the subway with Hunter. My parents would flip out. My mom already thought I lived in imminent danger, and she wasn't shy about telling me that. She kept offering up Syracuse as only an hour away, and Albany not much further. As long as I could come home for dinner once a week, my mom would have been satisfied.

I wished I had someone I could talk to. But I was on my own.

...

I was deliberately fifteen minutes late for the meeting at Hunter's studio. But when Hunter opened the door, his surprise was evident. "Kali! I didn't know you were coming tonight."

"Neither did I. But what the boss says, goes."

Fran was nowhere to be seen. He should have already arrived and explained that I was coming, paving the way for me to slip in while the photography session was underway.

"I guess Fran is late, too," I said.

"That's fine. I've got nothing planned for this evening." Hunter grinned. "Or tomorrow evening either."

So he *had* been putting Selina off. "You know, you shouldn't make Selina mad," I told him. "She could make things really tough on you."

"She could try. I don't like petty dictators in the workplace. She's not ordering me around."

I straightened my back. "She's in charge. Selina does whatever she wants."

"My contract says differently. I'm in charge of this project."

I knew he was going to cause problems! "You only have to deal with her for a couple of months. The rest of us are in it for the long haul. You have to make this work."

"I will. You can count on it."

"I am."

I had deliberately dressed down for this meeting, having run home first to change into jeans and a washed-out gray T-shirt. It was funny because Hunter was wearing almost exactly the same thing—a faded gray T-shirt and jeans—only his feet were bare. And very sexy, now that I got a good look.

He noticed my appraisal. "I've got a jacket I can put on for the photos, but it's a little warm tonight."

That wasn't why I was looking at him, but it would do for an excuse. I moved over to the windows that were catching the slanted sunlight. "Fran better get here soon."

At that moment, the buzzer sounded.

Fran arrived with a whirl of energy and motion, setting up lights and big white diffusers. He rapped out commands in his blunt Norwegian-accented English, as he directed us both around. I was a little worried at first, after seeing how Hunter had refused to bend to Selina. But Hunter lugged equipment and carried camera bags alongside of us.

Once they started shooting, Fran was in seventh heaven.

"Usually I photograph people in suits, talking heads," Fran said. "I wish I could work with more artists like you. Yes, bend down more," he said. "I want the shadow of the dial on your face. Selina sent me a billion texts this afternoon. She wants this, she wants that... why hire a professional if you can do it yourself?"

"Selina couldn't make it this evening," Hunter said solemnly.

"That's what she says. But this is better. Can you adjust the screen, Kali? Yes, that way." He titled his head at Hunter, as if assessing the angles of his face. "Can you give a bad photograph, Hunter? No, I don't think so. Now come over here. I want a profile shot."

"Selina said no profiles," I quickly put in.

"Just for me. That's it, that's good. Now look this way... yes, there. Very good. That's what we want. Sexy, with a bit of glamour. But happy, approachable. Selina says you have to be happy."

Hunter was down behind the sundial, the slant of the shadow across his cheek. He looked right at me over Fran's shoulder. "If you want me to be sexy and happy, stop talking about Selina!"

I had to laugh. Fran was intent on his work, firing off shots, talking a lot more than I was used to seeing. He really had a rapport with Hunter. It seemed like Hunter could create a connection with anyone.

They moved from the sundial to the bench. Hunter looked yummy sitting on the round balls with the sun casting nice shadows, relaxed and talking to both of us.

"How long have you lived in the city?" I asked Hunter.

"It's been ten years, now," he said. "I moved here when I was nineteen. Right after I finished my first commission, a sculpture for a prayer garden in Wycoff Hospital in Philadelphia. I thought I had it made. I was going to take New York by storm."

Fran snorted. "Who isn't? Why else do we put up with so much pain?"

"I meet a lot of artists and musicians living in Williamsburg." I could have added that they all needed drastic help. Many were living off their parents' monthly check. I had no respect for that.

"Aspiring artists," Hunter corrected. "There's a lot of people who like the idea of being an artist, but that's not how they earn a living. Fran here is a working artist. Now, with the SunTech contract, I'm another one."

"You've sold your work before," I said, thinking of his resume. He'd had several shows in galleries, along with large art installations and public art works.

"My last big piece was a pro-bono job for the park in Bed-Sty. It's not easy making it as an artist. But I couldn't work in an office, like you do, Kali."

I had heard that before, from my own dad. It was everything I hated about artists. They thought they were too good to work like the rest of us plebes. My dad had blithely changed jobs like he changed his clothes. That meant whether I could afford new clothes each year depended on if he was painting houses or directing plays at a local community theatre. I had watched my mom struggle to pay the bills as long as I could remember. I would never, ever ask her for money. I had to do it on my own.

I needed a man who was stable and reliable, which was probably why I wasn't attracted to many guys my own age. But I didn't like dating older men, either. I already had a dad—a playful, engaging dad. I wasn't looking for a husband who would try to mold me or make me fit into his life. So that cut out a lot of options, which is one reason I found it easy to turn down the men I had met since arriving in the city.

Remembering that helped to center my mind for dealing with Hunter. He was just another man who wasn't right for me, even if I was attracted to him. He was a work colleague, nothing else. A fun, sexy coworker.

It wasn't long before Fran got the shots he wanted. He clicked through the photos on his camera for both of us to see. There were plenty of good images for Selina to choose from.

I helped Fran pack up and when his phone buzzed, the photographer said, "That's my car. It's been real good, Hunter. Don't forget to call me about the casting. If I'm free, I'd love to get that shot you were talking about of the metal flowing into the mold."

It took all three of us to carry everything down for Fran. When Hunter and I were left standing in front of the building, Hunter laughed. "I'm not going upstairs without you this time, Ms. Jones. You might run off again."

I had to smile. "Okay."

We went upstairs talking about the project and the next steps that needed to take place in order to demolish the fountain. Hunter wanted to donate it somewhere, so we could generate more publicity for "recycling" the fixture. But neither of us could come up with any ideas of who might want such a monstrosity.

So I wasn't expecting the abrupt turn in the conversation.

"I know it was my fault you ran off last week," Hunter

admitted.

I was standing near the screen that hid his kitchen. He had already said that the platform on top of the bathroom was where he slept. I was suddenly very aware I was in this man's home, and now the conversation had turned personal.

"I didn't want to be a bother," I said. "I didn't realize it would be so dangerous."

"It's not, not really. But I kicked up a fuss running around looking for you. And those guys were looking for a wilding, so I made myself a good target for them to harass."

It made me feel better to know that he didn't blame me for it. "You handled it so well."

Hunter shook his head. "Not like I should have. And I shouldn't have gotten kinky with you without knowing you, especially in front of your boss. I didn't realize what a ball-buster Selina is."

"I thought you were teasing me."

"Yes. I thought you'd like it." He shrugged, admitting, "I really wanted to tell you, *bad girl*, for peeking at me in reception. And then running away. That does seem to be your thing, running away."

Bad girl! I couldn't look at him. I knew my embarrassment was making me flush, but there was nothing I could do about it. "It's not appropriate," I finally managed to say.

"It is if you consent. That was my mistake."

"Who would agree to let you say… *that*."

Hunter laughed. "Lots of girls."

"No one I know." But I remembered Brittany from college. Brittany had talked a lot about her freaky boyfriend and the things they did together. Once she told us that he had spanked her for breaking his iPhone, and she laughed when she said breaking it was almost worth it because then they had totally hot sex.

"I'm sure you do," Hunter said. "Selina for one, but she's on the giving end of things, not the receiving, I can guarantee it. Haven't you ever tried anything like that?"

"Like what?"

43

"Getting tied up with a scarf during sex? Blindfolded? French maid's outfit?"

"No!"

He smiled again. "No hair pulling?"

I shook my head silently. It was like I had no words at my command. This was not the sort of conversation I was supposed to have with a coworker. But his eyes held me there.

Hunter took a step closer. "It's one of my favorite things, taking hold of a gorgeous woman by the back of her hair, holding her and knowing she's mine…" He put his hand around me, on my back. I kept looking up at him.

"Just say no, and I'll stop," he said very low.

I remembered the feel of his hand when he had guided me on the subway, as we fled from the gang. He had touched my back like this as we got off the train car, comforting and in control. Now it raised goose bumps on my arms, remembering that and feeling him touch me so deliberately.

His hand slid up to my neck, his fingers curling around. He was right up against me now, our bodies touching but not pressed together. Close enough for me to feel unbalanced. His other hand went to my waist, steadying me.

He leaned in to whisper in my ear. "Like this."

He smoothed his hand higher on my neck, then let his fingers clench deep into my hair, twining and tugging at my scalp.

"Oh…," I breathed. His cheek was close to mine, his breath warm on my ear.

His fingers tightened in my hair, pulling my head back. My neck was exposed, open to him. I was trembling. Not that I feared him, exactly, it was an instinctive reaction. From feeling so vulnerable.

So I resisted, and he had to steadily pull my hair until I was looking straight up at the ceiling. His lips were hot on my skin as he kissed my neck, high up, where it was most tender at my throat.

His arms were so strong, holding me up, holding me in place

44

for him to consume. I couldn't help struggling as the sudden sensation was too much for me, too overwhelming. His lips pressed against my neck, then down under my ear. I couldn't see him, could only feel him as he moaned in pleasure.

"Delicious!" he murmured in my ear.

His hips were against mine, as he bent my back further. I was pressing into him, the rigid bar of his erection constrained by his jeans, against me.

I gasped, feeling a wave wash through me that felt almost like climaxing. What was he doing to me?

I could only hold onto him as he held me in place, kissing my neck. I had never felt so helpless or so turned on in my life.

Slowly his hand loosened, and I suddenly realized how tightly he had been pulling my hair. It hurt. But it didn't feel so bad, not when every nerve was zinging and my body tingled from head to toe.

As he pulled back, Hunter was also breathing fast, lingering near me, like he didn't want to let me go.

I was turned on, no denying that! Ready to go. For the first time in my life, I wasn't thinking ahead, stuck in my head, questioning things and considering—*what's the best thing to do?* I wanted this man, and I wanted him now.

"Nobody's ever done that to you?" Hunter whispered, almost smirking.

"No." But I didn't want to tell him "no." I wanted him to kiss my lips instead of my neck, and stop looking at me with those searching, piercing eyes.

"You liked it," he said.

I nodded. *Do it again*, I wanted to say. But he was so much calmer than me, not flipped head-over-heels like I was. I couldn't say a word, only stand there looking at him all hopeful and happy, ready to do whatever he wanted.

Chapter 6

Hunter

I was tempted to throw her down on the floor and take her right then and there. The way she smelled, no perfume or cloying shampoo, just pure woman. Luscious! The way she moved in my arms, how she drew in her breath so softly when I touched her. How she ground her hips into me. The honesty of her reactions, no longer trying to hide her reaction to me.

Everything I loved in one sweet package. Bold, confident and independent, but willing to roll over if she was coaxed along properly.

I wouldn't ruin that by rushing her. I had messed up once before, actually twice, because I let my dick get ahead of my brain. But I would be more careful now that I knew the treasure I had in my hands.

Literally in my hands, as I rested them on her shoulders, appraising her. She waited for my next move, a natural submissive.

It was undeniable—I was putting everything on the line for this. It could cause problems with my SunTech project, hell it could get me fired if anything went wrong! Everything I had worked for could be flushed down the drain…

But it was only a fleeting annoyance in the back of my mind. I had to have this woman.

Now.

He opened my mouth to tell her what to do, but a knock on the door interrupted.

My fingers tightened. That knock was very familiar. I was tempted to ignore it, but what was I going to do—seduce Kali while Minx stood outside knocking? It was only one brief instant that I hesitated, but my disappointment was so sharp that I had to take a second to absorb it.

"Sorry," I told her, giving Kali's shoulders a rub of assurance, realizing I was squeezing too tightly.

She nodded, turning away to gather herself and smooth down her rumpled T-shirt. I couldn't bear to look at her. What a rude awakening after such a heady start!

I opened the door, and was careful to keep my anger from my expression. I didn't want Minx to fall into full-on slave-role in front of Kali. This was bad enough.

Minx stood there flying her post-Goth look, drawn-on eyebrows and fuchsia hair, acting like she belonged here and eagerly checking out the strange girl in my studio.

"I won't need you tonight, Minx," I said. "I cleaned up this afternoon because the photographer was coming over."

I stood in the door to make sure Minx understood she was not coming in. But Minx was still looking past me at Kali. "Oh, did you text? I left my phone at home," Minx drawled.

I was angry that Minx had put me in this spot—so typical of her! Obviously she had gotten my text about putting her off until later and had taken advantage by coming so early. I couldn't just order her away as usual, not in front of Kali. I had to keep that part of my life separate from this project, or they might find out more about me than I wanted them to know.

"This is Kali. I'm doing some work for her company," I said. "This is Minx, my studio assistant."

Now Minx knew she had really messed up. She shot me a fearful look. "Sorry, I'll come back later."

"Tomorrow," I said.

Her expression fell, which is the last thing I wanted. I should have just let her leave without a word.

As the door closed behind Minx, I knew my scene with Kali was over. *Fini.*

Kali's feelings were clear. She didn't think much of Minx. I could tell she was putting two and two together, getting four as she should, and then going even further than that.

"My studio assistant." Then I could have kicked myself for repeating it.

"Yeah, I heard."

She kept looking at me, but I was saved when my phone rang. I pulled it out. "It's the car. It's waiting downstairs."

She smiled tightly. "Time to go."

I wished I had managed that better. With Minx, she knew all the rules up front. She had called me master and sucked my dick the second time I saw her at a party. It had taken no effort at all.

I wasn't so sure about Kali. She had definitely gotten off on the hair pulling. But that was one tiny step away from vanilla. She could have been imagining a house with a picket fence and two kids the whole time. Maybe that's what made her gasp.

I don't have a fucking clue what she's thinking!

Now Kali was folded into herself like an origami swan, giving nothing away with her slight smile as we walked downstairs. For the first time in a long time, I wasn't sure how to move forward with a woman. But I couldn't let her get into that car and drive away without having some hook in her.

I couldn't let her get away.

"I'm sorry we were interrupted," I said.

"Well, now I know what kinky means," she said lightly.

"Hardly. That's only the tip of the iceberg."

"I think the tip is all I need. I'm not a whips and chains, black-eyeliner kind of girl, if you didn't notice."

I knew she was talking about Minx. "I like that about you. Let me take you out to dinner and I'll make it up to you. Everything."

I opened the front door of the building for her, and she gave me a narrow look as she passed through. "What would your girlfriend say about that?"

"Minx isn't my girlfriend. Get that right out of your head. She helps me in the studio."

Kali glanced away. "Yes, I'm sure she helps you."

"She likes to be of service so she cleans my studio when I'm too busy. But she's more a friend than anything else. Definitely not a girlfriend. Definitely. Not." The car was waiting, and Kali was walking forward, so I asked, "How about dinner on Saturday? I can pick you up at 8."

She didn't answer right away. She reached for the car door, but I got there first and opened it for her. She stepped inside, graceful even in that.

I stood there holding the door, to make it clear I wasn't going to close it until she answered. I was already planning what I'd like to do to her on Saturday. If she let me.

Chapter 7

Kali

I had never felt so torn. All I could think about was Minx, who was everything I wasn't—wild, edgy and free. If Hunter dated girls like that, there was no way I could compete.

But I could still feel his hands on my hair and his lips on my neck. I had never felt anything like it! More like sex than real sex. I was heady from it, feeling like I could fly home.

I tried to get myself together, to say no, like I knew I should.

Instead, my lips curled in a smile I couldn't stop. "Okay. Saturday."

Hunter grinned down at me in triumph, closing the door. He looked smug, like he knew that he had won.

As the cab pulled away, I gave up trying to think straight. I rubbed the back of my head where he had griped me so tightly. My nerves were still thrumming.

Remembering the feel of his lips on me, a shiver went through me.

Chapter 8

Hunter

Over the next week, I worked in the sheet metal fabrication shop on the first floor of my building creating the twenty-four-foot long spear of the sundial and the triangular base. I also thought about Kali far too much, about the way she sank into my arms, letting me kiss her neck.

I'd had plenty of women who were kinky, and plenty who weren't but who didn't mind playing around. Kali was different. Sometimes I thought she was as vanilla and prudish as they came. There was definitely something holding her back. Maybe there was a clue in how modestly she dressed, as if she grew up in a very religious family. But when I held her and kissed her neck, she had caught fire.

I knew it was dangerous getting closer to Kali. It could mess up everything with SunTech if she found out that I made erotic art. Pornographic, my critics said. But it sold, and it kept me in the city, which is all I cared about. I never really thought I would have a chance at a big corporate job, and last year I even considered linking my erotic sculptures with my main website. *Am I glad I didn't!* There was no way Selina would have approved me if she knew the media could get hold of the graphic images I made.

No matter what happened with Kali, I would have to keep her from finding out about Hunting Art until after the sundial project was finished.

When I called the office to speak to Kali about the permits for the demolition on the plaza, I kept it professional. So did she. She was probably dealing with Selina at the same time. But hearing her was enough.

I didn't even want to play with Minx when she came by the

51

next evening. I made Minx clean my shower and scrub the toilet and wash the sheets so everything would be pristine in case my date with Kali went better than I expected. Then I told her to make me a grilled cheese sandwich. When Minx finished cleaning up, as I was taking the last bite, she stood in the proper submissive posture with her head up and eyes down, hands clasped behind her back, eagerly expectant.

I sent her away without touching her. Minx knew she was being punished, and I was too smart to punish her with attention. She would learn not to come over unless I told her to. She could have blown this entire gig for me.

I didn't tell her when to come next. I wanted her to know how much I disliked her little tricks to get more from me than I chose to give.

And I wanted to see what would happen with Kali.

Chapter 9

Kali

I thought about Hunter a lot over the next few days, wondering what would happen on our date. I had already let him get intimate with me, if you could call hair-pulling intimate. I hadn't even kissed him! The only thing I knew about kinky sex was from that book everyone was reading, but that was just a romance novel with a billionaire protagonist and his virgin lover. That had nothing to do with *my* life.

I knew Hunter wasn't the right man for me. I could never be the kind of uninhibited girl that Minx was. And he would never be the rock-steady partner I was looking for. It was sad because there was so much chemistry between us. I knew chemistry didn't mean compatibility, but it was really hard to ignore it. Even when I reminded myself over and over again that he charmed everyone. I was just one among many to him.

So I tried not to, but I thought about Hunter, wearing a groove of him in my mind. I found myself daydreaming about his hand clutching my hair, and my hips grinding into him shamelessly. His hands on my waist, holding me so firmly…

He texted me on Saturday afternoon saying: *I'm looking forward to seeing you at 8.* It was the first text I had gotten from him. I wondered how I would feel seeing his name on my phone after the project was over. I had a very bad premonition that it would all end in me deleting his number in tears.

I had never looked forward to any date with so many mixed feelings. The worst thing was that I felt like I couldn't talk to anyone. I was curious, but afraid to go further down this path. It was the same feeling I had when I moved to New York City—it was scary and thrilling because I didn't know what would happen next.

Wasn't this the sort of life I wanted when I moved here, something more unpredictable and new?

I just wished I could talk to someone about it, someone other than Hunter. But I hadn't spoken to my college friend Brittany in years, and we never had much in common other than our mutual set of friends. Nobody else would even begin to understand.

It also bothered me that nobody knew I was going out with Hunter. Not that I thought he would do anything bad to me. But I didn't know him, and he was… kinky.

So once I was ready, I ran downstairs to see Pam and Karen. Thankfully, they were home.

Karen answered the door. "Kali! Come in, so glad you came down. We were just fixing some spaghetti, would you like some?"

"I'm going out to eat."

"I can see that." Karen stood back to examine me. "You look great. Who are you going out with?"

I had picked out my best jeans and a silky shirt that draped over my breasts, exposing a tasteful amount of cleavage. Not to mention my high heels and best lingerie—not that any guy would see my underwear on a first date! I just liked the sexy way it made me feel.

I followed Karen into the narrow kitchen, a mirror of my own kitchen two floors above. The same mid-80's oak cabinets and battered Formica countertops, the same wood floor. Pam was stirring a big pot on the stove, an apron wrapped around her curvy figure. Pam was reserved—she was a medical researcher who worked at the VA Hospital in Brooklyn. Karen was lean and spare, always moving and talking, always upbeat. She worked in a big midtown hotel in the audio-visual department, setting up the equipment for conferences.

Suddenly facing them both, I felt embarrassed to mention my fears. "I'm going out with Hunter Munro, the artist who won our competition to redesign the plaza at SunTech. He's making a giant sundial for us."

"Nice!" Karen said. "Is it a date-date or a work-date?"

"It's a date-date. Our first. So I wanted to let someone know."

Pam nodded over at the stove. "It's always a good idea. You never can tell who you'll meet in the city."

"Anywhere!" Karen agreed.

I hesitated, not quite sure how to bring it up. "He says he's kinky." I looked between them. "Do you know anything about that?"

"What? Like ropes and whips?" Karen asked, wrinkling her nose.

"I guess."

Karen shrugged in wonder. Pam was turned away toward the stove, but I said, "Why do people always assume gay people know everything about freaky sex?"

"Oh! I'm sorry!" I exclaimed. "I didn't mean it like that. You two are just the only people I've gotten to be friends with since I came here. I don't know anyone else to ask."

Pam took one look at me and abandoned the spaghetti to come to me, touching my arm. "I didn't mean that. It's just a reflex. I know you're not prejudiced."

I nodded, wishing I hadn't asked them.

But Pam wouldn't let it go. "Have you talked to this guy about it?"

"A little bit. He's done a few things with me, and I'm not sure about it."

"Has he pushed you into doing something you don't want to do?"

"Yes. But he apologized. He said he shouldn't have done it while I was at work. Before I agreed."

"That's not good," Pam said flatly. "It's your choice what you do. You have the right to stop anything at any time."

"One thing I liked and the other I didn't." I liked the hair pulling, but I didn't like thinking about what he said to me, how he wanted to call me a "*bad girl.*" That was just too much.

"Have you slept with him?" Karen asked.

"No. I'm not sure he wants to have sex with me. Not in the usual way. And I'm not sure I want to do it his way."

"Well, you better be sure," Pam said. "If you let someone tie you up, you damn well better know they're going to untie you again. If you don't, you can get into trouble."

Karen saw that I was worried, and she reached out to give me a hug. "Just be safe, okay? You have my number, don't you? Why don't you tell him you're going to call me in a few hours? That way he knows someone is keeping track of you."

I thought that sounded like a great idea. Though I was sure that Hunter wouldn't hurt me. He would be stupid to try. I could nix his contract in a second if he got out of line. But it seemed like sound advice regardless of who I was dating.

By the time Hunter texted me saying: *I'm downstairs*, I had made up my mind that it wasn't going to work out between us. I couldn't get serious about a man who was the kind of person my friends had to warn me about. I would have to consider this a one-time thing, and that was the end of it.

I grabbed my purse and ran down.

One look at Hunter, and all my good resolutions flew away. He was so sexy, standing there on my stoop. His face lit up when he saw me. It was flattering. Especially coming from such a handsome man.

"Beautiful!" he exclaimed.

"Thanks. You look good, too." He was also wearing jeans, this time with a sleek button-down shirt. I was glad to see I had judged the tone of our date correctly.

I was very aware that Pam and Karen's front window was right next to us. Karen peeked through the curtain, getting a good look at Hunter. Then with a little wave, she was gone. Hunter never saw it happen.

"I thought we'd stay in your neighborhood. I know a great Afghan restaurant nearby. Do you eat meat?"

"Yes."

"Good. It's near the bridge. Do you mind a walk?"

"I love to walk." It was a pretty night out, and since it was Saturday, there were plenty of people on the sidewalks.

"You sure picked the right neighborhood to live in," Hunter said. "It's changed a lot since I first moved here. It used to be much more affordable, but then everyone discovered it."

"I'm lucky. My floors are slanted and the kitchen needs a desperate renovation, so it doesn't cost too much to rent."

In that way, we talked about what it was like living in the city and trying to succeed in a place where everyone came to try to succeed. Most of the people that I met came to New York from someplace else, trying to make a better life for themselves.

As we moved on to our past, I told him a little bit about my hard-working mom and dilettante dad, and what it was like growing up as an only child. He was surprised at that, saying I didn't seem spoiled at all. I didn't want to tell him that there was no money to spoil anyone in our family.

"My mom and I have a really good relationship," I told him. "We always have. I guess she treats me more like a sister."

In turn, Hunter told me about his roving childhood in city after city as his father chased jobs, all of them in trucking. "Sometimes he'd be gone for weeks. But he was hard to deal with, and we never seemed to make ends meet. My mom was working, too, so I took care of my younger brothers and made sure they got off to school and did their homework. I've been working summers since I was fourteen. One place was a metal fabricator. They let me sweep up and do odd jobs at first. That's how I got interested in metal casting, and when artists came I got to see how it was done."

"Where did you go to college?"

"High school was the most I got. I'm self-taught. My first piece was accepted in an outsider art show that got some press. There were paintings by prisoners and spray paint artists. People who never had any training. There's something raw and primal about that kind of art that I've always respected."

Dread was rising inside of me. This was the part I hated, that artistic passion that led so many people astray. I knew mom would hate the fact that I was dating a man who only had a high school degree. It proved even more that Hunter wasn't my type.

"What's wrong?" Hunter asked as I went silent. "The restaurant is only one more block."

"It's not that."

"Then what?"

I hesitated. "I don't want to offend you."

"You can ask me anything. How can we get to know each other if we tip-toe around everything? Besides, I'm not easily offended. Or surprised."

"Okay, since you insist. After a chaotic childhood like that, I'd think you'd want to pick a stable job where you know where your next meal is coming from."

His eyes opened wider. "I thought you were going to ask me why I want to dominate women. Your question is more interesting." He considered it for a moment. "I think people tend to recreate the environment they were raised in. I'm a child of uncertainty, so I'm comfortable with uncertainty. My youngest brothers were mostly spared the chaos because they relied on me until my parents settled down in Harrisburg. David just finished his college degree. It took him six years because he had to work his way through, but he's used to working hard because he always had to."

"That makes sense, I suppose." I sneaked a look at him. "So why do you?"

"Do I what?"

"Dominate women," I awkwardly echoed his earlier phrase.

Hunter laughed. "We're here. So that question will have to wait for dinner."

I liked the easy, confident way he spoke to the host and the wait staff at the Afghan restaurant. He had reservations for a table in the garden. Our low table was partly veiled by potted trees and vines climbing on the trellis. Over the top of the fence we could see the Williamsburg Bridge, with the curve of the suspension cable lit up by lights. Tiny Christmas tree lights were threaded through the trees, and our table was lit by several candles.

He had arranged for us to be seated in the secluded spot. It was a very romantic gesture, one I wished more of my dates did. There was no romance left in the world, so to find it in Hunter was the last thing I had expected.

"Do you drink wine?" he asked, and when I agreed, he ordered a lovely red wine. "Now, what kind of meat do you like?"

With that, he proceeded to grill me on my dining preferences. Garlic, onions, green vegetables, nuts, fruits, sweets… I felt like he was taking mental notes the whole time. His interest was a little overwhelming.

"Now you know as much about what I like to eat as my own mom," I finally said.

"Then you won't mind if I order for us?" Hunter gave me a smile and ordered several dishes when the waiter returned. "It's part of the culture that the dishes are communal. We can share."

The first dish arrived, with what looked like a pile of rice and a large flatbread. Hunter ripped off a small piece of the bread and filled it with the rice and meat mixture. "This is *pulao*. They mix rice with lots of different ingredients. This is lamb meat." He folded the bread over the *pulao* and took a bite.

I copied his example. I liked the taste. "Good. Different, but good."

"It's one thing I like about living in the city. You can try every food there is in the world if you stick at it long enough."

It was dangerously seductive. I imagined more dinners like this as we explored the world of food in the city. I liked listening to his voice and watching his hands as he delicately picked up each bite of food in his fingers. Maybe it was because we weren't using utensils, but it made the meal seem more intimate.

I was sliding down the path again, wondering if he could be a real romantic possibility. I liked so much about him. But there was an elephant in the courtyard, and I rushed into it to bring myself back to reality.

"So why do you like to… you know."

"Dominate beautiful women?" he asked.

"Yes."

"I like to be in control. I learned early on to take care of things, so that's what I do. That's why I create things out of nothing, from an idea and a feeling. Not only in my art, but in my life. I'm working with you tonight to create this experience, and who knows where it might lead? But if I play off you, your responses, then we can dance together in a new way for both of us."

That sounded promising. "So… is there anything in particular you like to do?"

"Other than hair-pulling?" He said it suggestively, like he was remembering the way he had kissed my neck in his studio. "I mostly take inspiration from the moment. But lots of people do have their thing. You could call it a fetish. Some men like breasts, while I love a fine butt. You, my dear, have a very fine butt."

I loved it. He made it easy to sit there and be complimented, like I was supposed to be admired and he wanted nothing more than to admire me. But at the back of my mind was doubt. A guy this good with words was dangerous. He was going to suck me in and make me fall in love with him while he dashed off to the next unique flower he came across.

"I like sex games," Hunter explained. "We set some limits and play."

"But isn't it about pain? S&M?"

"Did it hurt when I pulled your hair?"

I considered it. "Yeah, sort of, but it felt good."

"It can be about intense sensations, but it has to be done in a way that feels good. Nobody likes to stub their toe. But I bet I could give you the same amount of feeling in a way that would make you bliss out. It's all about building it up slowly, mixing erotic cues with the stronger feelings."

I blinked at him, considering that.

"Even more," he added, "BDSM is about power exchange. You give up control to me, and I take us on a journey together."

"How?"

"I'll show you." Just then our waiter arrived with two more dishes. Hunter waited until he was gone, to ask, "Will you do what I say for the rest of the meal? I won't do anything overtly sexual here in public or ask you to. And you can stop the game any time you want."

"Here? Now?"

"Why not? You're curious."

I remembered what Pam had said about the dangers of going home with someone and letting them tie you up. If I was going to try it, why not here with all the restrictions that would place on us?

"Okay. What do I have to do?"

Hunter laughed, but there was a wicked edge to it. "Just eat. Here—" He filled a small bite of bread with some blackened meat and sauce from one of the new dishes and held it out to me, right in front of my face.

I took the bite from his hand. "Mmm! I like that one. What is it?"

"Beef and dumplings in a curry sauce."

I swallowed and took a drink of water, and by the time I was ready for another bite of the delicious dish, Hunter was holding up a small prepared bite of dumpling and sauce in his fingers.

This time I realized what he was doing. He was feeding me. The first bite was easy, I hadn't even thought about it. But now for some reason it made me feel funny. Grown women didn't let themselves get fed like a baby!

He lifted the bite higher, his eyes intently on mine.

My eyes shifted quickly. Were people watching? There must be people watching. But the palm fronds of the plants were between us and the other diners. I could see them, but not very well. Maybe they could see me, but not very well.

Such a simple thing. But nervous excitement raced through my body. I felt alive. How could something so simple shake me up like this?

Maybe it was because of Hunter, staring into my eyes in that sexy, intimate way he had.

Slowly I leaned forward and took the bite of food from his fingers. As I was chewing, still watching him, he murmured, "Good girl."

I raised my hand to hide the food in my mouth. "You can't say that to me!"

"Why not?"

"It's demeaning. Belittling."

"I think you like it. It makes you all flustered and flushed, and I like you that way." He leaned forward. "But you're really such a *bad* girl. My bad girl…"

I felt oddly stroked and loved by the tenderness in his voice, but I shouldn't like it.

He might be right. It was certainly stirring up my insides like nobody's business. It was all too confusing to sort out right now, so I just went with it. If I couldn't handle eating a meal in a restaurant under his control, then I certainly couldn't go any further with him. And I really wanted to see if we could go further.

So I went with it, sipping my water and wiping my mouth with my napkin, trying the dishes he suggested or eating from his fingers when he offered me a bite. At one point he held out his finger that was smeared with the curry sauce I loved. "Lick it," he ordered quietly.

So I did, looking up at him as my lips closed over his fingertip.

He didn't have to say it that time. The words were in his eyes, amused and proud of me for not fighting him. *Good girl.* He was always ready with a bite when I was, or urging me to try a dish on my own, so it flowed along very nicely.

Dessert arrived, a big square of honey-dripping baklava. Hunter cut off a huge piece with a fork and held it out to me.

"That's too much," I protested.

"I think it's just enough."

I examined the large chunk on his upheld fork. I did love honey, which I had told him during his earlier cross-examination of my food likes and dislikes. It looked delicious, and I really wanted some.

"All or nothing," Hunter told me.

"Fine!" I opened up wide but could hardly get the baklava into my mouth. When I bit down, honey drooled from both corners of my mouth.

He laughed at me as I worked on the baklava to get it down to a manageable size. Even before I was finished, I had to laugh along with him. "You *are* sadistic," I told him.

"Oh, you have no idea." But he was laughing, too, so I couldn't take it seriously.

"My face is sticky now," I said.

"Here." He ripped open the foil package and pulled out a moist towelette. "Lean closer."

I put my face up to him and he carefully washed the honey from my lips and face. His other hand gently held my chin. Again I had the feeling of being a kid, of being taken care of by my parents. Of feeling safe and secure.

"There, all clean."

I smiled. "Now my lipstick is gone."

"Give it to me." Again, just the hint of an order wrapped in sugar.

I went into my purse and handed over my Bert's Bees lip balm, tinted just darker than my lips. He read the label, then sniffed it. "Do I smell peppermint?"

"I think so. There's something in it that makes my lips tingle."

"We're going to get along just fine." Hunter motioned me forward again. He carefully smoothed the shimmer over my lips.

"How does it look?" I asked.

"Perfect." His face was close to mine. He was going to kiss me.

"I want to see if that's really peppermint," he murmured, as he leaned in and kissed me. His lips were hot against mine, urgent, burning through my body.

I forgot to breathe, lost in his mouth as he kissed me. Then his fingers tightened in my hair, a reminder of last time, driving me higher.

Instantly I was ready for him. Maybe it was the long, slow build-up as he fed me and took care of me through the meal. But when he claimed my mouth as his own, I felt it in every fiber of my being. It was pure passion sparked by a single kiss.

Finally Hunter drew back, his fingers still tangled in my hair. "I can't tell if it's peppermint, but something's making my lips tingle."

His lips were shimmering now, too. It looked great on him. I could imagine him wearing guy-liner and rocking it in the clubs he probably went to. It was strange and wonderful at the same time.

"And now I have to replenish you." He stroked the tiny wand across my lips then handed it back to me. "There, you're perfect again."

I almost felt let down as he paid the waiter and we finally walked out of the restaurant. Out on the street, he suggested we walk around the neighborhood some more.

"How did you like your first scene?" he asked.

"What's not to like? It's different, but fun. I see what you mean by calling it a game."

I was a little heady from our kiss. I tried to focus as we talked about music and what we liked to read. We had completely different tastes. Hunter went to bars where the music was so loud you couldn't talk to anyone, while I preferred vintage pop—Backstreet Boys and R.E.M were my style. He read the Voice and the Free Press while I got the NY Times every Sunday and read every section in a long, leisurely ritual.

He also had a terribly casual view about his income, and was vague about the various odd jobs semi-related to the art field that he did to supplement his creative work. He said flat out that he didn't use credit cards. I had a feeling he had cash stashed under his mattress, if he had anything at all saved for a rainy day.

I was shocked when he told me he'd been living in his studio for nearly three years, and it wasn't even legal to live there. I couldn't imagine lying in bed at night knowing the fire department could kick everyone out at any moment.

Even worse, I kept thinking about our first kiss. It had been sexy and packing a punch, but it wasn't romantic. A first kiss should be romantic, shouldn't it? Not the punctuation at the end of a kinky dinner game. That wasn't the kind of first kiss you had with your husband. That was the kind of kiss you had with a one night stand. And I had never had a one night stand.

A panicked feeling was rising inside of me at every word Hunter said. We were worlds apart, but the blazing chemistry kept engulfing me in the tone of his voice and the way his hand grazed mine as we walked. He was nothing like my dream guy, in fact on paper he scared me, but I wanted him in a way I had never felt before. Like I was being pulled towards him by an irresistible force.

It was such a strange feeling, feeling that I could abandon all restraint with this unrestrained man. Nobody would know. Now that I was away from my family and my friends, I could do anything I wanted without having to worry that the entire town was going to talk about it. He wasn't the right man for me, but did that matter? Why move to the city if I was just going to do the same things all the time?

No, we weren't right for each other. But it was right for me right now.

Standing under a streetlamp in a pool of light, I suddenly made up my mind. Even though it was doomed to never go further than tonight, or maybe a week, or if I was lucky to the end the project. But I couldn't let him go without a real taste.

I knew I was playing with fire. I would have to keep telling my heart this was only a little fun. An exciting walk on the wild side that I could remember when I was older and sitting across the dinner table from my husband and teenagers who would try to tell me I didn't know anything about kids today.

"Do you want to come to my place?" I asked.

Chapter 10

Hunter

I wasn't expecting that. I had felt her moving further and further away from me as we walked after dinner. I thought it was the natural withdrawal that sometimes happened when I dominated a woman. People felt vulnerable when they were played with, and she had played wonderfully well with me during dinner.

"Are you sure?" I asked.

"Yes." Kali turned to walk back toward her street.

I didn't get surprised too often. People revealed everything about themselves if you just watched and listened to them. And everything she had done up to now indicated that she was *not* the type of woman who invited a man back to her place on the first date.

"You have to be honest with me," I said slowly. "I need to know what you're really thinking and feeling, or we can get badly off track."

"I want you to come home with me."

I didn't get it, but I wasn't going to argue—I wasn't that much of a saint. Even if I was getting a gut check. I tried to keep it casual and talk to her about her neighborhood on the way back, but she seemed distracted, so I let the conversation lapse into silence. She still didn't say a word as she let me into the front door of her building, and all the way up two flights of stairs to the top floor.

With one glance, I took in the minimalist décor of her apartment, clearly the beginning of a life in New York City. Some Ikea furniture with a convertible couch in the front room that looked out on the street, and a narrow galley kitchen with the bath and bedroom in the rear. She had chosen subtle stripes and polka dots as patterns.

I zeroed in on a few framed prints that held comic strips. It looked like they were on cheap newsprint. "What are these?" I asked.

Now she looked even more uncomfortable. "Just something I played around with in high school. A couple were printed in the school paper."

"You drew these? They're really good!" They were also framed very nicely, belying her dismissal of them. I read the cartoon about the girl and her cat who liked to sit on her head, and laughed out loud. "That's really funny."

"Thanks." Kali offered, "Would you like some wine or a beer?"

"Wine, please."

This was her idea, so I took the wine and sipped it with a pleasant smile. "Do you have any more work of yours?"

"No, I didn't spend much time on it," she said dismissively.

She led me into the living room to the couch. She turned slightly as she sat down, as if to keep me away. So I sat down at the other end.

"My friends who live on the first floor are going to call me in a little while to be sure I'm okay. They watched us come in."

"Very smart," I said. "There are men who will take advantage of you if they can. You have to protect yourself." I didn't even want to think about some stupid jerk hurting her. She was so curious and open. The idea of crushing her spirit sickened me, but some men would want to do that to her.

Now she seemed surprised. "You think I'm wrong to bring you here?"

"Me? We work together. That helps. Your friends are another thing. But if you were my sister, I would tell you to never bring a man home on the first date."

Kali glanced away. "This is my first time."

I smiled. "That's a compliment." When she didn't reply, I asked, "Why did you ask me back?"

"I want to find out more about this kinky stuff."

My dick began to swell in anticipation. But I pulled hard on the reigns. I didn't care about moving fast, but she did. This was all new to her. I wanted to be sure she understood what she was agreeing to.

"That sounds romantic," I said lightly.

"I don't expect it to be romantic." She considered it. "Can it be romantic?"

"Don't you think it was at the restaurant?" I edged over closer to her. "I was looking into your eyes, taking care of you, feeding you the best bites, making sure you were happy…"

"I guess."

"But?" Clearly she didn't want to answer, so I urged, "This is how you find out about the kinky stuff, Kali. We have to talk about it first."

"Talking about it isn't romantic. Maybe I'm not very good at this."

"I want to know what you want. What do you feel? What are you afraid of?"

I took hold of her hand. She held on, as if that helped her. "I… want what you did to me at your place. Only… more."

"'More' is very open-ended. You want to feel sensations, but not pain. Yes? And you liked being dominated, I could tell. What else?"

"I'm not supposed to get tied up."

"No, you're not. Because it's our first scene, and you should never get tied up on a first scene."

I was having to work hard to keep myself in check. I hadn't been so turned on by a woman in years, not since my first real submissive. *Claire.* The lovely Claire. We had both been so young, not quite sure about how to go about rough sex, but knowing deep inside that we both wanted the same thing. We had figured it out together, but she was like other high school girls and wanted a relationship, while I always wanted to try more girls.

I wasn't so sure about Kali. I wanted her, yes! Loud and clear on that one. But I still wasn't sure what she wanted.

"How far do you want to go? Sexually, I mean," I asked.

"I don't know. What's the usual thing?"

68

"You can do whatever you want. Some people have scenes without any sort of sex. Like we did at the restaurant. Sometimes people play with breasts or genitals. Or masturbate. Or use dildos. And of course there's oral and anal…"

"Oh."

She looked even more beautiful, a little lost and overwhelmed. So vulnerable. I loved it, but it also made me nervous. Did she really want to or not?

"If it was up to me," I said, my voice raw with honesty. "I'd take you right here and right now. And then I'd do it again. I want you so badly I can taste it. But it's probably not a good idea. As much as I want to ravish you within an inch of your life, we need to go slowly."

Now her eyes were fastened on me. "We do?"

"Yes, we do." I was already building our scene, though she didn't know it.

"Why?"

"So you'll come back for more."

She nodded, smiling slightly.

"Stand up," I said quietly.

I stood up with her, still holding her hand, turning to face her. "You can always stop me, at any time. Do you understand that? You just have to tell me."

She shivered slightly. "Okay."

"I noticed you like to be pushed. You can say no as part of the game. But say 'stop' if you really mean it. That's your safeword."

She nodded. It was as if she had taken the first step, and had released everything that had been holding her back. I could tell she was already feeling rather than over-thinking everything.

I ran my fingertip down her cheek. Then I pulled her close and kissed her again. But this time it wasn't playful. I let myself go in this kiss. I knew I wouldn't get nearly the kind of satisfaction I wanted from this scene, but I was going for much bigger game. I wanted *her*. I wanted her to give herself to me completely. And that couldn't happen in one night. Not with this girl.

So I kissed her in promise of all that was coming, the passion and romance she wanted, and the kinky sex I craved. That she would crave, as long as I held myself in check and didn't frighten the horses.

So I tried to calm my breathing, resting my forehead against hers for a moment. I could feel the fluttering pulse in her neck, where my fingers were clutching her hair. I hadn't even realized I was doing it.

Her eyes were dark with desire, with only the thinnest rim of gray-green around the edge. Large and shining with desire.

"Much as I love looking into your eyes, I want you to relax." I gently swept my fingers down her face, making her close her eyes. "Keep them closed," I murmured.

My hand continued down to her shoulder, sweeping down the curve, then further down, just grazing her breast with my arm. "I'm going to take off your shirt and your bra, but everything else will stay on." That would make a nice hard limit I couldn't let myself cross. And I needed a good hard limit right now.

She peeked, as I knew she would. Because she was a bad girl. I let her see it in my eyes, smirking at her.

"Oh!" Then she started to laugh, surprising herself.

"That's better." Now she was even more relaxed. I hooked my fingers in the hem of her shirt and slowly began pulling it up.

Her laughter stilled as she realized what I was doing.

"Close your eyes," I whispered.

I pulled the silky material up until it covered her face, making her lift her arms. But I left her shirt there covering her face, with her arms trapped, folded over the top of her head. Now her head and arms were covered by the ivory silk, leaving only the impression of her nose and cheeks and chin, like a veil pulled over her face.

She squirmed a little at first, holding her elbows over her head. She was exposed, but not able to see. Her breath made the silk flutter faster in front of her mouth.

I scooped her up, lifting her off her feet in one motion. She let out a little cry in delight and fear. But she couldn't do anything with her arms trapped over her head but kick her feet slightly.

I laid her down on the coffee table with her feet on the floor. I had been eyeing the coffee table since I came in. It was very low and sturdy, and the top was a bit scarred up so I didn't think she would care if a few other things happened to it. It was just tall enough to make her arch her back slightly to reach her feet on the floor. With her arms trapped over her head by the ivory material, in her pale gray bra with delicate embroidery on it, she was laid out for me to do with as I pleased.

I lifted her shoulder to shove away the small pile of magazines underneath her, so she could lie flat. And I caught the candle before it could topple off the edge.

The candle was my other inspiration. I checked to see it was ordinary paraffin. I clicked on my lighter, making her flinch at the sound. Lighting the candle, I laid it aside for the moment to turn back to my feast on the table.

I started with my hands because that was the best way to ground someone. I ran a finger lightly from the base of her neck exposed beneath the material of her shirt, down the center of her chest to her stomach and into the hollow of her belly button. I slipped a finger under the waistband of her jeans and gave it a tug or two, wishing I could pop open the button and continue all the way down. But I had set a limit and wouldn't break it.

With my hands circling her waist, I pushed them up her body to her breasts, cupping them over her pretty bra, then down under her body to her shoulder blades, lifting her slightly from the table. I wanted her to feel she was in my hands, that I held her.

She gasped at being lifted, and I watched her rapid breathing in her stomach, pulled taunt by the arched curve of her back.

I rubbed her with my whole hands, loving the feel of her ribs and the curve of her waist. Then I slipped my hand around and with a flick, opened the back of her bra. The tiny hooks on the two straps

71

slipped easily out of the fabric loops, and I was able to pull it off without undoing her arms from their silk bondage.

Her breasts were natural B-cups, full yet perky. I lowered my face to the center of her chest, blowing softly. Then I shifted over to one nipple, my mouth very close but not touching her, blowing. She made a slight sound as her nipples tightened from the sensation.

Cupping her breasts, I pinched her nipples between my thumb and the base of my forefinger. She gasped out loud, her hips bucking in response. Some women could learn to climax from having their nipples pinched.

She was breathing faster now, so I pulled her shirt slightly higher, exposing just her chin and mouth. I loved watching her lips quiver as she licked them, glad to be partly released.

I leaned over her, letting her feel my body against hers. I kissed her, enjoying how she couldn't see, how she was completely at my mercy, with just her lips free. And her lips eagerly responded, giving herself to me.

Stretched against her, my hard cock pressed against her hip. Humping was far more chaste than my usual fare, but like the first time I held her, it ignited me, making me grind against her harder. Her breath caught against my mouth, as she arched her back.

I almost couldn't stop, but I had other plans.

At the edge of my fingertips was the candle. The flame had melted a pool of wax.

I lifted myself, laying one hand over her crossed arms over her head, holding her down. She instantly tensed, fighting against me. I let her struggle, until she knew that she wouldn't be able to dislodge me. I could hold her down like this no matter how hard she tried.

"Hunter!" she gasped.

"Don't fight me, Kali."

Slowly she began to relax, and I waited for the perfect moment. Then I tilted the candle and let the wax drip onto the center of her stomach.

"Oh, Hunter!" She tensed, struggling against me. "It's burning me!"

I held her arms easily with one hand. Then I bent down and kissed her stomach, licking my tongue all around where the wax was hardening in a nickel-sized pool on her stomach. Then lower to her belly button, which I licked, then nipped with my teeth. I pressed my teeth together on the tiny bit of flesh, until she writhed hard enough to draw a sound of protest from her.

I let go and carefully positioned the wax between her breasts. This time when I tilted the candle, the wax ran from her chest down under one breast, leaving a trail of burning warmth behind.

She made another lovely sound, like the call of a bird. I felt like a falcon circling overhead. I liked to see her twist and try to get away, but I could strike and hold her. I dripped the wax here and there, breathing with her, tensing with her, kissing her breasts and belly between the burning drops. Biting her breasts and nipples until her rising exclamations and the sheen on her skin told me she was nearing a peak.

Her flesh was reddened around the hardening wax, but it hadn't burned her even though it probably felt that way. I figured she had no idea what I was doing or if it would leave marks.

But she let me push her further and further, until I dripped the wax directly on her nipple. Her guttural cry tore through me, and my fingers dug into her more fiercely.

It made my raging cock fight to get out of my jeans. I wanted to jerk her pants down and plunge into her there on the coffee table.

I put my leg between hers, separating them. She spread her knees and opened her legs as wide as her jeans allowed. I slipped in between and leaned into her, my erection pressing against her. It was still within the limits, but as I rocked, sliding the length of my dick against her, I felt the moist heat of her even through the double layer of our jeans.

I moaned, feeling as if I was almost slipping over the edge. Just from humping her!

"I can't stand it!" I muttered, stunned by my own runaway

73

excitement.

Kali was writhing under me. Twisting more frantically as her arms fought with her shirt. "Just do it!" she cried out.

"Do what?" I asked.

She scrambled off the shirt, grasping onto my arms. Her eyes were wild and bright. "Make love to me! I'm going to die if you don't."

I was ready. More than ready. *Limits be damned!*

But it wasn't right, and some tiny sane piece of my mind stopped me. It was a bad idea to renegotiate hard limits in the middle of a scene. We both were out of our minds with lust! Now was no time to make a serious decision.

I pulled back, breathing heavily. Trying to get a grip. If only she was experienced. Then I could trust that she knew what she wanted even in the heat of passion.

She pulled at my arms, her eyes imploring me. "Please, Hunter! Even if it's only for one night. I won't let it interfere with our working relationship."

I stopped cold, as if I had been smacked. "What do you mean, even if it's only for one night?"

"I know this is only crazy wild sex. I'm okay with it. I want to do it."

"Only sex?" Now she was lying back down, looking up at me. I was leaning over her, my fingers tangled in the ends of her hair. "What do you mean?"

"I know you have other women. Like Minx. I know I'm not your usual kind of girl. We're not looking for the same thing. But I want this. Even if it's only for tonight."

"What if I want to do it tomorrow night?"

She had to smile. "Then I'd say yes. But I don't expect a relationship to come of this."

There it was again; the slamming of a door inside of her, cutting me off from everything important. "Why not?"

She blinked a few times, as if it was so obvious she didn't know where to start. "I'm not kinky, for one thing."

"I beg to differ. You're loving this."

"I'm sure this is like twiddling thumbs to you."

"No! I love it! I adore the way you respond, with your heart and soul. So sensitive! So responsive. It's like playing with the wind."

Now Kali looked away, embarrassed. She was closing herself off more each second. She covered her breasts with her arms. Her shirt was still looped around one.

I helped her sit up. "You don't know what I want. We haven't talked about relationships at all. You're making assumptions based on one glimpse of one of my play partners."

"What is your relationship with Minx?"

"I'm not in love with her. And she isn't with me. We enjoy playing together. And she helps me keep the studio clean." I wasn't going to go into the deeply structured relationship I had with Minx, wherein we were always in Master/slave roles when we were together.

Kali was looking at me with rising skepticism in her eyes. I could see goose-bumps starting on her skin as her flush slipped away. This was *not* how I wanted to end our first scene together. It had spiraled out of control.

It was so unlike me.

For the first time, I felt like she might slip through my fingers. This girl was so different from the others that my usual thing wouldn't cut it. I was out of my depth with her. I wanted to grab her even harder, to hold her closer and make her understand what I meant.

But I couldn't. I forced myself to smile and relax, so I wouldn't frighten her. It took an effort of supreme will. Fear in a sexual context could be delicious, but the kind of fear she was feeling now was making her want to run away from me.

I had to finish the scene and give her the closure she needed after opening herself up to me. So I took her into the kitchen and carefully scraped off the wax with a butter knife. I made her laugh, and tickled her until she nearly screamed. Just enough so I felt more in control. I was weak to do it. But I felt like I had just run a marathon and had to turn around and run all the way back again before I was done. I needed a long cool drink of water, something to sustain me. So I tickled her and felt her wiggle in my arms as I held her, and shamelessly rubbed my denim-covered erection against her body.

Then I carried her to her room and helped her get out her nightclothes. I pulled back the bed and plumped the pillow while she stared at me. "Go get ready for bed. I'll clean up out there."

While she was in the bathroom, I swept up the waxy bits from the coffee table. The candle was out and I fixed the magazines, then turned out all the lights except for the one by the door.

Kali met me at the door wearing a long white nightshirt.

"You look like an angel," I told her.

I took her face gently in her hands and kissed her again. This time I restrained myself. She leaned into me, silently begging for more. I let her know I wanted her, then pulled back, kissing her on the forehead before I left.

"Go to bed. I'll talk to you tomorrow," I said, going out the door.

As aftercare for me, it sucked. Why did it feel like I was the one who just got whipped? But I couldn't lie down on her bed and cuddle with her, as much as I wanted to. I would end up having sex with her, and probably scare her because I would be too rough or too raw or something. It would only confirm her idea that this hook up would be brief and meteoric.

I wanted to draw it out as long as I could. I paused outside her closed door, wanting to knock, to return and hold her for a few minutes. But that wouldn't solve anything.

I went downstairs and outside, looking up at the darkened living room windows. I felt so disconnected from her. After playing her body like a fine instrument, reacting with her, taking her to the heights of ecstasy… I felt a crashing emptiness inside. I hoped she didn't feel that way, too. It wasn't a good idea to try to have a serious talk right on the heels of a scene. Emotions were too riled up, feelings needed time to settle before they were processed.

I slowly circled the block, unable to walk away. On the next street I could see the back of her building through a wide empty lot surrounded by chain link and graffitied plywood. A dog was barking in a building nearby.

Her bedroom light was still on.

I felt like a dirty stalker, but I couldn't stop myself. I had to be sure she was okay. I knew even simple scenes could pierce someone's psyche. Look at me! Here I was lurking outside an empty lot, watching her when she didn't know it.

Once again, Kali had shaken me so badly that I was reacting on primal instinct. First in the subway I had endangered us both by making a spectacle of myself searching for her, and now I was stalking her, unable to let her go, like a dog searching for my bone.

I am a dog, I thought to myself, giving my rigid hard-on a rub through my jeans. I had been hard for more than an hour with no relief in sight. But I was used to that. I was Mr. Control when it came to my own orgasm. It shouldn't be driving me out of my mind this way.

So I pulled out my phone. I wrote a text to her: *Do you need anything? I could come back if you do.*

I counted to thirty before a text returned from her: *I'm fine. I'm just going to bed now.*

I texted back: *Good girl.*

For nearly a minute I stood there looking at her window. And then it went dark. She really was going to bed. She would think of me tonight and tomorrow when she woke up. And when she found tiny bits of candle in her sheets or in her hair. She would think of me and how I had held her and done things to her that she hadn't ever allowed anyone else to do.

With another absent rub of my cock, I turned away. Now I could go home. But I would be back. I wasn't going to let this treasure get plundered by anyone else but me.

Chapter 11

Kali

It was the hottest thing I had ever done, and we didn't even go all the way! I lay there after he left, wishing we had made love. It was maddening, as I twisted from side to side. He was obviously excited. The whole time. That was one of the best things about it.

When I finally fell asleep, I slept so deeply I didn't wake up until very late. Stretching and yawning, thinking of what had happened last night, I pulled up my nightshirt and checked my stomach and breasts. There were little reddened marks where his teeth had bitten me, but nothing from the candle wax.

It was funny. It had felt like it was burning, and I was afraid I would have blisters this morning. I was so scared while it was happening. There were flashes of fire, some really painful, but I listened to his voice luring me forward every step of the way. And now I found I'd been right to trust him. Other than the wax shavings, you could hardly tell anything had happened to me last night.

Wandering out to my living room, I picked up the candle where he had replaced it on the coffee table. On the coffee table! I had begged him to make love to me on my coffee table! I could hardly believe that was me last night.

But it was so incredibly sensual. He was touching me constantly, kissing me, rubbing me, leaning into me and holding me down. It was more contact that I usually got when I had sex. Like he was making love to my whole body.

Why didn't he go all the way with me? I wondered. *I threw myself at him hard enough.*

Sex had never been a big deal for me. It was usually too fast for me to orgasm, and the few guys who got that far weren't around long enough to get to know my body. But Hunter took his time. Last night

79

was all about making me feel good.

If the few guys in my past had taken that kind of time to make me feel *that* good, I wouldn't have found it so easy to turn them down.

So when Hunter texted me, I couldn't help dancing a little in place. It read: *Morning! I hope you feel good today.*

Laughing, I had to text back: *No I'm a bad girl, remember?*

Yes you are, he texted right back. *And I'm the one who figured it out. You remember that.*

I had fun last night, I texted.

So did I. How about dinner tomorrow night, after work? I should be done with the demo crew by 6.

I hugged myself. He was asking me out again! He wanted me. Even if it was only for kinky sex games.

Well, I could do with a few more kinky sex games if they were all like that. Except I wanted the sex part, too. Now that I had gotten my feet wet, I was ready for a dunking. Our scene last night blew everything else I'd ever done out the window, and I was ready for more.

...

Later on, while I was doing my laundry and staring off into space, thinking about how gorgeous Hunter was and how he could have any girl he wanted, he sent me another text: *Do you have a private email where I can send you a note? Not work-related.*

I gave him my gmail account – KaliKaliKali. Then I kept checking the browser on my phone until his email popped up. It was from his usual address.

Hunter Munro – Hunter@Huntermunro.com
Re: relationships

You said something about relationships last night. What is it you're looking for?

80

H

I considered it, then sent the following email in response:

Kali Jones – KaliKaliKali@gmail.com
Re: relationships

I'm looking for love, like most people. But I'm not in a rush to find it.

~Kali

After a few minutes my phone pinged and another email came through.

Hunter Munro – Hunter@Huntermunro.com
Re: relationships

If you're going to be that short, we could have texted.

Tell me what you really want. Unless you'd rather sit down over dinner tomorrow and talk? But you seemed uncomfortable, so I thought it would be easier for you to say it in an email.

H

Well, if he wanted a real email, he would have to wait for it. I wasn't going to tap out something incoherently on my phone. So I closed the browser and sat back to think about it as I watched my clothes go round in the dryer. What did I want? An exciting career, a husband who was my partner in life, a nice home and two kids so they would have a sibling, unlike me.

But in the short term, I wasn't sure. I wanted to leave the door open. I wanted to see Hunter again.

As soon as I got home, I sat down with my laptop without even putting my laundry away. At first I tried to write about why I wanted to see him again even though it was so out of character for me to pursue casual sex. But all I kept coming up with was: *you smell so good. I like the way your hands feel on me. I want more….*

So I went back to his original question – *what do I want from a relationship?* I tried to describe my idea of the perfect relationship could be stretched to fit this situation. But when I read back my few tortured sentences, it wasn't right.

I went and put my laundry away. The routine chore put me back into the proper frame of mind. He said I had to be honest with him. And the truth would come out regardless.

So I sat down and wrote it out in a stream of consciousness, not letting my doubts stop me:

I want a man I can trust and depend on, someone who will be there in the hard times and laugh with me in the good times. I don't just want a dad for my kids. I want someone who wants to hang out with me and not run off all the time. I'm not going to settle, and I won't get married if I can't find someone who can be a real partner to me. I want to be in a relationship for the long haul, and not fear he'll give up when things get rough. My parents are still together, but sometimes I thought they wouldn't make it. I would hate to go through that with my own kids. If I can't find the right man, then I'll keep focusing on my career. I picked the green industry because I want to make the world a better place, and if I don't have a family, I will concentrate on that. But I do want love in my life. And I want to try new things—that's one reason I moved to New York, so I could get out of my hometown and the things I've always known.

I had thrown in that last sentence so even if he didn't want the rest of what I wanted, he would like that.

I emailed it without editing it. He wanted honesty. *There it is.*

Let's see how he responds.

Chapter 12

Hunter

I was putting the finishing touches on the sundial pattern when an email finally came through from Kali. Several times as I waited I had been tempted to text her again, but that would be admitting too much. I had asked her a question, now it was up to her to answer.

I read through the email several times. Husband, kids, nice house, career... she wanted it all.

Or did she? She had been hearing about those things in romantic movies and books since she was a girl. No, I needed to look deeper. *Someone who wants to hang out and not run off all the time...* There was something real in that nugget. Her own experience, maybe with a boyfriend who didn't pay enough attention to her? A lot of girls liked being submissive because they could be in the spotlight. Exhibitionists, attention whores, you name it and they flocked to the scene so they could show off.

I knew that wasn't Kali. She was too modest, if anything.

Her line about the green industry reeked of something she repeated to herself over and over, like a protective chant. I didn't believe it. She wasn't like any corporate public relations person I ever met. No one could be more the opposite of Selina Stern, and she was a paragon of the breed.

So there was a nugget of truth to unearth in that.

The last thing was nearly the last thing she had written. It was the only thing in the email that spoke to my life, and she knew it. She wanted to try something new, ie. *me*. And kinky sex. But she was still convinced that I couldn't give her what she wanted.

That's okay. I knew better. I knew she didn't know what she really wanted. The city would blow all of her preconceptions out of the water. You couldn't stay the same and be exposed to so many different things: different cultures, different expectations, and stresses that came with so many people and such tight quarters.

She would figure out what she wanted soon enough.

I would be glad to help. I would rather see her learn to live before she met some idiot and got pregnant, like my mom did with me. When my mom decided to keep me, that's why she married my father. She wouldn't have ended up with my dad if that hadn't happened. Her life would be a lot better right now if she hadn't gotten pregnant back then.

I wasn't going to let that happen to me. I wasn't planning on getting married and having kids. It was tough enough on my own. Most days it felt like I was scrambling up a sheer cliff with my fingers and toes.

Making art was my thing, and I had sworn a long time ago that I would give up everything else as long as I could continue creating new things. I didn't even try to make a bargain with the devil that I would be successful—the process was my passion, and I couldn't live without it.

I wouldn't.

The one thing I didn't like was lying to Kali when she asked how I made rent money. That's when I should have told her about my X-rated sculptures. But I had already decided I wouldn't tell her about Hunting Art until after the project was finished. Now I had to protect her because it wasn't just my job at risk. She could get into trouble, too, if anyone found out she knew about it and was dating me.

After that email she sent, I knew she would really hate Hunting Art. Traveling to kink conferences and erotic art festivals around the country to sell sculptures definitely didn't fit with her idea of a traditional relationship.

I didn't dare send her an email in response telling her that I was a confirmed bachelor who would rather blow up the conventions of society than live according to them. She would run away.

I couldn't stand that. So I set to work. I would create a romantic date for Kali that she would never forget.

I would crack her open to see what made her tick.

Chapter 13

Kali

I kept checking my email, but Hunter didn't respond to my note. It bothered me, but I had made my choice when I refused to sugar-coat my desire for a husband that I could depend on. In fact, his silence showed he didn't want the same thing. If he was the kind of man who wanted to be in a serious relationship, he would already be in one. Instead he was chipping around with freaky girls like Minx, who probably didn't ask much from him but a good time.

As I went to bed that night, I told myself that I would have to deal with a lot worse if I wanted to see Hunter again. Could I really have sex with him knowing he was doing these things with other women? My body screamed *Yes!* while my mind crossed its mental arms and shook its head sternly *No!*

"One step at a time," I told myself as I climbed into bed. I could do one step at a time. And when it got too bad, then I would end it. By then, maybe I would be disgusted with his perverted ways and not care anymore. Or I maybe would be a rag-doll left in a gutter after he had used me up. But I hoped I had enough good sense so that wouldn't happen.

It wasn't the usual Monday as I dressed for work with an eye to our evening date, choosing a tailored sleeveless dress. The A-line skirt flared at the bottom, and it was a luscious dark teal, so it would translate well into evening. I hadn't asked him a thing about what he had planned, so I had to cover all of my bases.

By the time I saw Hunter at work, I was able to smile pleasantly as if there was no open-ended email hanging in the air, as if I didn't remember writhing under him as he dripped hot wax on me.

In front of the others, he acted like there was nothing between us, which I appreciated. I didn't want my boss finding out about us now. Selina would be furious if she knew we were seeing each other. Ever since Hunter started pushing Selina away, she had alternated between being cloying sweet and ordering him around like he was the bus boy.

Hunter didn't seem to care either way, and it was slowly driving Selina crazy. She kept handing him over to me to deal with the permits and the contractor doing the demolition, and then stepping back in abruptly to take over, messing up our perfectly good plans. Selina would love to find some way to undermine Hunter with Mr. Ryan, and the fact that he and I were dating was a big juicy secret she would use against us both. It was critical that we were discreet.

I was pleased to find that I worked well with Hunter. He was very quick on his feet when it came to getting around the inevitable red-tape roadblocks that kept cropping up. I had to stop myself from watching him and catching his eye, he was so distracting. I kept thinking of the way he had touched me, never letting go of me while I was blindfolded, keeping us connected.

By the end of the day, I was so ready to go to dinner with him. I had managed to whisper at one point, "Let's meet at the deli at the end of the block instead of in the plaza."

He nodded, and nothing else was said. But when I hurried up to meet him after work, already getting excited, my heart fell when Hunter said, "I'm sorry, but I just got a call that the Conservancy Garden may be able to take the fountain. They want me to be up there in an hour so I can meet with the director before the gates close."

I wasn't able to swallow my disappointment. "Oh… well, that's good. If we can recycle the fountain, we should do it. Where's the Conservancy Garden?"

"It's in Central Park, on 5th Avenue and 100th Street." He checked his watch. "I'm hungry so I'm going to grab a bowl of noodles. I know it's not what you had in mind, but do you want to join me? Then we can go up together to the garden. It should be pretty at sunset."

I smiled, feeling better. "That sounds nice."

He explained on the way down to Delancey St. that the director was making a special trip up to the garden from the park headquarters on the west side. But instead of listening, I kept watching his mouth, when he spoke and the way he gestured. It still thrilled me the way he had faced off with those thugs on the subway. And then during our scene, how he had kissed me when my eyes were covered, until everything spiraled away into bliss. All of the things I had forced from my mind during work hours. Now I could indulge myself.

He took me to a tiny storefront Chinese noodle shop that was filled with steam. Several small round tables and rickety chairs were next to the refrigerated display cases for pastries. A counter cut off the back half where the kitchen was going gangbusters turning out food for the steady stream of customers that came and went.

Hunter didn't ask me this time; he went ahead and ordered two bowls of noodles and chose several buns from the display cases. The woman tending the counter couldn't speak English, but that didn't seem to slow either of them down as they smiled and thanked each other.

Hunter set everything down on the table, including a bottle of water that he opened and placed by my side. "I noticed you drink water instead of soda. That's good. It's better for you to not drink soda."

"Yes, doctor."

"That's 'yes, Sir' to you."

I made a rude noise before I could stop myself. Then covered my mouth with my hand.

"I'm sure I can make you say it, with the right encouragement," he said.

"No way," I said automatically.

He laughed and deftly took a bite of noodles, as I looked down in confusion.

"I'd love to hear you call me Sir because you'd have to force yourself to do it." His voice lowered. "Just the thought it of makes me hard."

I looked around quickly, but nobody was listening. Leave it to Hunter to fluster me with only a few words. I had to stoop over my bowl and bite off the noodles, letting the rest slide back into the broth. It was the most awkward food you could possibly eat on a date. But it was delicious with bits of shrimp and spices. I had no idea what they were, but it tasted good.

The buns were even better. I bit into one, and it was filled with shredded BBQ pork that was somewhat sweet. I could have made a meal on those pork buns alone. The other one had a dense custard cream that, funny enough, wasn't as sweet as the pork. I ooh-ed and ah-ed over the unusual tastes.

"I love to watch you eat," Hunter said. "You don't hold back, do you? I hate it when people pick at their food. Why eat out if you're going to order and then sit there staring at it?"

I picked up the bowl to drink the last of the broth. "I like to try new things."

"That's what you said in your email."

I swallowed and wiped my mouth with the paper napkin. "You never did answer it."

"Didn't I?" He stacked up our bowls.

"No." I stayed seated though he was making motions for us to leave. He had managed to distract me from the conversation about relationships we were supposed to have over dinner. "Since I told you what I want, now it's your turn. What are you looking for?"

"I'm not looking for anything particular. I take what comes along." He leaned over and touched a light finger to my lips. "And I'll definitely take you."

It sent a shiver up my spine. The way he was looking at me, like he wanted to slurp me up like he did with the noodles… everything else flew out of my head. For a moment, I thought he was going to kiss me right there.

But instead he said, "We're going to be late if we don't go."

We headed over to the subway. As we headed down into the station, it brought back vivid memories of when the gang had chased us. Hunter's posture changed as if he was remembering it, too. When we got onto the train car, he squared his shoulders, glancing around at every man nearby as if assessing their potential for causing problems.

"That was the scariest thing that's ever happened to me," I said quietly.

He understood. "It was off the hook."

Hunter was standing right in front of me, and I was against the door, so he blocked me off from everyone else. The car had a lot of people standing nearby, but it wasn't packed.

Feeling him so close, rocking in time with the train, I couldn't think of anything except how he had stood between me and the gang. Exactly like this. I remembered how I had rested my hand lightly against his back, too afraid to look at the approaching men.

Hunter had kept me safe. He did what he needed to do.

It made me weak in the knees. I wished he would kiss me now. But he was too keyed up to let down his guard. And he was probably right. Now I knew how quickly something could get out of hand.

Getting off uptown, we walked several blocks to Central Park and entered through the wide iron gates just minutes before seven o'clock. At the bottom of the flight of steps was a broad avenue of trees. Running down the center of the promenade was a grassy plot surrounded by hedges. Along each side were flower beds filled with spring blossoms and trimmed bushes. It looked lovely in the rosy twilight.

As we walked down the promenade toward the back, Hunter said, "Look at that!"

At the end was a small gray fountain sitting in the middle of a broad circle of grass. It was lost in the midst of such an expanse. And the trickle of water spouting from the top was not impressive either.

"Our fountain would look so much better!" I exclaimed. "It's huge compared to that thing."

Hunter was nodding, his eyes alight. "And it's a better color for this setting. It will anchor the avenue of trees without being overpowered like this one."

A middle-aged woman wearing a dark green work shirt walked up and introduced herself as the director of the Central Park Conservancy. She liked what she had seen in the photos Hunter had emailed her, and when they marked off how much bigger the fountain was, she was delighted.

"My only problem is that we don't have anything in the budget for moving it," the director said. "We have the pavers and the manpower to widen the base for it, and the plumbing was run a few years ago, so that's fine. How much would it cost to move such a massive object?"

"I spoke to Mr. Ryan about that," Hunter said. "He's offered to donate the cost of moving the fountain up here to the Conservancy Garden. We can dismantle it into sections for easier transport, so it's only a matter of a big truck and a forklift to unload it once it's here."

That was the first I had heard of this, but I saw the opportunity and added, "We'd like to take photos of the move and let some of the papers know about our donation of the fountain to the Conservancy Garden. It will be good publicity for Central Park as well as SunTech."

The director was enthusiastic about the deal, and Hunter looked very happy to find a good use for the fountain. They talked about the timeline and details of the move which would have to happen very quickly to match the plaza renovation timeline. It got quite dark before they wrapped it up.

As we were walking back to the subway, Hunter said, "It's a good thing you came tonight. I wouldn't have thought of the PR angles like you did."

"You did all the work on this. Mr. Ryan must be thrilled."

"He will be when I tell him."

"But I thought you said he would donate the transport up here?"

Hunter grinned. "I got him to agree to that before I started calling places. I didn't want that to be a problem if a community park or green space wanted it. I wasn't expecting Central Park to have budget issues, but parks are underfunded."

I glanced at him, struck by his delight over the whole thing. He was the one who had made this happen. He had done outreach to all sorts of parks and public spaces, trying to find a place that could use the fountain.

I remembered he said his last project was a pro bono piece for a park in Bed-Sty. There was something really admirable about that. His motive in finding a home for the fountain was even more altruistic than mine—even though more publicity for the project would bring more publicity for him, he hadn't considered the PR angle until I brought it up.

He hesitated when we reached the top of the subway entrance. We both looked down into the black maw and neither one of us made a move to step down.

"It's such a nice night," he said. "Our date's been busted up and we both have work tomorrow. But what do you say about walking a little further down to the river? There's a water ferry there we can take directly to Williamsburg."

"That sounds perfect."

He gave me a sideways look. "I think secretly you like being on the subway with me. You like it that you were afraid, now that it's over."

I looked at him quickly, but there was no judgment in his eyes. "You're probably right." To change the subject, I asked, "So why didn't you answer my email? For real."

"You might not like my answer," he said slowly.

I felt a chill. Here it was. "I thought you said honesty was the most important thing."

"It is. But some people don't like it when they get it."

"Now I'm really curious. What did you think of my answer?"

He grimaced. "I don't think that's what you really want."

"What do you mean?"

"You don't know what you want."

"Oh, really? So you know me better than I know myself?" I felt a little irritated. "That's funny coming from someone I met two weeks ago."

"Ten days," he corrected absently.

That irritated me even more. "So tell me what do I want?"

"I don't know," he admitted. "But I do know that those things—a husband, kids, a nice house—those are things you've been *told* you want. It's the story you tell about yourself, that you tell other people, because it feels safe. It's not really you."

"What do you mean? It's not really me?"

"It's a front you put up, your way of getting through the world. You want people to think you're a nice person, a *good girl*. So you do things to please other people. But all the while, you're hiding behind your façade of niceness, judging people and hoping they don't see you in there making calculations about what they want and what you're willing to give in exchange."

My mouth fell open. "How can you say that about me?"

"Maybe it's unconscious, this pretty way you have of dealing with people. So innocent, so guileless." He looked at me harder. "But I think you know what you're doing. You think things out. You rarely do anything by impulse. Even what happened with me the other night. You thought that through, put everything on the scales, and made the choice to ask me back to your place."

Pinned, I felt pinned like a dead butterfly. Every scallop and color block catalogued, and put in my proper place according to size and type.

He's right, I thought helplessly. I couldn't have spoken for the world. I felt naked and exposed, even more than when I had been lying naked on my coffee table with my shirt over my face. My shirt over my face! No wonder I liked it. To be hidden from his prying eyes. To be able to relax and not have to think and wonder…

His arm went around my shoulders. It felt better than anything I had ever felt before. "It's okay, Kali. Everyone has their shining

94

armor they wear when they battle life. But you can't get lost in thinking that the way you learned to deal with other people is really *you*. You're in there, struggling to get out. To find out what's important to you. Maybe it's SunTech and the environment. I don't know about that. I think it might be something different. You have to give yourself space and the freedom to make mistakes, to take alleyways and go down side paths. Because sometimes that's the best way to find yourself."

I let out my breath in a long stream. Why did it feel like he could see right inside of me? Like he had ripped off my protective shell and was calmly surveying the grubby worm that squirmed in front of him.

But his eyes were compassionate. Like he really cared about me. Like he saw potential in me that no one else had ever seen.

And those words… *maybe it's SunTech and the environment. I don't know about that…*

"How do you know?" I managed to get out.

"Because I've been there. You have to strip everything bare to be a real artist. And it's not easy. But easy isn't always the best."

"You think it's easy to get a job in New York?" I asked, my throat tight.

"Why did you choose public relations?" he countered.

"Well, I'm a good writer. My teachers always said I had a way with words. I wrote a few articles for the school paper."

"Like the cartoons you drew," he said.

"Yes. But I didn't want to be a journalist. It's a dying field, with so much competition. I knew I'd never make a living that way. So I chose copy-writing instead. I majored in communications."

Hunter gave me a look. "Don't be too sure you've found your career path."

I shrugged, feeling way too exposed. "With Selina as my boss, how could I be sure of anything? Every second, I'm afraid she'll fire me."

"You don't show it. Keep it up. She'll go for your jugular if she thinks you're vulnerable."

I took a deep breath. Things felt so different now for me. In only a few blocks, the heady romance of our date had slipped away and turned into something much deeper. A true intimacy. He understood me. And he liked me.

Something eased inside of me, letting go. I didn't have to guard myself with him. I didn't have to pretend to be something I wasn't.

I wasn't sure if it was real, but it felt glorious. He stayed silent, letting me feel it. My throat was so tight I couldn't have spoken at that moment.

We crossed the walkway over the FDR Drive to the edge of the island, and it was like we stepped into another world. The open air and the sound of the lapping water, the moonlight and tiny streamers of glowing clouds far above were a relief after the closed-in canyons of the city streets. The muted sound of traffic was behind us, and in front nothing but the black river that sparkled on the surface with a million lights.

We boarded a little yellow ferry taxi. We were among a couple of dozen people taking the ferry back to Brooklyn.

As the lines were cast, and the boat smoothly turned into the river, Hunter asked, "Are you cold?"

As the wind picked up, I shivered. "A little."

"We can go inside."

"No, I like it out here. Let's go to the back."

I went to the corner of the railing at the stern on the side closest to Manhattan. Behind us was the much lower dark outlines of buildings in Queens and Brooklyn. In front, Manhattan spread from side to side with crowded skyscrapers. Lit windows made a checkerboard pattern everywhere I looked.

Hunter put his arms around me, surrounding me with his warmth. I leaned back into him, feeling how solid he was. My head rested in the curve of his chest next to his breastbone, and he nuzzled my hair with his face.

Finally!

The way he held me, and breathed deep of me, made me close my eyes and sigh in pleasure. It felt so good!

I didn't dare speak, my heart was too full. I turned my face up to him, to his questing lips. Then we were kissing, and I was twisting in his arms, reaching up to touch his face with my fingertips.

For the first time, we kissed like lovers.

His lips were soft and eager on my mouth, as he pulled my waist closer to him. I stroked his face as he kissed me, loving the roughness of stubble on his cheek. Then his hair, so silky that my eyes opened in surprise as I caressed the back of his neck.

It was heaven! Everything I had dreamed of. His own passion drove me higher and higher—

Hunter suddenly broke off, glaring over my shoulder at a guy who was leaning against the railing too close to us. I could feel his body changing to defensive in an instant, as he shifted to stand between me and the stranger, curling his arm around me protectively.

But the guy didn't take a hint and move away. I could feel Hunter getting tenser, like pressure was building inside of him.

"Come on," Hunter murmured to me.

He took my hand and led me inside the ferry. But the bright lights made us both wince, and when he opened a door, I followed him inside instantly without realizing where we were going.

It was a tiny bathroom, not much larger than the one on an airplane. There was barely enough room for both of us to stand in front of the toilet, with a sink on one wall. There was a hatch overhead that was lifted up, letting in a fresh stream of air. It was not as bright in the bathroom with only one dim light bulb.

He cupped my face and kissed me again. Suddenly I didn't care that I was in a bathroom. I didn't think about anything. I needed to touch him, any way I could.

Kissing him was like waltzing to music only we could hear. By turns tender and fiercely eager, he kept pausing as if to try to cool us both down, as we stood there breathing each other in, our foreheads pressed together and his hands gently stroking my cheek.

His eyes searched me, wondering and amazed, as if he was surprised to be so overwhelmed. I felt the same way. It was sudden, almost shocking how quickly I wanted to dive into this man.

Hunter saw it, like he saw everything with his piercing eyes. He reached down to my dress, pulling it up, letting his palm trail over my naked thigh. His teeth caught his lip, and I let out my breath in a long release, lifting my face for him to kiss again.

"Please, Kali," he murmured in longing. "I must have you."

He ran his hands over my butt, squeezing and lifting up my skirt.

It felt so good. "Yes," I breathed.

"Are you sure?"

"Yes!"

Suddenly it was all movement, like we couldn't do it fast enough. He helped me pull down my panties and they ended up somewhere, I had no idea where and I didn't in the least bit care. All I wanted was his skin on mine, his hot, musky smell, the way his cheek scraped against me as he pulled me against him, lifting my leg high. I braced my foot against the wall behind him, shamelessly opening my legs for him as he pulled out a condom and tore it open. He smoothed it down on his erection, letting me see it for the first time. I gave him a stroke through the condom as he slid it all the way on. So long, and fat enough that I couldn't touch my finger and thumb around it ...

He drew in his breath with a hiss. So I stroked him again.

Hunter pushed my hands away, grabbing my thigh and pulling me against him again. "I must have you," he demanded, as if he couldn't stand it another moment, not being inside of me.

I arched my back and lifted myself for him, letting him press just a bit inside. I was more than ready. I'd been primed for days by him. But he was so big that he had to ease inside me with gentle pressure.

I grabbed his shoulders to brace myself, my butt resting on the edge of the sink and one leg against the wall. He slowly sank all the way inside of me, drawing a deep moan from me. We were locked together, his arm around my waist and holding up my leg, his fingers digging into my thigh. I could hardly move, I was pinned against the walls of the tiny space, as he began to plunge into me again and again.

He moaned out loud, throwing his head back. I held onto his neck as I panted faster, tension building inside of me, muscles straining to hold on, ready to burst. Never had it happened so fast! So hard, so fast…

Then he was staring into my eyes again, piercing me inside and out, demanding I surrender to him. "Yes, Kali," he growled. "Give it to me!"

Unable to look away, mesmerized by his eyes, my climax ripped through me. I cried out, on and on, as I came. Until I couldn't see him anymore. Until the bursting lights tore me away from myself.

He made a strangled sound. "Kali!" he cried out.

It almost made me come again, with pleasure washing through me. I wasn't sure how long it went on. "Kali," he kept murmuring into my hair.

We clung together, supporting each other, breathing heavily. I was flushed and moist now, and his neck was sweaty. I gave his skin a kiss, loving the fresh saltiness. I wanted to kiss him all over, like he had done with me the other night.

He was still deep inside of me. Impaling me like I would never be able to break free.

All of a sudden I remembered where we were. There were people sitting on the seats just on the other side of the door; a barely adequate door with a large crack along the bottom.

Embarrassment shot through me. "Oh, no!"

"Oh, yes!" He laughed out loud at the shock on my face.

Chapter 14

Hunter

I thought she was even more beautiful, all bashful and ducking her head when we finally left the bathroom. The boat was docking and there was only one guy who was close by watching us as we came out, but nobody else seemed to have noticed. I stared at the guy until he backed down and looked away. I wasn't taking any chances with Kali again. Everyone would know I was in complete control.

Even if I wasn't.

I didn't want to admit it to myself, and I didn't want Kali to know, but I was shaken. I never came like that, surprising myself, unable to hold back. I was known for fucking for hours if I wanted to.

It was shocking. I wanted her so bad I could taste it, like the tang of blood on my lips. My hand tightened on hers, feeling not at all like the conquering hero, even though she had just given herself to me in the bathroom of a ferry taxi. Instead I felt like she was about to float away from me, and there was nothing I could do about it.

"Do you need help?" Kali asked an older woman who was trying to push a wire handcart over the lip of the ferry onto the Brooklyn dock.

I called my mind back to order and lifted the handcart over the ledge, carrying it up the dock. It was too bumpy to pull it on the uneven boards of the dock. Kali walked next to the old woman, patiently listening to her explain something about feeding the cats in Gracie Mansion Park.

Kali was truly a sweet person. There was no reason to be nice to a crazy old cat lady, especially while she was dealing with her own embarrassment over their very public sex. But it wasn't a show she put on for the world. She had been gracious to the Chinese woman at the noodle shop, smiling and putting her hands together in a slight bow, imitating the woman's thanks to them for coming to her shop. And then she had stood with me in the park long after it got dark talking to the director of the Conservancy Garden, when she had thought she would be relaxing with a drink on a date after a long day at work.

I took hold of her hand again, even though I wasn't big on hand-holding. But I wanted contact with her. Actually, to be honest with myself, I needed to connect.

But it didn't help. As we walked to Kali's apartment, I felt myself pulling further and further away, in spite of our touch. She barely spoke, and only glanced at me a few times. I knew it was a natural reaction on her part to distance herself, especially if she had never done anything that wild sexually. For me, a little public sex was nothing. For her, she was confronting preconceptions about exhibitionism and slut shaming that every girl got growing up in America.

It was remarkable how open and uninhibited she was when we were playing together. But she was in new territory, so of course she would naturally withdraw to regroup.

But for the life of me, I hated it.

And that bothered me even more. I didn't want to care this much, so my own defenses snapped into place. I could hardly keep holding her hand, but I knew if I dropped it, she might never come back.

By the time we got to her place, I didn't feel like myself at all. I kissed her forehead, and then gently her lips. "I won't come up tonight," I said. "But I'll see you tomorrow morning at work."

She blinked at me like she did when she was confused. "Okay."

Then she hesitated as if she thought I was going to walk off. But I waited at the bottom of the stoop for her to unlock the door and let herself inside. Once she went through the inner door, I finally turned away.

Screwed, I'm seriously screwed, I thought. She had been as distant as I had felt there at the end, and I hoped I hadn't messed everything up. Why did I jump her on the ferry? Part of me desperately wanted to go upstairs with her, and curl up in bed with her, and wake up tomorrow with her.

That was the part of me that had let go of everything and came inside of her like a geyser. My dick throbbed in remembrance.

The other part of me, the sane part, said I needed to get a grip. Fast. I was letting my balls take over my brain, and that was a sure road to ruin. It was crazy to rush into things with her, especially when it involved the biggest project I ever got. This could be everything for me. Was I that volatile that I was going to self-implode right when I could reach for the brass ring?

I swore to myself I would take a break. No matter what happened, I wouldn't see Kali tomorrow. I needed to get some distance on this thing to get control of myself again.

Chapter 15

Kali

I really wished our evening hadn't ended that way. It had been
going so well, until I made love to him in a restroom! Our first
time...

Romance had left the building for good.

Not that it wasn't the most intense thing I'd ever felt. It was
thrilling and awful at the same time. Just thinking about it made the
muscles between my legs twinge, as if my body remembered and
was shamelessly begging for more.

But it was a public restroom! Why couldn't I hold out until we
got back to my place? It would have been so much better to lie with
him on my bed afterwards and float in that wonderful feeling of
bliss, rather than getting all freaked out because people were
watching us as we came out. And the way that old lady had winked
at me as we walked up the dock, she must have been listening, too.

Humiliating!

I knew from the beginning that I would get wild sex from
Hunter. I knew this wasn't the start of a life together. And now I had
proof. He could have waited fifteen minutes. If he wanted to make
love to me like a real lover, he would have waited until we got to my
place. But he didn't.

And then he left.

I knew full well that I couldn't handle casual sex with him. I
needed to get out now, before my heart got crushed.

But I couldn't stand the idea of not seeing him again. Not
kissing him again. Never feeling his arms hold me so tightly...

I was suddenly crying and didn't remember how I got started. It
hurt so bad, but thinking about him felt so good...

One more time, I bargained with myself. *I have to touch him one more time.*

It was bound to fall apart sooner rather than later. Look at what happened tonight! We both weren't happy in the end. If we were happy, he would be here right now, lying in bed with me, his arms around me.

I turned off the light. One more time, I promised myself. *If* I could get it.

Chapter 16

Hunter

I realized the next day at work that it was going to be hard to keep it cool with Kali while I was working with her. I kept admiring her curves as she leaned over the plans on the table, or the way she kicked off her heels when she sat down, sometimes dangling one off her foot to show her high arched instep. I hadn't even explored her feet yet, or her legs, or even her pussy…

No, I had been greedy, rushing to take her the first second I could, like a stupid teenager. And I was paying the price for it.

I found myself thinking about Kali rather than my project, and had to drag myself back again. But I did it. If I couldn't control myself, I shouldn't control another person.

By the end of the day, my concentration had returned. I had closed the door on the Kali-room in my mind, and focused on getting the last details in place for the demolition crew to start.

She also seemed to relax as the day went on, and we worked well together until it was past six. Then we ran into each other waiting at the elevator. There wasn't anyone else around, and Lindy had already left the reception desk.

I was determined to keep my promise to myself. I wouldn't see her tonight. But I was tempted, very tempted. She was looking at me expectantly.

Suddenly I recognized this moment. I knew what would happen if I was friendly but didn't say anything about getting together. She would feel snubbed, and she would be off balance from my sudden lack of pursuit. It was the first crack of the whip, the first call to heel.

Hell, I did it with Minx like second nature. Our entire relationship was built around me pushing her away and her crawling back to give me more. The only thing that made it okay was the fact that she was merrily polyamorous and was having sex with other people, including her girlfriend who she lived with. If I ever thought Minx was falling in love with me, I would end it immediately. I didn't want to torture someone for real, I only wanted to "torture" them.

So I hesitated because it was a habit with me, and because I knew I needed to get control of myself. But her smile faltered as she realized I was pushing her away, and I knew there was a difference between getting control over myself and controlling her.

"How about dinner tomorrow?" I asked.

Kali's face lit up and that made it worth it. "Sure."

"We'll meet at the deli then, after work."

We took the elevator down together talking about what we needed to do for work. But I split off from her outside, saying, "I've got a few things to do in the city. But I'll see you tomorrow."

I didn't want to get on the subway with her for the ride home, and have those protective feelings surge up inside of me again. I didn't think I would be able to resist walking home with her. Then she would invite me in, and there was no way I would be able to keep my cool, not when I had just barely recovered it.

That way lies madness…

She gave me a little wave good-bye. It felt strange as I turned around and walked away without even touching her hand, but there were SunTech employees passing right by us. Selina must have her own network of spies, so I had to keep it absolutely professional at work or I could myself. I had to be careful—the ways I could screw myself were multiplying with every passing day.

It was tough to walk away from Kali, but I made myself do it. And after I got home, I forced myself to go over the plans for the demolition. I didn't let myself think about Kali until I was lying in bed in the dark, and then I finally let go and masturbated over how luscious her body was, and the heady feeling of being inside of her.

I came almost as quickly as I did on the ferry. It was kind of galling, like I was thirteen years old again.

But I fell asleep instantly, so it worked out okay.

The next day the crew came in to set up the plywood barricade around most of the plaza. They left the portico running along the inner curve of the building open with an entrance to the sidewalk on either side. The center of the plaza was encircled by plywood, so everyone had to walk along the curving front of the building to get to the doors to the building in the center. Typical of most construction fencing, there were a few strategically-placed diamond-shaped holes in the blue painted wood so that people could see inside.

It was good, hard work, and I helped out. I only spoke to Kali once and saw her another time after that as she left the building for lunch. She was smiling as usual, and both she and Debby, the graphic designer, waved to me as they passed by.

I took a few minutes in the afternoon to make two phone calls to set up our romantic date. It was the same plan I had to cancel on Monday after I got the call from the Conservancy Garden.

I was going to show Kali that those clichés she thought were her real desires were nothing more than props people used while they pretended to live life. Romance was the last thing she was expecting from me, so she would have to look at me in a different light.

I was hoping it would make her start thinking about the roles *she* was playing in her life, and whether those roles fit as well as she thought they did.

I was feeling like myself again by the time work was over. I went to the deli early so I could buy Kali a flower. A single perfect red rose.

It felt like I waited outside the deli for a long time, but it was only a few minutes after six when she finally walked up. I met her and presented the rose to her with the appropriate flourish. She laughed in delight. But I still held back from touching her, afraid that a SunTech employee would pass by.

I had never imagined that I would be nervous, but one look from her laughing eyes threw me off balance again. Two days of hard work getting myself under control, and all I wanted to do was kiss her and never stop.

"Here's our car," I told Kali, as a black limo car pulled up.

"For us?" she asked in surprise.

"Yes, tonight you can put your heels back on. But I do love how much of a walker you are. I'd usually rather walk or bike than anything else."

"I thought I was plenty outdoorsy, swimming in the lake, cross-country skiing in the winter. But I don't think I ever walked this much since I came to the city."

We got into the towncar and I ordered, "The Beekman, please."

Kali took off her sneakers and tucked them back in her bag in place of her high heels. She was wearing a form-fitting gray skirt and jacket with a tiny ruffled edge on the lapels. The jacket gathered at the back of her waist, with a pleated flare of silvery gray fabric pointing down to her butt. The skirt did things for her ass that I didn't think were possible.

She curled up on the seat facing me. "What's the Beekman?"

"It's a surprise. I hope you like it."

The car took us all the way up to midtown via 2nd Avenue, stopping at 46th Street. "The Beekman Hotel," the driver announced as he pulled up.

I noticed that her brows drew together briefly, a fleeting frown. She didn't like it that I brought her to a hotel. As we walked through the lobby, she was reserved, letting me guide her but not smiling into my eyes the way she did before.

I could have told her then that we were going to the restaurant on the 26th floor with the most amazing 360-degree view of the city. But she thought I was taking her to a hotel room. She was pre-judging me because I was kinky and she thought this was only about sex. I was going to let her keep on assuming things, just to show her that she didn't know me at all.

It's true that on Monday I had considered reserving a room for after dinner, but her comfort was my main concern. I had decided to wait to see if she liked the idea of a neutral space for our first time having sex. But it turned out our first time was in the bathroom of a ferry taxi. And she said she wasn't kinky… little did she know herself.

Now, seeing her reaction to the posh hotel, I knew I wasn't going to ask her if she wanted to take a room here later. That would have to come from her, if she wanted it.

"This way," I said. I took her to the bank of elevators and pressed the button marked Top of the Tower. She noticed, and looked at me curiously again.

The doors opened and when we walked forward, the view opened up as the windows lined every wall.

"Ooo…," she breathed, turning one way and then the other. We were up in the midst of the towers of Midtown, some buildings taller, others lower. To the south was the dip of the skyline over Greenwich Village and Soho, with the SunTech tower glinting at the edge. Then further down was the giant tower cluster of downtown, with the Freedom Tower taller than the rest.

The lowering sun gleamed against the windows, creating brilliant refractions here and there. As we sat down at our table, Kali pointed out the tiny figures and cars passing by in the street directly below us.

"Have you ever been to a place like this before?" I had to ask.

"No! It's exactly what I thought the city would be like." Kali was charged with excitement, eager and looking at everything outside instead of the huge menu the waiter gave to each of us. But as the waiter began to go through the specials, she turned to give him her entire focus. I smiled at that. Whatever she did, she did with all of her being.

"Yum," she murmured after the waiter left. "That encrusted sea bass special sounds delicious."

This was the point where I would usually take over, guiding her choice or better yet, choosing for her. But that wasn't the game we were playing. This was a romantic date. So she picked out her own meal, including a glass of White Zinfandel. I did give the waiter her order since that was traditional date behavior.

"Have you been here before?" she asked.

"No, I usually prefer ethnic food." I gestured to the windows. "This place is for the view. You have to dine at least once in your life looking at the skyline of the city."

"Just once?" She looked around at the business crowd in the restaurant, with a few obvious tourists and dating couples sprinkled in. "I bet some of these people eat here all the time."

He shrugged. "If you're rich enough, you can eat out every night and not go to the same restaurant twice in the same year."

Our soup arrived, and it was time for me to start. Nobody could understand the anticipation I felt. This was real power, being able to dig into a person's soul. "Tell me more about growing up in Jefferson. You said you didn't like it?"

She shrugged. "My mom works at Jefferson College as an administrative assistant. It's one of the most expensive places you can send your kids to in the country. I ended up going there because of my mom, but I didn't fit in. The others came from all over, but it was like they spoke a different language that they all understood. And the money... you have no idea what money can buy. Talk about spoiled, these kids are spoiled. The cars, the clothes, the toys. Then there was me, bringing homemade sandwiches for lunch and working in the cafeteria part time."

I grimaced in sympathy along with her. It was clear in those few words. "Did your old friends from high school go to Jefferson, too?"

"No. Most of them didn't have the grades or a mom who had enough pull to get a full-ride scholarship. I made a few friends at Jefferson, some were study buddies, so it wasn't all bad."

"What about your dad?" I asked.

She looked up at me. "He fancies himself an artist. But he doesn't make much. He's dabbles in a lot of different things. Music. Acting. Woodworking."

It was the way she looked at me, with her voice gone hard and cold. This was the diamond at the heart of where it had all gone wrong for her.

"So he wasn't very supportive when you were growing up?" I asked.

"Not in the traditional sense. Oh, he's a lot of fun to be around. But he was never able to contribute much financially, and my mom had to struggle my whole life. I would never ask her for money now."

I smiled. "Let me guess. Your mom thinks journalism is a dead field and you could make more money in public relations."

Her chin jerked. "What? I guess so. We did the research together."

"That's what I thought." There was a lot more going on here than I first thought. But I couldn't push too hard. She was already resisting me.

Her eyes narrowed. "What about your family? Did they support you in becoming an artist?"

Now it was my turn to shrug. "I didn't need anyone's support. My mom depended on me because I took care of my brothers. I know what it's like to be different because we dressed different and spoke different and didn't know what all the other kids were into in whatever podunk town we were in at that moment. I'm not going to run away, so stand and fight was my only option. I got into a lot of fights. It made me independent. Rely on myself."

"Really? I'm trying to imagine you in a fight."

"You would have seen it for yourself if those guys in the subway had jumped me. Haven't you ever gotten into a fight?"

"No, not even close."

"That's right, you don't have brothers or sisters. My brothers and I scuffled all the time, over any little thing. They still do sometimes, more in a joking way now."

"You sound close to them."

"My younger brother David especially. I practically raised him. I had to put him in line a lot." I grimaced. "My dad was gone most of the time, but he wasn't above taking a swing at me if I thought I was being cocky. But what kind of authority can a father have when he's never home? I had to be the man of the house because he wasn't there."

She was nodding. "My dad was gone all the time, too. Out doing his thing. He's so flighty, you'd think it was his choice to give me my name."

"I've been meaning to ask you that. Is Kali short for something?"

She laughed and covered her mouth. "I should make you guess."

"Is it Kalista?" I figured that was the most likely candidate.
"Nope."

"Kaliope?" I guessed hopefully.
"No!"

"Well, I know you're *caliente* but I doubt your mom would name you that."

"My real name is Kalico, spelled with a K. My mom says there's a reason for it, but I've never been able to get her to tell me."

"Really? A mystery… I love that. It's the perfect name for you, my sweet Kalico-cat spelled with a K."

We talked through the whole dinner, taking our time over everything, including a shared dessert that she picked out. This time it was a berry tart with whipped cream.

The only time I slipped out of romance-mode was at the end. I speared the last fat blueberry on my fork and with teasing eyes, held it out to her. She knew immediately what I was doing. She opened her mouth and stuck out her tongue slightly, urging me on. I popped the berry into her mouth and she bit into it.

"Yummy!" she said around the juice.

Maybe it was a romantic gesture, after all. But feeding her felt like control to me, like power. Like I wanted to do more.

I took her downstairs. As impatient as I was, I would never suggest we get a room. I knew now that she wouldn't be comfortable in a fancy hotel room. I didn't want to do anything that would remind her of college and feeling like she was out of her depth surrounded by rich kids.

The doorman got a cab for us and opened the car door. She thanked him as she got inside, as sweet to him as she was to everyone.

In the cab, she brushed the rose against her lips, absently looking out the window at the moving lights. I wanted her closer than that.

I lifted her hand and began to kiss her fingertips. She murmured and turned to curl up against me, leaning her head on my shoulder as I kissed the back of her hand. I went nice and slow, letting her feel every touch, every tiny lick. Then I turned her hand over and nibbled on the flesh of her palm, as she squirmed and made soft sounds, not quite moans, as I tickled and bit her.

From her palm, I moved to her wrist. The flesh of her arm was sweet, firm and softer than velvet. I felt more than heard her indrawn breath as I let my stubble scrape along her skin. Her head was thrown back, her mouth opened with her quickening breath, as I buried my mouth in the crook of her arm, the choicest part, where I would bite into her flesh and feed from her if I was a vampire. I could feel the pulse of her blood under my mouth, feeling how vulnerable she was.

It felt like we reached Kali's apartment in a flash. She looked similarly dazed. We were both riding a euphoric high. And I was only kissing her arm! My dick was raging hard and demanding attention, my balls clenching in anticipation. Like, telling me to get inside her. *Now*.

Somehow I got through the mechanics of paying for the cab and getting upstairs with her and behind a locked door. I could hardly restrain myself, I wanted to throw her down and take her right there, with all of our clothes on. But I couldn't lose control like that. I did that the first time we had sex, and it had taken two days for me to get a grip again.

I hooked a finger over the button in the center of her jacket and pulled her closer. She took a step, looking up expectantly. Waiting to see what I was going to do.

Flicking open the button, I pulled her jacket down over her shoulders. She was wearing a silk shell underneath. I turned her gently around and unzipped her skirt, pulling it down. I wanted to get a good look at that ass.

Full and round, with deep curves, nothing hidden by the panties she was wearing. Two perfect dimples on either side at the top. What a butt! I could imagine it turning red as I smacked her, gently at first, then harder and harder as she writhed in my lap against my cock...

I smoothed my hand over one butt cheek, and she shivered, wrapping her arms tight over her chest. I remembered that she was a novice, and a spanking was not the place for me to start tonight. But I would give her a spanking soon enough. She would see it wasn't anything like what she thought it was.

With her back still turned to me, I tugged down her panties. She almost stopped me, but I pulled more insistently, and she let go without a word.

She really liked to struggle against her submission.

Facing her back, I lifted up her shirt, pulling it over her head. Then I undid her bra, sliding it down off her arms. She was still wearing her high heels, but nothing else.

Slowly, I turned her to face me again. Her arms were hiding herself, one over her breasts and her other hand cupping her crotch. She was looking up at me, wary because she was naked and I was completely clothed. It was the quickest way to make someone feel vulnerable.

I felt better already. No matter how much she fucked with my mind, I could fuck her body and make her belong to me.

"You can say no any time, remember?" I asked. "Only you like to say no, don't you? So say 'stop' if you really mean it."

She nodded.

"Repeat it," I murmured. "Stop."

"Stop."

"I'm going to bind you now."

I put a hand on her arm as she looked up at me wordlessly.

"Come on." I took her hand and led her into the bedroom, grabbing my messenger bag on the way. It was stuffed with everything I needed for work. And something else.

My hand closed around the soft bundle and pulled it out. The coils of thick nylon rope had been dyed a gray-green color. I held it up to her face, looking from her eyes to the rope.

"I thought so. It's exactly the same color as your eyes." I had bought the rope a few years ago, attracted by the shade, but I had never used it before. When I had found it again in my rope bag, tucked away forgotten in the bottom, I had turned it over in my hands thinking of Kali's eyes and how I would tie her up with it. It was as thick as my little finger, and as soft as a silk scarf.

Picking up one hand, I wrapped two loops around her wrist and tied the end in a knot that wouldn't slip. I left the long tail of the rope hanging. Then I tied a loop from another piece of rope around her other wrist. Her breathing quickened.

Looking deeply into her eyes, I moved her back against the bed, pushing her down to sit. She held onto me with her gaze. I pushed her down to lie back, going with her, so I laid sprawled half over her.

"I'm going to finish kissing the rest of your body," I told her. "I did the top half last time…"

"Oh…," she breathed.

I covered her face with kisses and nibbled her neck, chest and arms, slowly pulling each wrist up until she lay with her hands reaching out to each corner of the bed. One at a time, I tied them tightly. She resisted a little, but was lulled by my kisses. She hissed every time my teeth sunk into her, pressing her flesh in my mouth. Love bites were almost as good as kisses, in my book.

Then I started down, kissing her belly, finally able to go lower, to stroke the soft skin above her silky pussy, to kiss the top of her thigh, blowing gently on her short reddish brown hair, but not touching her cleft, not yet. I wanted her to go wild, and I couldn't let her do that unless her legs were also tied. I had two more ropes I'd cut, silvery green ropes that looked so beautiful against her fair skin.

I kissed all the way down her leg, taking my time, exploring every hollow and curve of her leg down to her ankle. Then her sensitive feet. She tried to pull away when I pushed my tongue between her toes, but I quickly wrapped the loops of rope around her ankle and tied it to the bedpost with a few twists.

"Hunter?" she asked, jolted into awareness when she felt her leg was suddenly held in place.

I stroked her waist with my hands, firm and soothing. I lulled her back again, slowly straightening her free leg and when I reached the bottom of her foot, massaging it to relax her, then tying the knot before she realized what was happening.

I got up and stood by the bed looking down at her. She gasped, feeling herself completely bound, laid out naked for me. She was breathing faster for me, tugging against the ropes.

I felt a rush like I had never felt before. She was completely in my power, and her eyes said she knew it. I could do whatever I wanted with her. She couldn't help showing a tinge of fear when my fists opened and closed, showing my eagerness to get my hands on her. I would do it. I would make her white flesh turn pink and then red, swelling slowly as I made her nerves sing.

I leaned over and grabbed each of her wrists, digging my fingertips in. My nails were nice and smooth, just long enough for her to feel the scrape of them against her skin. I dragged my nails down her arms to her shoulders, leaving faint pink lines trailing behind.

"Ohh...Hunter," she breathed, stretching into the sensation. "That feels good..."

I kept going down, trailing my fingertips all the way down the sides of her legs to her feet. She shivered as I made goose bumps rise on her skin. It would get her blood going, bring it to the surface, and make her eager to feel more.

Then I leaned over between her legs and kissed her pussy, not so softly this time, more insistently. Her lips were like a folded flower, pink and fresh. I licked up to find the tiny bud of her clit, letting my tongue swirl around it before pressing my mouth into her, shaking my head back and forth slightly.

Her reaction was incredible. She cried out, high and piercing, as she fought against the ropes. But she couldn't close her legs. I pushed her knees further apart, and dived in again, licking and sucking on her until her cries rose with force. I pressed on and on, as she gasped out, saying no a couple of times, but never stop... so I never stopped.

When she came, her hips bucked, pressing herself against my mouth. I dug my fingernails into her sides below her breasts, raking them slowly down her waist and over her hips, all the way down her thighs and down to her calves. I dug in, wanting to mark her. Wanting to claim her as my own.

Her cries rose louder, urgent, guttural, as if wrenched from deep inside of her. I could feel the rhythmic clenching in the muscles of her thighs, my own cock jerking in sympathy, as the pain prolonged her orgasm. I held on for dear life, as her hips heaved beneath me.

I clawed my way up, no thought of anything but getting *in*. She was dripping wet from my mouth and her cum. I had barely the presence of mind to roll on a condom before I put the tip of my cock against her.

"Do you want it?" I growled.

"Yes!"

"Beg me for it, Kali."

"Oh, yes, Hunter, *please. Please....*"

"Say 'yes, Sir!' Kali." I was holding myself back by sheer force of will, but I wanted it all.

"Yes... yes, Sir!"

I pushed against her, sliding my cock inside with one long, heavenly push, all the way to the hilt. She cried out again. It was almost too much for me.

My hips thrust wildly against her, driving into her, pinning her to the bed. It went on and on, with waves of pleasure carrying me higher and higher, an endless motion. I would never stop, never let her go, stay inside of her forever…

My own cry rose with hers as I came deep inside of her, my cock pulsing, our bodies pulsing together. Locked together forever…

As I realized I was breathing in synch with Kali, I also realized I was lying on top of her, completely relaxed and probably crushing her with my weight. I shifted slightly off her, regretfully letting my dick slide out of her. She let out a little sound, rubbing her cheek against my hair, as if she didn't want to let me go.

My arms tightened around her, my throat clenching up at the sudden feeling that she trusted me. She had let go completely, and so did I. I was supposed to be the ever-ready guy, but it felt like I wouldn't be able to come again today. She had drained me, taken everything I had to give. Because she gave me everything she had.

I wanted nothing more than to lie there cuddling with her, but she had been tied up for a while and struggling against the ropes. I needed to check to see if any knots had tightened. I touched her hand and it was cool. It needed more blood flow.

So moving carefully, I untied her wrists, leaving the other end of the rope tied to the bed. That would make it easier to tie her up next time. When I unbound her ankles, she moaned and curled into the fetal position. "That feels so good…"

I chafed her wrists and ankles, warming them up and making sure the circulation was flowing nicely. Then I helped her to the bathroom to wash up. She was still a little wobbly. By the time I pulled on her nightshirt, she was yawning. She plunged into bed, shifting over so there was plenty of room for me.

"No need for aftercare tonight," I said with a slight laugh.

"Who needs any care after that?" she mumbled through the pillow. "That was nothing but care! It felt like you touched me all over."

"I fucked you all over, that's for sure." I was still smiling. "And there's more to come. There's a party this weekend I want to take you to."

She shook her head, her face still buried. "I'm going upstate this weekend to see my parents. Didn't I tell you?"

"No." I stood next to the bed looking down at her. "Can't you go up on Saturday morning?"

She turned her head to look at me with one sleepy eye. "I'm sorry, Hunter. I would love to, but my parents are expecting me. It takes four hours to get there and if I go on Saturday, the whole day is wiped out. As it is, I have to leave work by three to make the train."

Kali put her head back down with a yawn. It was settled. I had the sinking feeling there was no way I could budge her.

She looked so peaceful lying there, snuggled into the pillow, a slight smile curving up the corners of her lips. That wicked curve of the corner of her mouth.

Even though I knew, rationally, that I couldn't expect her to give up plans for me, it bothered me. The fact that I wanted to try to convince her bothered me even more. Why didn't she say something sooner?

It was stupid to question it. I should accept it for what it was. But the questions were there, and I knew I was lost in Kali again.

Deep down, we fit together hand in glove. At first it was her quiet beauty, that dressed-down, corporate gray, flashing-out-at-moments kind of beauty. Then it was her fighting spirit that refused to let me walk all over her without her consent. Then it was her valiant poise when we were being pursued by the homeboys. I wanted a woman like that, one who could face down the enemy hand-in-hand with me, trusting me completely.

Plus she blew my mind sexually. I was supposed to be blowing her mind. But she swept me up in her response and carried me along like a tsunami. I *wanted* to be carried off by her. I wanted to surrender to the maelstrom, for the first time in my life.

But I couldn't. I was always reaching for her, but she wasn't reaching back.

So I did the only thing I could do. I turned off the lights and

119

took her apartment key from her key chain. I went outside and locked her in, slipping the key under the door.

Chapter 17

Kali

I didn't know what to think when I woke up the next morning and found out that Hunter hadn't stayed the night. I must have passed out on him. But it was his fault for driving me out of my mind.

I found the key on the floor and put it back on my keychain. All of my clothes were scattered around the living room where he had tossed them, with my bra hanging over the back of my desk chair. Gathering up everything and throwing them in the hamper, I got ready for work.

My body throbbed in a lot of new and different ways. There were long pink streaks down my sides and my legs where he had scratched me. In places he had dug deeper, leaving faint red flecks of blood embedded in my skin. And my wrists and ankles were chafed by red rope burns, reminders of what we had done. My cheek had a pink patch where it had been rubbed raw by the stubble on his face.

The way he had tied me up spread-eagle on the bed—I couldn't believe that was me! But it felt so natural, moving from one thing to the next. I rubbed the slightly raised scratches on my skin. If someone had done that to me when I wasn't aroused, I would have hated it. *I'm sure of it.*

Hunter had touched me everywhere; I couldn't deny him. And the focused, intense look on his face made me feel like there was nothing else in the world except for me.

Only I knew that wasn't true. I was one among many.

When I saw Hunter at work, both of us smiled like we were getting away with something.

But Hunter was fully back in work mode and busy with the demo part of the project. I didn't need to be so hands-on during this stage, so I barely saw him for the next two days. He didn't ask me about my weekend again. I wished I wasn't busy. I would have liked to meet his friends.

By the time I left the office with my overnight bag on Friday, I was worried. My self-bargain for "one last time" looked like it was the truth. We had exchanged a few flirty texts, but that was it. I had no idea what he was feeling to cause such a distance between us.

Maybe for him, this was normal.

It was only on the train heading north that I really started thinking. Four hours was a long time to think, and the time served me well. I had been floating around in a euphoric fog for the past week. But Hunter had admitted that our romantic date was not his usual thing. He did it for me.

He gave me romance so I would let him tie me up.

And it was true that our lovely dinner and sharing our pasts had made me comfortable with him again. I had bargained with myself to play with him one last time. Then I would have to ask him the hard questions—what about Minx? What about other women? What about his future? Could he see having a relationship with me?

Now I had gotten my "one last time," and it had been more than I had hoped for. But it was looking more and more like it was just another game to him, not the beginning of a beautiful relationship.

He said it himself: "I fucked you all over."

Not—*I made love to you all over.* He wasn't making love to me. He was fucking me. That meant sex, not love. It was all play to him; playing sex games.

It was full dark when the train pulled into Utica, the closest big town to Jefferson. My mom was waiting on the platform, her arms wrapped around herself for warmth in the chill night air. I ran over and gave her a hug, and was struck by how small she felt. She had always been very lean and spare, with deep worry lines in her face aging her prematurely.

Jenny Jones had struggled, and you could see it. I could see it now like I never could before.

"Where's dad?" I asked.

"At the village board meeting. There was some kind of problem with the sidewalks, and he has to go make his case, of course." There was a bitter edge to my mom's voice. It was because of my dad. If it wasn't the band taking up his time, it was some volunteer project or civic group that he was involved with.

It was a familiar feeling, that my dad was out of my reach. When he was around, he was the most engaging and playful dad a girl could have. But looking back, I mostly remembered long hours talking alone with my mom in the evenings as we baked or crafted together.

I usually checked in with my mom at least once a week. She was worried about me living in the city. I had told her about my dinner dates with Hunter, but I hadn't gone into many details.

"So tell me about this new guy," my mom said, while we were still on the train platform. "You've gone out three times, right? That's usually when it fizzles for you."

"It may be the same with this one." More like a nuclear explosion than a fizzle, but I couldn't tell my mom that.

"Oh? What was it this time?"

"I don't think he wants a relationship. He's so good-looking. He can get any girl he wants."

My mom gave me a sharp look. "How do you know?"

I realized I was going to have to tread carefully or I would end up confessing the whole sordid thing. And I couldn't imagine forming the words to tell Jenny Jones about kinky sex. Or her reaction if I tried. My mom would never get over her horror at the thought of her little girl getting tied up.

"He's gorgeous, mom. Plus I met his girlfriend. Minx. I'm not sure if she's still in the picture."

"You don't know? What on earth have you been talking about?"

"Everything else." I gave her a rundown of Hunter's background and career.

As expected, Jenny didn't like it one bit. Our family knew what it was like being on the less-advantaged side of the class divide, so my liberal mom would never say Hunter was not our kind of people. But the thought hung between us unspoken, and from the frown on her face, she was troubled by her own reaction.

"Even if he does want to get married," Jenny said, "it sounds like he isn't ready for it."

"Go ahead and say it—he sounds like dad."

"Well… yes, in that he may not be willing or able to take on a steady job to help support a family." Now my mom looked even more upset. "But you like him?"

I sighed. "More than any other guy I've ever met."

Jenny was silent as she turned onto our street and slowly drove past the large grassy square that was meticulously maintained by the village. Much further down, nearly outside the town on a back street next to the canal, there was our little clapboard house. It had steep gables and ancient trees in the front yard arching over the roof of the porch.

Suddenly I was back in reality, and all the weird, crazy stuff in the city seemed far away.

My home was a doll's house, picturesque and old-fashioned with wood trim and banisters, with the kitchen as large as the living room, and only two bedrooms and a bath upstairs. I loved our house with a passion that nearly rivaled my mom's, who had worked a second job at the pharmacy to get us a real home. My dad had done a lot of the repairs on the house, painting and finishing the floors. It had fallen into disrepair after foreclosure, but together they had brought it back to life.

My mom and I hung out like we usually did. Jenny gossiped about the college and her friends in town, and I was grateful I didn't have to say much. She had messages from some of my old friends to come to the Tavern on Saturday to see everyone.

It was ten o'clock when my phone jingled with a text. I grabbed it from my bag, and a smile spread over my face as I read the text from Hunter: *Did you get home ok?*

I texted back: *Yes. How's your party?*

Not much fun without you. Sleep well.

My smile faded just a bit. So he didn't want to talk. But I was glad he reached out even though he was busy.

My mom was watching me. "A lot of emotions just crossed your face really fast, Kali. This guy has turned you upside-down."

I covered my face with both hands. "I know!" Then I dropped them. "I know…"

After that, I didn't want to talk about it, so I wished my mom a good night and went upstairs to my room. Even though I didn't live here, it was still my room. It looked caught out of time, with my college-self still imprinted here. For the first time, I thought it would be better if my parents turned it into something else. Space was very precious in our home. But Jenny would resist the idea. She once said that she went and read in my room every now and again, because it made her feel like her little girl wasn't so far away.

I thought it was sweet when she told me that. But now, looking around, it just felt weird. I had changed so much already that I knew the *Kali* she was remembering wasn't really me anymore. Things had changed the day I found out the job at SunTech wasn't in Albany, as we both thought, but in New York City. Jenny wanted me to decline the interview, and I told her no way!

The idea of moving to the city was bigger than I had ever dreamed. All I wanted was to get out of Jefferson, as far away as I could. But New York… I went through with the trip to New York for my interview in spite of all of her objections. And that single-minded determination must have helped because I got the job.

Things hadn't been the same between us since. How could it? I only came home for a couple nights every couple of months.

But tonight felt like old times. Comfortable, but narrow and boring.

I lay awake in my bed under the eaves that night, wondering what Hunter was doing at the party. What kind of party was it? Was Minx there? Did he take another girl? The thought of him tying up Minx made my teeth clench. The thought of him having sex with

Minx made me want to scream. I couldn't stand not knowing. What if he was touching some other woman "all over" like he did with me?

Now that image was stuck in my mind—Hunter tying up Minx, who looked incredibly hot with her slinky, tattooed body. I wasn't sure I could ever let him tie me up again. All I would think about was him doing it to Minx, who was more exotic and more experienced than me. The thought of it made my stomach sink in dread. There was no way I could compete with that.

I hated being compared to other girls and judged inadequate. I'd rather not compete at all. And how could Hunter *not* compare me to his other women?

It was a long, fitful night and I didn't get much sleep.

The next morning my dad was cooking pancakes in the kitchen when I went down. He greeted me with a hug and gave me a stack of three, the way I liked it.

There were no worries about straying into sensitive Hunter territory with Danny Jones. Instead my dad asked a ton of questions about the sundial project. I had sent him bulletins the whole way through the contest, and he had picked out the sundial early on as a favorite. He said the design was "a brilliant use of space." I didn't bother to tell him that I was dating the sculptor. If it was over, I didn't want to get him excited that I was dating an artist. And I knew my mom would never tell him anything we had talked about privately.

As we ate together, my dad told me about a set he was building and painting for the next production at the Jefferson Community Theater. After a hiatus of several years, the JCT was again his current passion, and he mentioned the casting and directing decisions he was involved in. He also crowed over his victory at the community board meeting the night before, winning some point about the sidewalks that I couldn't quite understand.

It was a little sad. I had been disillusioned about Danny Jones since fifth grade. Before then, I had always seen his projects as grand adventures that proved my dad was meant for bigger things. He always told me he never got the chance to truly spread his wings, and I believed him.

Until one day my mom called him a big fish in a little pond. And I thought that meant he was a big man in town. I told one of my friends, who laughed at me, and he got all the others to laugh at me, too. When I told Jenny, she explained what it really meant. That my dad was a nobody who would never be successful because he wasn't good enough.

I remembered the horrible feeling in my stomach, realizing my dad wasn't magical. He wasn't on the verge of something big, like he always said. People in town laughed at him. The loveable loser. A man who couldn't support his family, who made my mom work twice as hard to take care of us.

It wasn't a fun trip home. I spent the rest of the weekend thinking about Hunter, torn between wishing I could see him and kiss him, and thinking it would have been better if I had never met him. On the outside, I smiled and talked to a few of my old high school friends. They said they were jealous that I was living in the city, but strangely they didn't ask me questions about it. Instead they brought me up to speed on all the doings in the village, as if nothing else existed but their own little world. I could finally see how I had grown up constricted inside a small circle of social intrigue and round-robin betrayals.

More than anything, I noticed a difference in my parents. They had never been close, but now they rarely spoke to each other. They led completely separate lives.

It was sad, really sad. Now that I was back home, I remembered the struggle it had been to get here, into this house and to pay for my education—even with the scholarship it had been hard. I got my first job at sixteen and had been working ever since.

How could I choose hardship for my future, for my children? When I knew the cost. I had watched my parents' relationship deteriorate from the moment I was aware of such things. How could any relationship survive when the struggle was that difficult? When only one person was willing to pull their weight? Even a rock-solid commitment would have a tough time winning through adversity like that.

Jenny didn't have to say much. But on the way to the train, she said quietly, "Don't make the same mistake I did, Kali. Make sure you choose a man who will work hard to make a good life with you."

My lips pressed together briefly. "I know, Mom."

My mom looked very lonely as she waved good-bye. I got on the train to go back to the city.

I knew that the rest of my life depended on decisions I made now. I had to be sure I didn't make a mistake.

Chapter 18

Hunter

I had an awful weekend. I wasn't used to being denied by a woman. I knew if I could see Kali in her hometown, then I could decode her like the Rosetta Stone. But that wasn't possible.

I checked the train schedules and knew when she'd be pulling into Penn station. I didn't want to ask her out over the phone. I needed to see her face when I spoke to her. I needed to find out what she was thinking.

When I ran into Kali at work Monday morning next to the construction fence, a bunch of people were around. She asked for an update on the progress of moving the fountain up to Central Park. I felt like the blue plywood wall was standing between us instead of next to us.

She gave me no chance to ask her out, and by the time the truck arrived to pick up the fountain, I knew it was going to have to wait. Maybe she was backing off because I had withdrawn after our last scene. But that usually made women chase after me more. Kali definitely wasn't chasing after me. If anything she was as polite and distant as I had been last week. Maybe she had talked to her friends at home and had thought better of going down the kinky brick road with a dark, handsome stranger.

A crowd gathered to watch the sections of fountain being loaded by a forklift onto the back of a semi-truck. I was in the thick of it, directing the workers to keep people out of the way and making sure the rigging was secure. I couldn't let anything go wrong, not with several reporters standing near Kali and Selina, taking photos of the move.

When we were done, I went up to the Central Park Conservancy Garden in the truck. None of the reporters came with us, so Kali didn't either. The reporters would come back in a few weeks once the fountain was reassembled and hooked up, with the new cobblestone plaza laid around it. I helped the efficient Central Park crew as they unloaded the pieces of the fountain and laid them carefully behind cyclone fencing near the fountain's final resting place.

Finally, as I left the garden, I texted her: *Want to watch the sunset at my place? You have to see the view from my roof.*

There was a longer pause than usual for her reply. Finally it came: *I want to talk not play.*

We can do that, I wrote back.

Not at your place. Or mine. I know what will happen.

So I wasn't kidding myself—she was putting on the brakes. I couldn't argue with that. I kept trying to put the brakes on myself, only I wasn't having much luck. Maybe she would.

I checked my watch. She should be leaving SunTech right about now, and I didn't want her to wait in a park for me while I grabbed a subway back downtown.

How about Katz's on Houston & Ludlow? I asked. *I can be there in 30 min.*

Ok, she texted back.

...

By the time I got there, she was already seated at one of the side tables waiting for me. Usually I went directly to the counter to order, but the tables were separate and more private, so it was a good choice.

"Is this really where Harry Met Sally was filmed?" I noticed that she didn't get up to greet me with a hug and a kiss.

I glanced up at the placard dangling over one of the center tables. "Yes, that scene where she fakes an orgasm."

"I can't wait to tell my mom. It's one of her favorite movies. She always makes me watch it whenever it's on TV."

I was suddenly glad we were meeting at the restaurant instead of my place. She was right, I wouldn't have been able to keep my

130

hands off her. Her delighted laughter made me want to take her in hand, and make her beg for more. It was exactly the wrong time for me to get lost in a lustful haze staring into her eyes and remembering how she looked spread out naked for me to use as I wanted.

I ordered the pastrami sandwich for her, because it was the best. But she quickly requested no mustard to the waiter.

"It's not the same without mustard," I said.

"I hate mustard." She smiled at the waiter as she handed back the menu.

"Okay, good to know."

There was an awkward silence as I tried to figure out the best way to pierce the wall between us.

She toyed with a fork. "So how was the party?"

"Not bad," I shrugged. "It was a birthday party for a friend of mine."

"Where was it?"

"At a local fetish club."

She blinked. "Do people have sex there?"

"Not like intercourse sex. We do BDSM. And we hang out with our friends."

"Which one did you do?"

I hesitated. She noticed, so I quickly added, "It wasn't much of anything. I gave my friend her birthday spanking. She's a Domme, so usually she's the top. But she does bottom to certain people, and she asked me months ago if I would do it for her at her party."

Kali looked at me for a few seconds. I had a hard time figuring out what she was thinking. She was so reserved.

The waiter came up with our root beers. Kali waited until he left. "What's her name?"

"Heather. I've known her for a long time. Practically since I came to New York. She's one of the friends I want to introduce you to."

"So tell me what you did. I want to know more about your life is like."

131

I figured I might as well take the plunge. Kali would have watched the scene if she had come to the party. Maybe this was better. "I put her over my lap and gave her thirty hard smacks, alternating on each butt cheek. Plus one to grow on."

"Over your lap? Was she naked?"

"She was wearing a g-string. It's not the same if you spank someone through clothing." I noticed Kali pulled back slightly. "It wasn't sensuous! Everyone was standing around egging me on and laughing at her as she begged me to go softer. But she didn't use her safeword, and I knew she wanted a really hard spanking to mark her birthday."

The waiter returned with our sandwiches and placed them on the table. Kali stared down at hers as if she had never seen such a thing before. The image I had just placed in her mind was apparently throwing her for a loop. To me, it seemed so tame. Innocent, almost, in the context of the scene. Like hugging someone.

"Have you ever had sex with Heather?" Kali suddenly asked.

"Sure. But that ended years ago."

"So you stay friends with your lovers?"

"I try to. Sometimes it's not possible. But there are only a certain number of parties and events, so you're bound to run into your past."

Kali shook her head slightly as she removed half the meat from her sandwich so she could fit her mouth around it. I took a bite of my own pastrami with mustard, watching her.

We ate for a while, until I couldn't stand the silence any longer. It would be better if she would just talk, but if she wouldn't, I would have to drag it out of her.

"Didn't you see any old boyfriends when you went home?" I asked.

She swallowed. "I saw my grade school crush at the hardware store, if that's what you mean. He used to be the cutest boy in school, but now he's fat and kind of slow. It was weird how he wanted to talk to me, when he pretty much ignored me when we were kids."

"No one more recent than that?"

"Hmm, come to think of it, Johnny was at the Tavern on Saturday. I dated him in my Junior year in high school. He's married now and his wife was at home with their two babies."

I felt an absurd stab of jealousy. "So you see how it happens."

Kali shook her head. "I didn't say two words to Johnny. Not quite like spanking your near-naked ex-girlfriend as she lies over your lap."

I met her eyes, trying to will her to understand. "It wasn't sexual for me, Kali. I don't feel that way about Heather."

"What about Minx?"

"What about her?"

She laughed shortly, but she wasn't amused. "Did you see her this weekend?"

"Yes. She came over to clean the loft."

Kali looked away. "Oh. Right."

"We didn't have a scene. I didn't even touch her. I didn't want to."

"I'm sure it satisfies her or she wouldn't be scrubbing your floors."

I didn't know what to say to that, because she was right. Minx had fallen at my feet and kissed the ground in front of my toes, begging me to punish her for coming over before without permission. She said she would take anything, do anything, as long as I forgave her. She was trembling, wracked with emotion, as I ordered her to leave on Sunday. My denial was winding her up to a feverish pitch. I knew she would follow through on her promise, and there were all sorts of dirty, demeaning things I could make her do.

But I didn't want to.

"I only want you, Kali. I don't want those other women."

"But there are so many women in your life. And you're still doing very intimate things with them. Hunter, I can't be in a relationship with someone who's seeing other women. I have to trust you."

I nodded. "I can understand why you feel that way. But we've only just started to date."

"Will it be different later? You like to be free, I can tell, to do whatever you want."

"To be honest, yes. I've done that for a long time."

"So you don't mind it when Minx sleeps with another man? Or if I did?"

"You?" Suddenly it all fell into place. "Not you. I don't think I could stand it if another man touched you."

Now she was really looking at me. I was finally reaching her.

"You don't know what you've done to me," I confessed. "I think about you all the time. If you don't want me to see Minx anymore, then I won't. I won't get kinky with any of my friends. I want to explore this with you."

"You want a real relationship with me?" she asked.

"I want you to stop pulling away from me. It's driving me crazy."

Her mouth fell open, as if I had just said something shocking. "I see."

I didn't understand. "What do you see?"

"It's all a game to you, isn't it? I'm something to conquer, to win over. And then what? Do you really want to get married and have kids?"

I was at a loss. "I don't know. I never met anyone that made me want that before."

She refused to even meet my eyes. I had almost had her! "You're stuck in your idea of what's right for you," I told her, "instead of seeing what we have together."

"It's the chase," she said slowly. "I'm running away, so that's why you want me. But as soon as I stop running and try to have a real relationship with you, then *you're* going to run."

"No, I won't." But I wasn't sure about that, now was I? I was supposed to be prying into her brain to figure out how she ticked, not the other way around.

She sadly tried to smile, but it didn't work. "You know I'm right, Hunter."

"But this is different."

"I'm just harder to catch than girls like Minx. Because I want more than sex, Hunter. You're the one who said I should figure out what *I* want. And one thing I know for sure—even if it *is* fantastic, mind-blowing sex, that's not enough for me."

I didn't know what to say. It was true that I quickly grew bored when women chased after me. I loved the pursuit, the subtle game of luring a woman in, but so few were elusive. At some point they threw themselves at me, and that ruined everything. Then I spent the last half of the relationship trying to peel them off and keep them at a distance. I was doing that now with Minx.

But nobody had ever turned me on like Kali did, with her quiet reserve and proud, independent ways. The secrets she hid inside of her.

Kali stood up. "Thanks for dinner, Hunter. I'll see you at work tomorrow."

I snatched hold of her wrist, keeping her from turning away. "Is that all? When I know you want me as much as I want you?"

"You're not going to break my heart, Hunter. It's already hard to leave now." Gently, she twisted her arm to get me to release her. "We don't want the same thing."

As she walked away, I felt like I couldn't take a deep breath. How could she walk away from me? I wanted to run after her, to shake some sense into her.

Suddenly I knew how the women in my life had felt, when they had cried and begged me to not break up with them. I acted sad and wise, just like Kali was being with me.

She didn't care about me. Or she couldn't walk away. Like I had walked away from those women who I didn't care about.

It felt like a knife in my gut. Twisting and torturing me.

I had to sit there and not run after her. Like the more pathetic girls who ran after me.

It took a long time, but when I finally left, I had one clear determination—I wasn't going to lose her. That wasn't going to happen.

If she needed proof that I wanted more than sex with her, then I would give her that proof. Whatever it took.

...

When I saw her the next day, she wouldn't meet my eyes when she spoke to me. It was like she was a different person. My Kali had gone back to visit her hometown, and a different Kali had returned. That was some powerful stuff happening upstate. I wished I knew what it was.

I had to fix this. Fast.

But I barely saw her all week. I was stuck in my studio creating the numeral medallion patterns for the sundial. They had to be sent to the foundry where I would make the molds the following week, so working nearly around the clock, I carved twelve medallions out of slabs of clay.

When my brother Drew texted to say he was coming into the city on Friday and wanted to get together, I was irritated. I was too busy working! And I needed to figure out what to do about Kali. I didn't want family problems dragging me back into that old familiar pit of never-ending pain.

Then I realized this was my chance. Kali wanted proof of my sincerity. I would ask her to meet my brother. I would bring her into my life, and share the ugly secrets of my past. I would make myself as vulnerable to her as I wanted her to be with me.

The thought of exposing myself that way sent a shudder through me. She would judge me. How could she not? It might even change her opinion about me.

But it was time to man-up. How badly did I want this? Enough to expose myself and risk more rejection?

Whatever it takes, I swore to myself.

I knew Kali wouldn't let me speak to her alone, so I texted her, *I want you to meet my brother tomorrow. I want you to be part of my life.*

Then I waited.

Chapter 19

Kali

Every night, I lay there numb, thinking about Hunter. It was impossible. It had been doomed from the start. Sex games weren't enough. Not for me.

As hard as I tried to put on a pleasant face when I had to deal with Hunter at work, I knew my effort showed. How could it not? One look at him was enough to stop me in my tracks, as much as I tried to ignore the fluttering in my breast. My traitorous feelings made me want to reach out to him, to hug him so I could feel like everything was okay again.

So when I got his text, it floored me. He was asking me to meet his brother!

That was real life. That wasn't just casual sex.

It was a chink in the wall, letting in light. Maybe he did want a real relationship with me.

Then again, maybe the second I stopped running away, he would lose interest.

Even if he did want a relationship with me, what about everything else? Just like my parents, we weren't compatible. Did I want to be worn out at forty after working twice as hard as I should have? I *knew* that way laid heartbreak.

But in the end I figured, I had nothing lose by meeting his brother. It would tell me a lot about Hunter. It could confirm everything I had seen so far, and then it might be easier to say good-bye to him.

And if it really wasn't too good to be true, if Hunter did want to get serious with me, I couldn't miss out because I was too scared to go to dinner with him and his brother.

Finally I texted him back. *Ok where and when?*

He instantly sent back the name and address of a restaurant. *I'll meet you at the deli at 6 to walk up together.*

The next day at work, I stayed away from Hunter. But whenever I saw him, his eyes lit up with pleasure. It was really hard to resist him. He could make a connection with me from across the construction site with a dozen people around, and somehow manage to make me feel special.

I met him at the deli on the corner after work. Hunter said, "I'm glad you decided to come."

"Why did you ask me?"

"Because I want you to know me. And I want to get to know you. I'd like to come meet your parents and see where you grew up. I think that tells you a lot about a person."

It sounded perfect. But I couldn't help thinking of the last time we had stood here, setting off on our date where he had ticked off the romantic gestures one by one: rose, limo-car, surprise destination, restaurant with candles, white tablecloths and an amazing view.

Was he playing a role again now, or did he really mean it? Looking back, I was sure that date was designed to get me into bondage later that night.

So rather than listen to any more of that kind of talk, I asked him questions about the next phase of the project. The demo was complete and the raw space was ready. The patterns for the sundial and medallions had been sent to the foundry today along with the pattern for the unique ball-bench that he had packed into a crate. He would be staying all next week in Pennsylvania monitoring the creation of the molds. The dial part of the sundial would be poured into a special form that was twenty-four feet long. Meanwhile the construction crew would start laying the new pavers in the plaza and set the bolts for the installation.

Our work conversation carried us on our walk up to 6th Street to a row of tiny restaurants. At the bottom of every tenement building, down a short flight of steps, were Indian restaurants. One after the other. The narrow, deep interiors were filled with mirrors, tiny lights and a rainbow of silk hangings.

"There's so many!" I exclaimed as we walked by more than a dozen.

"There's a lot of people who need to eat."

As Hunter turned off the sidewalk and went down several steps to a glass doorway on the basement floor, I asked, "How can you tell them apart?"

He grinned. "I've been to every one of them, and this is the best. Drew loves Indian food."

Before I knew it, I was shaking hands with Drew Munro as Hunter introduced us. Drew looked a lot like Hunter—tall and handsome, but he was bulkier and heavier in the face. He also had blue eyes, but they were mild in comparison. Whereas Hunter was lean and hungry, almost predatory in appearance, Drew was the kind of solid, ordinary guy you saw in Home Depot.

Drew seemed surprised to see me. "Uh, hi, there. You're Hunter's friend?"

"I work for SunTech. We're doing the sundial project together."

Now Drew looked even more confused, shifting his gaze to his brother. Hunter nodded, and said, "It's all right. I'm dating Kali, even though she's not sure she wants to. My bad reputation, and all."

Drew raised his brows. "I can understand that."

I wanted to pounce on his comment but if I put him on the defensive, Drew wouldn't tell me anything. So I sat down and we chatted for a while about Drew's job as a fireman and his life in the firehouse. He had taken the train up from Harrisburg and was going back that afternoon.

It felt to me like Drew was a blurry mirror-image of Hunter. He was solid, reliable—a fireman, for Christ's sake! He saved lives for a living. What a noble, wonderful job with health insurance and a good retirement plan. I felt awful for thinking it, but who wouldn't?

But I didn't have a smidge of attraction for Drew. It was like he was made of mud for all the electricity I felt from him. But I could feel Hunter sitting at my other side, wound tight with sparks coming off him in a never-ending display.

The two men discussed the menu options and Hunter ordered for me as usual. After the waiter left, Hunter turned to Drew. "Let's get this over with, Drew. I know you've got something to tell me or you wouldn't be here."

Drew's eyes slid to me, as he hedged, "It's about dad."

Hunter nodded. "Yeah?"

"He lost his job again."

Hunter hit the arm of his chair with his fist. "Damn it!"

Drew glanced at me again. "He was drinking at work. He'll have a tough time finding another trucking company willing to hire a driver who was let go for drinking and driving."

"Was he arrested?"

"No, the company found the bottle. He won't be charged."

Hunter let his breath hiss through his teeth. "We have to be grateful for that."

I stayed very still, feeling like an intruder. This was serious stuff. Drinking and driving! Fired from his job! Hunter looked like he wanted to strangle someone. Maybe his dad.

"What did mom say?" Hunter asked.

"What can she say? She only works at the A&P thirty hours a week, so after taxes it barely covers the lot rent and utilities."

"And you don't get unemployment for being fired." Hunter sighed. "They need money."

Drew nodded. "I can give them $100 a week until Dad gets another job."

"Who knows when that will be?" Hunter dragged his hands through his hair. "I can do the same. I figure I'll have a year and a half, maybe more, before the funds from this project dry up. I'm hoping to pick up more work from the publicity that Kali's creating for it. Maybe dad can pull it together by then."

"I hoped you'd say that. David is paying off his student loans and doesn't have an extra dime to spare."

After that, the two brothers dropped the subject and they dug into the food. For such different men, they seemed very much in synch. They shared the different dishes and after a while the mood lightened. I really liked Drew—he was sensible, capable and honest. In some ways, he seemed much older than Hunter, as if he had already solidified into the form he would have for the rest of his life.

"Do you have a girlfriend?" I asked Drew at one point.

"Yes." Drew lit up and suddenly he looked a lot more like Hunter. His girlfriend was an EMT, someone he had met on the job and their friendship had eventually turned into romance. They'd known each together for more than two years and he said they were talking about when they would get married. He was very tender about her dream wedding in the mountains in the snow. Drew said their biggest problem was that his job took him away for four days at a time, and that was hard on their relationship.

I finally asked the question I had been dying to broach all evening. "What about Hunter? Am I like the girls he usually dates?"

Drew opened his eyes wide. "I don't know. I haven't met any of his girlfriends since high school."

"You haven't?" I slid a look over at Hunter. "Not in, what, twelve years?"

Hunter was watching us, letting Drew answer. "No. He doesn't talk much about the women in his life."

So it really did mean a lot that Hunter had brought me to meet Drew. But otherwise, it didn't sound so good. He hadn't brought home a serious girlfriend in over a decade? What was up with that? "How about his high school girlfriends?"

"Hunter was real popular. With all the girls. He was the envy of the other guys. One time he tied up this girl in the computer lab and the teacher walked in, and it was the talk of the school. I had guys high-fiving *me*..." Drew trailed off when he saw Hunter's frown.

"That's what I thought," I said.

Hunter leaned closer to assure me. "It's different with you."

Drew agreed, "That's for sure. I never figured I'd be talking about dad in front of a girlfriend of yours."

Girlfriend! I bit my lip hard.

Hunter shrugged. "It's not much fun letting Kali hear it." He turned to me. "But you need to know who I am for us to be together."

I couldn't have said it better myself. It really made me look at Hunter with new eyes. Maybe he was serious about me. Maybe he was willing to take my hand and walk into the future together. To see if we fit together.

It took my breath away. Who would have thought eating Indian food with two brothers could be the most romantic thing I had ever done? But it felt like Hunter had slain a dragon for me, opening himself up like this.

After we were done with dinner and standing on the sidewalk outside, Hunter turned to me in front of Drew. "Will you give me another chance, Kali? Come meet my friends this weekend. Get to know me better. That way you'll be able to decide."

The look in his eyes stopped me cold. For a moment, I could see how much this had cost him. He looked as if he had been stripped bare.

I was ready to say anything to make him stop looking like that.

Drew was also expectant, so much like his brother, but lightyears different.

"How can I turn you down when both of you look at me like that?" I asked.

I reached out and took Hunter's hand, and he grabbed onto me with a fierceness that seemed to claim me through his handclasp.

Drew was beaming. "That's great! He's really not so bad, Kali. He just needs a little understanding and patience."

Hunter smacked his brother on the shoulder. "You make me sound like a dog!"

"You *are* a dog!" Drew shot back.

Hunter laughed, but I felt an inward twinge. Could a playboy like Hunter really change?

•••

I did my best to not let my hopes get too high. Meeting his brother was huge, but Hunter's real life was here in the city. He went to fetish parties and his friends were part of that world. If I wasn't comfortable with that, it could tear us apart before I knew it.

On Saturday night, I felt like I was going down the rabbit hole with Hunter as we entered the side door of a big brick building in the east 20s. There was no sign. The door opened straight off the parking lot, without even an awning to protect it from the softly falling rain. It was a utility door, while the fancy glass doors around the corner were for the real patrons of the building. Not for us.

We went down a long flight of concrete steps, then rounded a corner and went down a long corridor with a low ceiling. At the back end was a window where a nice-looking blond woman was taking money. She handed over a sheet of paper with the club rules. I scanned it and saw things like "no intercourse or oral sex," "no play for pay," "no drugs or alcohol on premises," "must be 18 or over to enter."

That told me what I couldn't do. It was up to Hunter to show me what could be done.

We went through a black steel door with the word "Paddles" spray-painted in stencil on it, and down another short hallway. It opened up into a narrow room with a bar down one side and banquettes along the opposite wall. The ceiling was very low with exposed ductwork painted black. Signs on the wall advertised ice cream sundaes and smoothies. There were people seated on the stools and on the benches and several called out greetings to Hunter.

Almost everyone was wearing black. Hunter had told me to wear black when I had asked what would be good. So I had on my shortest black skirt that came to mid-thigh, bought in a Manhattan boutique, and a black button-down shirt with the sleeves rolled up and the neck opened. I got the idea from stills I had seen of the old movie, Secretary. I did a search for kinky images, and that was the only one I could identify with. That girl really knew how to rock the sexy librarian-look while her wrists were locked to a bar over her

144

shoulders.

Sounds were coming from around us, from nobody I could see, but cries and moans filled the air, coming from everywhere. The strong beat of the music couldn't drown it out.

I followed Hunter from room to room, until I was twisted around and not sure about the layout of the Paddles. All of the walls were painted black and the lighting was dim. Hallways turned abrupt corners and opened into small and medium-sized alcoves.

People were playing together in couples and threesomes, with others standing nearby watching. There was something outrageous everywhere I looked. Some people were tied up with their wrists locked to chains dangling from the ceiling or attached to giant wooden X's. Two men were bent over small padded tables with their buttocks exposed and were being struck by two women holding wooden paddles. Naked people, people crying out in pain and pleasure, people of all shapes and sizes dressed in lingerie or black leather. Exposing their genitals and breasts to everyone. Like a Halloween costume party for the Adams family crossed with an orgy.

"You look a little dazed," Hunter told me when we had completed our first circuit.

"All these people are having sex in front of everyone," I whispered. "I could never do that!"

"It's BDSM."

"But they're naked."

"Well, I guess it is sex for some people. For others it's more of a spiritual, ecstatic thing."

"What is it for you?"

"I'm just kinky. I'll try anything once. I've even done the hook pull a couple of times—that's really intense. It's what the Lakota Indians do in their Sun Dance, piercing hooks through the skin of your chest." He pulled back his shirt to show me the slight puckered scar. "One on each side. It sends endorphins rushing through your body. It's a high like nothing I've ever felt. It puts you in another world. Opens your eyes to what's real and what's not."

I reached out to touch the scar, as if by touching it I could feel a little bit of the sensation for myself. His skin was hot, and my fingertips cool. "I couldn't do that. I'd be too afraid."

"You'd be surprised at what you can do. And it's a good thing to surprise yourself, push your boundaries a little. As long as you make sure you're safe."

"Putting hooks through your skin doesn't sound safe to me."

"You have to know someone before you let them push your boundaries. And make sure they have the skills to do the things they're doing to you. I wouldn't let just anyone pierce me with a hook, and you shouldn't either."

It was such a solemn charge that I could only nod.

He smiled, giving my cheek a stroke with his fingertips. "Come on, Kalico-cat, I'm going to introduce you around. I've told them I met you through a job, but don't mention SunTech."

I nodded, not sure why he wanted to keep it a secret, but too overwhelmed by everything that I didn't question it.

It turned out Hunter knew everyone. Those covert glances meeting mine as he had shown me around the club turned out to be polite friends waiting for the signal that they could come over. Hunter introduced me to everyone as his girlfriend, and they all looked surprised by it. He put his arm around my shoulder or my waist, he kissed my hand as they talked about things happening, people they knew, and events that were going on.

At least five different people told me that Hunter had mentioned me to them. One second I felt like I was in a dark underworld filled with strangers, and now everyone was smiling and practically fawning over me. Hunter was a popular guy. I felt like I was with the Prom King, while I was wearing some old rag of a dress.

Hunter only used my nickname, and nobody else used their full name, though I did overhear someone refer to him as Master Hunter. Some had a Sir or Daddy or Lady or Mistress attached in front of their names. Others had playful made-up names like Ponygirl and

146

Bunnybrat.

"Scene names," Hunter explained when I asked about it. "We use them online and for playing. Most people don't talk about kink because they can get fired or sexually harassed. It's a real problem. We used to be called sick or crazy."

"I had no idea."

"Yeah, most people still keep it a secret, and use these scene names. But some people like it because they can take on a persona that way, and let go of their ordinary life and have fun."

When Hunter introduced me to a stout motherly woman named Popcorn, she gave me a huge hug, pressing the large black beads of her necklace into my chest. "I'm so glad to finally meet you. Hunter said you couldn't come last weekend. Had to go see the parents, hmm? Well, it's good to stay in touch. He says you're new to the city?"

"Yes, less than a year."

"And you've already found your way to us! Imagine that."

"It was Hunter... he brought me here. He takes me all kinds of places."

Popcorn smiled fondly at Hunter who was partly turned away, listening to a heavyset man speaking to him in a confidential tone. "Hunter has been having a love affair with the city for the past decade. No girl can compete." She appraised me. "But you might. He talks about you differently."

"Really? Because I wondered... I'm not his type, you know."

Popcorn waved her hand. "Hunter doesn't have a type. Which is helpful because everyone wants him. But he's a good boy, he doesn't let it go to his head."

I grinned to hear Hunter called that. "Good boy! I wonder what he would say if I called him that?"

Popcorn cackled. "He would like it because you'd be starting something *he* would get to finish!"

I considered the friendly woman. "How long have you known him?"

"I was one of the first people he met in the scene. We were so young. We had just started the TNG right about then, and he was a big part of that."

"What's TNG?"

"The Next Generation. It's a group that's for people under thirty-five. My friends and I kept seeing the younger people come and go because they didn't want to hang out with folks their parents' age."

"So this lifestyle is a big part of who he is?"

"He's a pillar of the community." Popcorn seemed to have no idea that she was saying something that I might not like. "I think he's been to every kink conference in the country, and some internationally."

I didn't like the sound of that. If Hunter was used to spending every weekend at underground sex clubs, I wasn't sure there was a future in that for me. As nice as everyone seemed, it was downright odd to be chatting with a woman named Popcorn while a guy was lying on the floor ten feet away getting absently stepped on by a redheaded woman in stilettos.

Still, the welcome was reassuring. Several people complimented me on being with Hunter, saying in little asides, "He's a great guy," and "You're so lucky he's your first master."

Hunter handled it well, always attentive towards me, and making sure I was all right, but giving me the space to talk to other people without hovering over me.

At the opposite end of the spectrum, I saw several couples were literally chained together by a leash that was attached to the collar of one of them. When I spoke to one couple, the chained woman waited until she was invited into the conversation, and then after that spoke like anyone else. It was disconcerting, not the least because the woman's breasts were hanging out of her peek-a-boo top, looped by tiny decorative chains. Her body wasn't in the best shape, which made her apparent comfort at being exposed even more surprising.

But it was amazing how quickly I was getting sort of used to seeing people in all states of dress or undress. Some men and women were completely naked—one middle-aged Latino guy had only a cuff and chain around his ankle, and he held the end of the chain himself as he followed a stunning brunette in a shiny black corset and thigh-high boots. So far, that was the closest thing to what I imagined the patron of an S&M club would look like.

When Hunter put his arm around me and asked, "How are you doing?" for the dozenth time, I said, "I'm think I'm on sensory overload."

"You're not a voyeur."

"I hope not!" I considered it. "Are you?"

He shrugged. "All men are. But I don't go peeping through windows, if that's what you mean."

"No, I don't think that. It's funny, but being here and meeting everyone, I do get the feeling you're a good man. You're not going to hurt me."

"No, I won't." His voice changed from joking to perfectly serious. "And I can't stand the thought of someone hurting you."

I looked into his eyes. He meant it; he would do whatever it took to protect me. I had felt it before. There was a bond growing between us, tying us together tighter and tighter.

He cupped my cheek with one hand. "You want to give us a chance, don't you?

"A chance for what?" My fear at what he would say made my throat tight.

"For whatever we can make it. This is too strong for us to ignore. How can you walk away, not knowing what we can have together? We have to try."

I made myself say it. "I want a real relationship. Love, partnership and sharing our lives. Do you really want that?"

"When I think about you, I don't want to leave your side. I want to help you through the hard times. Be with you for the good times."

"What about this?" I looked up at the club. "I'm not sure I want my social life to revolve around sex clubs."

"Mine doesn't. So I don't see how it could for us together. This is just fun stuff for me."

I couldn't say no, I didn't want to. And he could tell. His hand slid around the back of my neck, his fingers reminding me of that first time he had taken hold of me and shown me that he could set me on fire just from pulling my hair.

My body responded instantly. Warmth spread from my groin to my belly, filling me in a sudden rush. It didn't matter that we were standing in a black-painted basement surrounded by half-naked people.

"Do you want me to touch you?" he murmured, his lips close to my skin, taunting me.

"Yes," I breathed. "I do."

"What do you want?"

"I want you to touch me."

He smiled slowly. "Sir..."

"Sir," I breathed.

He kissed me, which was better than words. He seemed released by my agreement, like his pent-up passion burst out in one all-consuming rush. I drowned in his kisses, squeezed in his arms until I was breathless.

"Yes!" Hunter murmured, as he finally eased his crushing grip. "Yes... you *are* mine."

I nearly swooned. Why did it make my feel so loved and desired? He said it like I was the only thing that mattered to him.

He seized hold of my hand in a tight, possessive grip, like I was already under his control. I felt blinded, reeling from the wave of lust he had shot through me with his kisses and his words, as he led me through the club. He took me down a narrow hallway. At the end was a door blocked off by a waist-high padded bench. I could reach out and touch the old, worn bricks on either side. He turned me so I faced past his shoulder, down the hallway, with my back against the padded leather.

Several faces peeked around the corner, and one man with a

scruffy beard hiding his mouth came and leaned against the wall at the end, frankly watching. "There's people there," I whispered.

"You said you couldn't imagine getting naked in a place like this."

My eyes widened. "I can't!"

"Do you trust me enough to let me push your boundaries on that?"

My arms went to cover my breasts, as if I was already naked. "I can't!"

He gave a little laugh. "Either you're a closet exhibitionist in deep denial, or you were brought up by the Amish."

My mom's primly buttoned-up clothes sprang to mind. "My mom is a very modest person."

"You've never skinny dipped? Living out in the country like that?"

My head tilted. "Down to my bra and panties."

"Never naked?"

I shook my head.

"Okay, so bra and panties are your limit." His hand went out to the first button on my shirt.

My eyes slid to the unsavory man leaning down the hall. "What about them? Will they come closer?"

"Not if they know what's good for them." Hunter shot a warning look over his shoulder, and the leaning guy nodded. "Jake will keep everyone back."

"Jake is the one I'm worried about!"

"Don't judge a book, Kali. Jake is the kind of guy I'd want on my side in a fight."

He was so certain, that I relaxed in spite of myself. "I trust you."

"So do you want to play?" he asked.

I forced myself to not look behind him. "Yes, I do."

He leaned in like he was going to kiss me, his hands sliding down to my wrists. "Put your hands behind you on the bench."

A shiver went through me. Why did his quiet order turn my insides to mush like that? Was it the tone, the way he was sure I would obey? I did obey without thinking twice.

He ran his hands through the back of my hair, pulling and stretching me to stand tall. He rubbed my neck and then my shoulders, loosening me up. "Close your eyes," he whispered. "You're in my hands now."

I closed my eyes, glad that I couldn't see the watching faces at the end of the hallway. He ran his palms down my chest to my waist, tightening and lifting, so I was off my feet for a few moments. Then down my hips to my thighs.

He hesitated, then his hands rose again, under my skirt. "These have to come off." He pulled on my nylons.

My eyes flew open. I started to try to help him, but he ordered low, "Put your hands back."

I swallowed and put my hands back, not sure how I felt about it.

"Close your eyes," he added.

I did. It was an odd, helpless feeling as he tugged down my nylons. I twisted slightly to help him pull them down over my buttocks. It was far more intimate somehow than simply undressing myself. He moved very slowly and deliberately as he slid them down my legs, then gently lifted each foot out of my pumps one at a time to pull off the nylons.

I peeked and saw him kneeling in front of me, carefully rolling up my nylons and tucking them in his shirt pocket. Closing my eyes again before he could see, I felt comforted by that. I didn't like the idea of them discarded and lying on the floor of this place.

Hunter ran his hands up my bare legs, and I shivered again, feeling the chill air of the basement floating along the concrete floor. He kept going up, pulling up my narrow skirt along with his hands, all the way until my skirt was bunched around my hips. I shifted uneasily, thinking of those watching eyes at the end of the hallway. I really wanted to push my skirt down. Fighting myself, wanting to push down my skirt, but not wanting to remove my hands from the bench and disappoint him.

I opened my eyes. He was standing back watching me, clearly enjoying my inner turmoil. "You don't like that."

"I feel so exposed!" Even though he was blocking me from view, the fact that my panties were showing made me blush fiercely in shame. My mother always made me wear tights when I was little so my panties didn't show while I was playing. All those multi-colored tights that I loved, that kept me safe.

"Not any more than a bathing suit." He bent over, examining my pale blue panties, "Pretty. Nice and lacy."

My hand slipped off the bench, wanting to hide myself. "You can see through them."

"Barely." He leaned over and kissed me through the lace. "Juicy! I wish I could really make you squirm, but it's not allowed."

I gasped. The men at the end of the hallway, and a couple of women, were crowded in watching them. He rubbed his mouth against me through the lace, making me throb from his hot breath.

"Hunter!" I protested.

He laughed, low in his throat, a sexy sound that promised more evil to come. "You really are my delicate little flower. I didn't realize they still made them so sweet in the country. Maybe it *is* modesty…"

"Now you're laughing at me!" I blurted out.

"Yes." He was laughing up at me, still nuzzling me.

Somehow I kept my hands on the bench, even as my irritation flared. "I don't like being made fun of."

Instantly his smile was gone. "I was teasing. I would never think bad of you." He stood up, putting his arms around me, brushing back the hair around my face. "I think you're adorable, Kali! You make every second worthwhile. I'm laughing because I'm so happy someone like you exists. It reaffirms my faith in mankind."

I put my hands to his head, sinking my fingers deep into his hair as he kissed me. Like he didn't want to stop. I melted into his arms.

As he pulled away, he whispered, "Put your hands back down."

With a tremulous smile, I did.

His fingers went to the top button on my shirt. "I laugh when I'm with you because you take all the seriousness away. I feel like it's easy when I'm with you."

I watched him open my top button. "I'm sometimes very uneasy with you. I never know what you're going to do."

"Same here. But I like that about you. Most people are so predictable."

More praise. *This is getting a little embarrassing.* Then on second thought: *Maybe it's just part of the scene. Softening me up.*

He undid the next button. "I'd like to strip this off you all at once, like a warrior taking his woman. Then carry you out there over my shoulder to display you to everyone, to show them what I've won."

My mouth opened round. "You wouldn't do that!"

"I will. Someday. I promise you that." He put his hand over my eyes. "Close your eyes, you bad girl. I'm going to have to bind and blindfold you if you can't obey. Would you like that?"

I shook my head.

"You need to answer me when I ask a question, Kali." Again with that tone of command in his voice. More real than play-acting.

"No, I wouldn't like that." Again I felt that terrible conflict. I shouldn't be the obedient little woman, but it thrilled me deep inside. And that scared me. It broke the first rule my mom had taught me when I started to date: you don't do what boys tell you to do. I could hear my mom's voice in my head, saying, "If he's pushing you, then he's only thinking about himself."

Hunter finished unbuttoning my shirt and slowly slipped it over my shoulders. He pushed it all the way down to my wrists, holding my hands in place against the bench. "Keep them there."

Now with the shirt stretched tight between my wrists behind my back, I felt bound. It was easier to keep my hands on the bench, like I had no choice now. I took a deep breath, keeping my eyes shut so I didn't have to see the people watching us.

But after what Hunter said about showing me off to everyone as his prize, for some reason I didn't mind their searching eyes so much. He thought I was special, and that's all that mattered. So what if they were judging me? They would also value me just because he did, and they valued him.

It made me lift my chin higher, ready for whatever he did. And glad I was wearing my pretty sky-blue lingerie set. It looked good with my pale skin and dark hair. Having my skirt bunched around my hips made me feel even more undressed, for some reason. Disheveled and wanton. Words I had never felt before.

He leaned in and murmured, "I'm going to touch you all over." He drew his hands up the outside of my thighs.

I gasped. One of his hands was silky soft and the other rasped and scraped me, making me wince away. He smoothed his hands back and up my buttocks, where he slowly began to squeeze.

"This won't cut you. But it may leave some scratches."

"Hunter!" I gasped, as the prickly hand dug into my butt cheek, tiny shafts of pain lancing out.

Somehow I kept my eyes closed. "What is it?" I asked.

"A vampire glove, and this other hand is bunny fur. I know which one you like best."

I wanted to focus on the furry hand, but the bitey glove was too much to ignore. He stroked my whole body up and down, pausing to pinch or buff certain tender parts like my inner thighs or running a finger inside of my bra. He followed it up with the fur, drawing it under my arms and then tickling under my ear. All the while, the prickles taunted me, pinching and scraping, making me dance on the end of his string as I twisted against the padded bench.

He kept urging me on, to take it, to give in to the feeling, sounding more excited as I writhed harder, pressing me and pushing me right to the edge. I remembered it was this way when he was biting me while I was tied up. It was almost too much, but it felt so good! It sent little zings through my nerves right down between my legs, making me pant and squirm harder. I had to give into it, to let it pass through me instead of fighting it. There was nothing but pain and softness as he explored every inch of my body all the way down my legs to each toe, which he pricked and soothed, harder and harder as he stroked me like a prized possession.

I focused entirely on the sensations, jerking and twitching to his hands, only occasionally hearing the sound of a whip or a cry echo into their hallway. Even that made me feel isolated, like there was nothing else in the world but this, now, in his hands. In a bubble together, linked together by a thousand singing nerve endings.

Suddenly his furred hand was on my crotch, pressing in, rubbing back and forth as he held me against him. I tried to stifle my moan with my teeth. I twisted my hips but couldn't get away from him and he rubbed me with his whole hand until I was gasping.

"Yes, Kalico!" he whispered hoarsely. "Come for me."

His relentless fingers had learned what I liked, like he learned everything else about me, watching my every move so he already knew the rhythm and pressure that would send me right out of my mind.

"Yes, give it to me," he growled in my ear.

I cried out as I climaxed, shockingly quick. Me, who usually didn't get a chance to orgasm during sex because it was over too fast. But I threw my head back, letting the waves wash over me, as he ground his rigid hard-on against me, making me come again before the waves fully receded.

When he was done, I was limp and half-lying back over the padded bench, my arms tangled in my shirt. If he wasn't holding me up, I knew I would have sunk down to the sticky floor.

I couldn't bear to lift my head from his shoulder to see all those people watching me. I had never expected to orgasm in front of those watching eyes! My face burned. It was so awful I was almost overcome.

But he held me and murmured soothing things under his breath, telling me how perfect I was, how beautiful, how free! How much he loved making me feel good. Gradually my shame eased away, and I breathed more easily. There's no way I couldn't say I didn't like it! It defied all reason that I did like it, but it couldn't be denied.

Hunter pulled down my skirt and pulling up my shirt over my shoulders, buttoning it for me. I felt like a little girl again, washed clean and empty inside. "Are you okay?" he asked. "Would you like some water?"

Suddenly I caught sight of the end of the hallway. Five or six people were still watching! But when Hunter jerked his head, they began to fade away. Along with Jake, there were a couple of women who gave me lingering looks, but they also turned and were gone by the time the two of us emerged from the tiny hallway.

"I need the bathroom," I said.

Hunter smoothly led me through the club to the bathroom. I went in and took stock of myself in the mirror. My hair was wild like I'd just fallen out of bed after I'd been made love to good and proper. My makeup was more or less intact, which was the benefit of not wearing much. I replaced my lip balm.

Not bad, I thought to myself. My orgasm had left my cheeks flushed and my eyes sparkling. The top several buttons were now undone on my blouse, showing off a little of my bra and much more cleavage than usual. Hunter had buttoned it that way, so I didn't touch it.

I cleaned myself up in the stall and tucked my guilty damp panties in my purse. I felt particularly slutty when I came out sans underwear. But after what I'd just done, it was a well-earned feeling. I still felt that curiously empty and light feeling, like I had poured myself out at his feet.

I couldn't wait to get back to Hunter, but a girl entered the bathroom before I could leave. It wasn't until the girl said, "Hi, Kali," that I realized it was Minx.

Hunter's submissive.

"Oh! Hi," I said lamely in return. "I didn't know you were here."

Minx was wearing an uber-short flared skirt in red plaid and a tiny white top that was tied in a knot, pressing her small breasts together to form cleavage. Her hair was magenta tonight, and her lipstick was neon green to match her fluorescent green collar. I thought she would be really pretty if she got rid of the freaky get-up and let her hair go natural.

"I saw your scene," Minx said.

My stomach clenched. Maybe it was the bitter look in Minx's eye, or her tone of voice, but I knew what was coming. What did Hunter say? People were so predictable.

"Very sensuous. Not his usual style," Minx said.

"He never used the bunny fur on you?"

Her lips curled. "No. I'm not into bunny fur."

I turned to the mirror to check my lip balm. "Don't knock it 'til you try it."

"I think it's a little too wet for me to try it now."

My mouth fell open. *She was so crude!*

Minx laughed right in my face. "You really have no idea what you're getting into, do you?"

Now I was getting angry. "What do you mean?"

Minx instantly was contrite. "I'm sorry, Kali. We should try to get along, you know. We'll be seeing a lot of each other. And Hunter doesn't like drama."

Hearing her talk about Hunter in that familiar way made me want to scream. "What's going on between you and Hunter?" I demanded.

"You know. He broke up with me. He says he wants to see only you." Minx smiled. "But he's polyamorous at heart. He won't be able to stay with just one girl. You'll have to share if you want to keep him."

"I'm not a sharing kind of girl," I retorted.

"Why not? It's not like it makes any difference in the long run. If a guy wants something on the outside, he's going to take it." Minx sniffed. "Girls, too, for that matter. My girlfriend didn't like it at first, but she realized there are some things I need that I can't get from her. She's glad to let Hunter be my master so I'm with someone she trusts."

"You have a girlfriend?" I asked in confusion.

"Yeah—Bonny. Didn't Hunter tell you? We've been together since college. But Hunter is my master, and nothing can change that. I don't mind taking a break if that's what you two need. It's important to set a good foundation for your relationship, and anyone can see that you've never done this before. But when he opens it back up again, I'll be waiting. I'm really good at sharing, don't worry. I won't take anything away from you, I promise."

Minx sounded sincere, but what she was saying was so awful that I could only leave the bathroom without another word. It sounded like a threat, but I didn't think it wasn't meant to be. Clearly Minx thought that Hunter would be playing with her again soon.

When I rejoined Hunter, at first I expected him to ask about Minx. He saw everything, so of course he saw Minx go into the bathroom after me. But he didn't say a word. Minx sneaked out when his back was turned and rejoined a pretty blond at a table on the far side of the social area. Usually Hunter was so observant, but Minx had gotten around him real neatly.

It made me think that Minx probably knew Hunter pretty well. So maybe she was right about him.

But that didn't mean he was going to "open up" any relationship of mine. There was only so far I could go with this kinky stuff.

I remembered what Minx had said about Hunter not liking drama, so I didn't tell him about talking to Minx in the bathroom. He would be angry at her for interfering in our relationship. He might even say something to her, and then Minx would have the satisfaction of knowing she had gotten to me.

Instead, I smiled blandly at Minx and her girlfriend as we headed out. Hunter nodded and said a pleasant hello/goodbye to them both, and then we were outside hailing a cab.

"So did you have fun?" Hunter asked.

Thinking back on how he had ordered me to come, and the fireworks that had blown through my mind, I said, "Yes, I did."

"Do you want to come again?"

"Not next weekend. But I could come again," I said.

Much to my relief, Hunter seemed satisfied with that. He went home with me, and he stayed the whole night in my bed, just like a boyfriend should. We ate chocolate chip mint ice cream that he fetched from around the corner and we made love twice, with only a little hair-pulling and arm-holding, mingled with long, deep kisses that never seemed to stop. Then we fell asleep in my bed.

I was in heaven.

Chapter 20

Hunter

I hated to leave, but I had to go. "I'll be back on Friday," I told Kali, kissing her good-bye on Monday morning. I was going to pack my suitcase and fly to the foundry in Pittsburg to oversee the creation of the molds for the sundial.

Kali was prim in her buttoned-up corporate suit, but her expression was adorably sad. Big round eyes and tremulous lips that I kept having to kiss rather than leave. Silent, wistful sadness that I couldn't resist. I wanted to sweep her up and carry her off with me everywhere, and never let her out of my sight.

"You're killing me!" I exclaimed, taking one more last rough kiss. Her eyes sparked in arousal. "That's better, Kalico-cat. I'll text you later."

I caught myself whistling on the way to the subway. It was my father's happy whistle that he would let out when he came home from a long trip. Suddenly I was ten years old again, feeling relieved that my dad was home and would take care of the pesky problems in the house that I couldn't quite handle, like the leak under the sink or my mom's sad face.

Jesus, I'm letting her in deep, I thought. It was a lot really fast. But I had gambled everything to get Kali, letting her meet my brother and my friends as my girlfriend. They had been shocked at the way I acted with her, I could tell. None of the usual Master/slave rituals. Nothing of my sadistic side. That would scare her away, and I had barely gotten her back again. I wasn't going to risk blowing it.

So when I saw Minx slink into the bathroom after Kali, no doubt to whisper all sorts of insidious things to her, I bided my time. When Kali emerged, she didn't say a word about it, much to my surprise. I liked it so much that she wouldn't let Minx manipulate her, that I wanted to make her happy. We had pancakes and the Times on Sunday morning and a long walk along the river that afternoon, ending up curled on the couch together.

Mostly I sketched her in every way possible. I nearly filled a whole pad with Kali—Kali sleeping, Kali drinking her coffee in the back window, Kali in the shower, Kali getting dressed. I kept taking off her clothes so I could draw her. She always laughingly protested, then she would stretch out like the cat she was named for, luxuriating in the feeling of my eyes on her. As I sketched her, my dick would harden, as if I was claiming her by capturing her lines on paper. I decided to do a whole series of sculptures of Kali lying in bed, my favorite poses, some in bondage and others with her hair tousled and sleepy eyed.

Plus there was sex, lots of it. I kept it mostly vanilla, but I couldn't help the rough stuff creeping in. As long as I could sink inside of her, I really didn't need anything too kinky. Kali kept blowing my mind with her response. But I longed to spank that luscious ass, and was very proud of myself for holding off. Minx had nixed that possibility this weekend. Whatever Minx had said, she was trying to unsettle Kali, because that's what Minx did. But Kali held her own without any fuss. She'd been trained to do that for years from growing up poor in a town that served a wealthy clientele. Her desire for safety and security was part of that, something I was only beginning to understand.

So I shelved the spanking for later, and was more than happy with a little mock-force as she lowered her lips to my cock, putting my hand on the back of her head or holding her wrists and tweaking her nipple so she writhed against me. That, and I asked her to do things for me—fetch that pencil, bring me that cup. I liked it when she served me, and she took to it like it was second nature.

I didn't leave her apartment the entire weekend, hoping to satiate myself on her so she wouldn't hold so much erotic power over me.

But I couldn't think about anything else but Kali as I packed my bags and flew to Pittsburgh. I should have been thinking about my project, but Kali kept creeping into my mind, and I'd find myself daydreaming about touching her and doodling her face on any piece of paper that came to hand. My balls ached for release that only she could give me, and my cock swelled every time I remembered burying myself inside of her.

Instead of satisfying me, our weekend together was like a drug, and now I was addicted to her. In an effort to get mastery over myself, I restricted my calls to her to once a day, and I managed to stick to my self-imposed regime. But I kept sending her little texts: *thinking of you* or *xxoo* at night as she went to bed. I liked that contact, liked seeing my phone light up with her return texts, as mushy as my own.

My lonely nights in my Pittsburg hotel room were torture. This was crunch time: the molds were critical. If anything went wrong, the whole project would go off schedule. When I couldn't be at the foundry, I walked for hours along the river, up and down over hills, finding myself in some dicey areas of Pittsburgh. But I had to wear myself out to stop my racing thoughts. I should have felt on top of my game, but I felt disconnected and adrift. Kali sent me photos of the flagstones being laid on the plaza, but it wasn't the same as being there to watch over the work.

The only time I could focus was when I was at the foundry. There I was alive. I took over the old workshop where molds were made from the patterns. First I had to create wax patterns from the original bench, the numeral medallions and the parts of the sundial. I had made the mock-up of the twenty-four-foot spear from flattened sheet metal so it would have a slight wavy texture similar to the surface of the bench. The time-consuming part was working over the wax patterns once they created them, rubbing out the seams and the tiny pockets where bubbles had been caught. Then the wax patterns were coated in ceramic and fired in the foundry's huge kiln to remove the wax and set the molds for the bronze.

After I inspected the mold of the bench to find it was perfectly formed, my first thought was to call Kali and tell her. I took a photo of it and sent it to her before I even thanked the foreman.

As much as I wanted to push through and cast the molds of the sundial, it would take another week for the bronze shipment to arrive, so I would have to come back later for the casting. Before I left, I looked over some samples to decide what finish I wanted when they poured the bronze into the molds. In the original proposal, I had intended it to be polished bronze. But I decided the molds were good enough that I wouldn't have to grind off imperfections, so I could leave the metal raw. There were some interesting chemicals the foundry could rub on the inside of the molds to give the surface patina a textured look. It was something I would have to consult with Ryan on.

By the time I flew back to New York, I was seriously on edge. I had hoped that time away would let me get a grip on myself, but I was a junky rushing to get my fix. Running to get my girl. Like nothing else mattered.

I reached Kali's place before she returned home from work, so I waited on the stoop outside. The blinds in the window next to me moved as someone looked at me, but nobody came out and told me to leave.

I saw Kali coming far up the block, her swaying hips and slender ankles in her heels, her hair shining naturally in the sun. I was down the steps and walking towards her before I realized what I was doing, like a magnet pulled me towards her. Then Kali was in my arms kissing me, and I was myself again.

"I'm glad you're home, Hunter." Her smile was pure pleasure, without a shadow of the struggle I had been going through.

As we walked back up the steps, I kissed her hand, unable to speak at that moment. I wanted nothing more than to get her alone.

Once I bolted the door, I felt much better. Why was I feeling so freaking defensive? Like someone was going to dash in and carry her off? It was an absurd, primal instinct. Nonsense. But there was no arguing with my gut.

She belongs to me.

I took her into the bedroom and began unbuttoning her shirt. She started to help, but I lightly smacked her fingers away. So she stood compliant, smiling slightly as I undressed her, removing her suit and nylons, bra and underwear. I even took off her earrings and necklace, laying them carefully on the small dish beside her bed where I had seen her place them at night.

She was embarrassed, as she always was to be undressed while I was fully clothed. But I liked her this way, naked and vulnerable. Ducking away from my eyes, every shy dip of her head or twist of her body turned her curves into magnificence.

My cock throbbed, already rock hard. She did that to me. Without even trying. Maybe it was the smell of her skin, maybe it was the way she moved. I couldn't get enough of her.

"Really, Hunter," she finally said. "I've been standing around outside in the hot sun all day supervising your crew. I'm a mess. I should take a shower."

I nuzzled her neck. "Um… I can taste the salt on you."

She couldn't get away from my nibbling teeth. I only had one arm around her, but it was enough to hold her in place. I lifted her hand and kissed down under her arm. She tried to wiggle away, but couldn't.

I held her arm, stretching it high as I took a deep sniff of her underarm, breathing in her heady scent. I liked sweat, I liked making my submissives sweat as we worked through a scene together. She didn't smell like chemicals or artificial flowers. She smelled like a real woman.

I couldn't get enough. I threw her on the bed and kissed down to her pussy. Again she tried to put her hands down, saying, "No, Hunter!" But I persisted because she didn't say stop, burying my face in her soft reddish hair, licking up her sweet saltiness. I buried my tongue inside of her, making her moan as she threw back her head, finally letting me do what I wanted.

I licked and lightly flicked her cleft with my tongue, taking my time, building slowly until I was moving so fast she writhed from side to side. When she came, all of her muscles clenched, fighting me as I held her down on the bed.

Then when she was limp, I warmed up the water in the shower and carried her in. I soaped every part of her, using the purple nylon scrubby on her fingers and toes as she braced herself against my back, letting the hot water stream over them. I washed her hair and took careful note of the brand so I could get some for my place. And the type of razor and toothpaste she used.

"Do you trust me?" I held up the razor.

Her eyes went round. "You're not going to cut me with that!"

"No! Never let anyone draw blood unless you're in sterile conditions."

She nodded, looking a little dazed. I wasn't sure if that was TMI right now, or not. But the thought of some jerk hurting her because she didn't know anything made my vision turn red. I had to teach her to protect herself.

"I want to shave your pussy. It will make you even more sensitive. And I love the way it looks."

"Like a little girl?" she blurted out.

"No, like you're completely naked and exposed. Like you can't hide behind anything, not even a little fuzz of hair."

"I thought women got waxed when they wanted to get rid of the hair down there."

"You can, once I shave you and it grows in a bit. It's easier to wax if the hair is shorter."

She was staring at me amazed. "Well, aren't you the expert."

I laughed. "That's not the first time I've heard that."

My laughter seemed to make her more comfortable. She smiled back, no longer looking at me like I was showing her my pet tarantula.

"Okay, I guess so," she said.

"Sit there, on the front edge of the toilet." I positioned her on the lid, then pushed her shoulders back. "Lean against the tank. Now here's the hard part." I put my hands between her legs and slowly forced them open.

She gasped, almost sitting up.

"Stay there," I ordered.

She froze, as I knew she would, then relaxed back where I had originally placed her. She really liked to struggle against her submission. I loved watching it. That was the thing I wanted most; that moment when a woman gave in to me. With some women, they wanted it so much that the lack of resistance made it not so much fun for me. Even Minx with her high-spirited nature had never been as exciting as this simple tussle in Kali's bathroom over shaving her pussy.

Now she was reclined back on the toilet, her knees as far apart as I could place them, covering her blushing face with her hands.

"Beautiful!" I told her, stroking her with my fingertips. I was hard and raging to get inside of her, but I told myself sternly that it would have to wait. "Do you have some small scissors?"

She told me where to find her nail kit, and I took the tiny scissors and kneeled between her open knees. She twisted, breathing faster.

I clipped the fine hair close to her skin, being very careful. I didn't want to accidentally cut her. I let the fuzz fall on the ground, and when I was done, I gathered it up and threw it away.

She was looking down inquisitively, so I went and fetched her hand mirror. "Haven't you looked at yourself?"

Her eyes shifted away. "Sure, when I was like fourteen."

I held the mirror so she could see her genitals. With the hair mostly gone, the outer lips were pink and full, protecting the short inner lips that were even pinker.

"Wait 'til you see yourself shaved." I took the mirror away, and reached for the soap. I lathered her up, which she liked. Then with her legs spread wide, she made little hissing noises as I pulled each section taunt and slid the razor over her skin. It left behind pearly smooth flesh.

167

With every stroke, I felt as if I was branding her. I had to leave my mark on her. Removing her hair, exposing her most tender, private parts to my razor and prying eyes; that made her belong to me. I would know tomorrow and every day afterwards when I saw her at work that her pussy was naked because I liked it that way. And she would keep it that way for me.

I threw the razor aside and opened my zipper. My cock was jerking with tension, so ready to get inside her that only my determination to take her mind before I took her body had restrained me.

She was languid and suffused with the erotic charge of letting me shave her. I rubbed against her creamy wetness. With a hard push, I slid partway inside, but that wasn't enough. I had to get all the way inside her, nothing would stop me. I held onto her hips and took her hard and fast, as was my right. She held onto the back of the seat, turning from side to side and biting her lip from crying out too loudly.

When I exploded deep inside of her, crying out as I came, I finally felt back in control. It was frightening how much power she held over me. But I could only ride this wave where it took me, keeping myself in hand as best I could.

Chapter 21

Kali

I was sitting on my front stoop, sketching on a sheet of paper Hunter had left behind.

I had protested at first when he was constantly picking up his pencil to draw me. But it hadn't taken long before I found it easy to fall into a relaxed pose, feeling his eyes travel along every curve of my body, knowing he was capturing my essence with his quick, sure strokes. It was pure luxury to have his entire concentration on me. I saw myself through his eyes, through his pencil, and knew how beautiful he considered me.

And it awakened something inside of me.

Something I didn't even know was gone. But it had been a part of me a long time ago.

I don't know exactly when it started, but suddenly everywhere I looked, my doodles were back. In the margins of my work notebook and on my calendar. On printed out emails and post-it notes with phone numbers on them. Even on the ripped-out sketches of me that Hunter left lying around. Just as the art poured out of him effortlessly, my own began to flow.

How could I resist, when his lines danced across so much endless paper?

I used to draw all the time, creating fantastical creatures that filled entire pages. It started when I was little, with crayons and colored paper. My dad had framed a few of my early works himself. He had hung them on the walls of his workshop when we bought our house. Funny how I didn't think anything of that until now.

Like they had been lying dormant inside of me, these little creatures reappeared, dancing along after me.

Only now they had grown, and combined in new grotesque

ways. I didn't know where the grinning beasts and frightful women-animals came from. But there were no end to them inside of me, apparently.

I was sitting on the stoop because I couldn't take another step. There was something about the brick building across the street. I had been walking home with my groceries, when the cracks in the façade caught my eye. Suddenly I could see my little creatures inside the building. Literally forming the walls of the warehouse. And that made me think that all of the city was like that, made up of tiny ugly parts that came together to function as a whole.

I plunked down right there and pulled out the latest sheet I'd taken from Hunter's stash, and on the back of the floating sketches of me, I had started to doodle. Now I began to fill it with the image of the warehouse in front of me. A warehouse built of tiny, active creatures.

It was absorbing, and I was caught in a torrent of creation. My pencil flew, capturing the creatures I saw, linking them together like a jigsaw puzzle that created the ordinary warehouse in front of me. Somehow it was both—fantastical and realistic, like the creatures really were hidden inside and only someone with the sight could see them.

I was putting the final touches on it when I heard my name.

"Kali?" It was Pam and Karen, looking at me expectantly from the sidewalk. "We don't want to interrupt," Pam said. "It looks like you're busy."

That broke the spell. I realized my butt was aching and cold from sitting on the stone step. And my hand was cramped from holding the pencil so long.

"I'm finished," I said.

Karen came up and took a look down at the sketch in my lap. I had used my purse as a support, but I couldn't press the tip in so it had a very light, airy quality to it. It was a like a dream of the building.

"Cool!" Karen exclaimed. "I will never look at that old

warehouse the same way again. Come look at this, Pam."

Pam's eyes also lit up when she took the sketch, looking from it to the warehouse across the street. "It's a little creepy."

"Yeah, like it's real," Karen agreed. "That's why I like it."

I laughed. It was nice to get a reaction from them. I took the sketch back and looked at it with new eyes.

It was good. Provocative. A little crude.

I didn't care. I liked it. And I liked how I felt when I made it.

"I didn't know you could draw," Karen said.

"Not really. It's just something I do for fun," I said.

"I saw you with that guy last night," Karen said. "The one with the dark hair. Is that him? The freaky one?"

"Yes, that's Hunter."

"So you're still seeing him?" Karen asked. "What's it like?"

Pam glanced upward at the windows in the front of the building where other tenants could be listening. "Let's go inside."

I got up and followed them into their apartment. I wanted to talk to them about it. I usually talked to my mom about the guys I was dating, but she wouldn't understand any of this.

And at work, I couldn't breathe a word about a new guy in my life. I lived in constant fear that Selina would find out about me and Hunter, and somehow get me fired me for it. Selina would *hate* it that I got the man that she was pursuing. Hunter kept brushing off Selina's flirtations, as she vacillated between coming on to him aggressively and being frosty mean. I tried my best to ignore it when the two of them went at each other, but sometimes I thought Hunter enjoyed beating Selina at her own game.

I was playing with fire in every way possible—both my heart and my career. But I couldn't admit that out loud. It would make it too real.

"So tell us," Karen urged.

"It's like nothing I've ever done. Not just the sex, but that's crazy enough." I was sore and tingling all over my body because he couldn't stop touching me last night. And I didn't want him to stop.

171

"Crazy how?" Karen pressed.

"Embarrassing things. Nothing fazes him. It's like he takes me someplace new every time. And I have to admit there's something really beautiful about being able to let go. Relax. Let someone else take over. No wonder sex was so blah before him. I was thinking about how to make sure *they* were happy. But with Hunter, he's completely focused on me and my pleasure."

"Wow," Karen said softly.

"That sounds really good," Pam agreed.

"Yeah, but I can't help wondering if it's too intense? Like a flash in the pan. How can a man like that, who looks like he does, who's used to having all kinds of women, be satisfied with just me?" Minx had told me the truth. It was the distant light of a train bearing down on me as I willingly let Hunter tie me to the tracks.

"Is he dating other people now?" Pam asked.

"No, he broke up with Minx, the girl he was seeing and he said he wouldn't touch anyone else. But Minx says he does that when he's gets someone new, and then he opens the relationship back up."

Pam shook her head. "If you want monogamy, then that's that."

"I do want it, I know that much. Now I'll have to see if he's secretly expecting something else will happen. I can't imagine why he would—I'm such a doofus when it comes to these things."

I told them about visiting the Paddles and how strange it was to see ordinary people dressed up and doing such intimate things in public.

Surprisingly, Pam said, "I went to a club like that a few times with an old girlfriend."

"Who?" Karen asked. "Why didn't you ever tell me that?"

Pam shrugged. "Deanna. I did it because I loved her and it was fun to do together. She was a top so she planned everything out."

"It is fun and different," I said. "But I'm afraid that for Hunter, it's who he is. I want a family. I don't want to go to a costume party every weekend."

"I wouldn't mind going to one," Karen put in. "Let's go check it out, Pam."

Pam looked at her. "Really? You want to do that? I don't even know this place."

I put in, "It's real friendly. Minx was there with her girlfriend, and I saw other women playing together."

Pam and Karen were looking at each other speculatively. I was starting to feel like I was intruding on an interesting development.

I got up to leave. "I'll let you know what happens with Hunter."

"Just remember," Pam said, "the bottom line is if you don't like it, don't do it."

I wasn't even out the door before Karen was saying, "Okay, tell me more about what you did with Deanna…"

Grinning, I headed upstairs with groceries and my sketch. I felt like a sexual instigator stirring things up. It was funny, coming from me. But it made me feel a whole lot better to know that calm, thoughtful Pam had enjoyed a kinky relationship and came out the other side without any harm done.

Yet Pam never told Karen about it… but that also made sense. I didn't want to tell anyone about the things I did with Hunter. My thighs rubbed together, and I was so tender and sensitive down there, all naked. I was thinking about Hunter. Just like he said I would.

I cut the edges of my warehouse drawing and used a magnet to pin it to my refrigerator.

Too many good things were coming out of this. I was on the ride now, and nothing was going to pry me off until it was over.

Chapter 22

Hunter

When I got back to her place, the sketch on the fridge was the first thing I saw. Usually I only had eyes for Kali. Usually I'd be pulling off her clothes the first second I could.

But that sketch...

She was watching me warily as I homed in on it. It was whimsical and a little disturbing, one of the better combinations I had seen in a long time.

"I like this!" I exclaimed. "When did you do this?"

"This morning, as I was getting back from the store. It's the warehouse across the street."

I looked out the window at the drab old building. She had transformed it into something magical.

I pulled it off the fridge to look closer. It was done in ordinary pencil. I would have to get her some real tools. The shading would have blended nicer with softer lead.

I turned it over, and on the back were a couple of my sketches of Kali. On one of them, her head had been cut off. I raised a brow at her, and she blushed.

"I'm sorry," she said. "I wanted to cut off the doodle I had started on the back. I didn't think—"

"Never apologize for your art!" I told her.

She looked really uncomfortable. "It's not art. I was just fooling around. I don't even know why I put it up."

She made a move to take the sketch, as if to toss it away.

I held onto it more firmly. "Who taught you to disrespect your own work this way?"

She shook her head wordlessly. But she wasn't trying to grab the paper anymore.

"This is really good," I told her, looking her right in the eye. "Better than good. You've got a real eye."

"Oh, no. I'm not that good. You should have seen some of the others in my class who were so much better."

"In college?" I asked. It would be typical for the professors to suck up to the rich assholes with no talent and overlook the local girl.

"No, in high school. I took drawing my first two years, but I wasn't nearly as talented as some of the others. That's one reason I started doing cartoons. My simple outlines don't look as bad in a comic."

"They look great here," I pointed out on the sketch of the warehouse. "Was it a teacher who put you down?"

Surprised, she shook her head. "No. Everyone was very nice to me. I always got A's. I just knew... I wasn't any good. It was never going anywhere anyway. Drawing was just the elective I decided to take."

"What did you take your last two years?" I asked.

"Cooking. My mom said it would be smart to have a practical skill I'd use for the rest of my life."

I didn't let her see my excitement. She was finally giving me the goods, and she didn't even realize it. "Your mom, who's your best friend?"

"Near enough," she admitted.

"What does she think of our relationship?" I asked.

Now Kali looked really uncomfortable. "I don't really talk to her about it."

"Even when you went home?"

"I told her I didn't think it would work out." Seeing my expression, she said, "We ended up breaking up after that, remember? You were busy spanking your ex-girlfriend the night I was hanging out with my mom at home."

I nodded, knowing that the walls were cracking even if she didn't realize it. "So you haven't told her we're back on."

"I haven't had time."

175

I wanted to point out that she'd been hanging out all week alone while I was in Pittsburgh. That would be the natural time a girl would call her "best friend" to tell her about her new guy.

But I had a feeling this went deeper than even Kali knew. I had to be careful when I breached the walls inside of her. She was a fighter, but she would close down if I pushed too hard.

So far, the physical exploration had been easy, except for corporal. She resisted any sort of blows. Even when I gave her a love tap on her butt, she protested. I liked pushing her resistance, but I had to be sure she really wanted what I was doing. She needed to be curious and ready for the experience, and then I could play with her wariness.

Opening herself up sexually must be having an effect on her. I looked down at the sketch in my hands, proof there was more hidden inside of her.

"Since I have to fly to Pittsburgh tomorrow for the casting," I said, "I won't be back until Friday. But I was thinking, I could fly straight to Syracuse on my way back—it's not far from your hometown. Then I could meet your family next weekend."

"You want to go to Jefferson?" she asked dubiously.

"Sure, you met Drew. Now I want to know more about your family. How you grew up."

"It's out in the boondocks. You'll have to rent a car to get there from Syracuse."

"I'll figure it out, don't you worry about that."

She didn't seem thrilled with the idea, which bothered me and made me more determined than ever to go to Jefferson. Her past held the key to Kali. She was so busy guarding herself right now that she couldn't let go emotionally with me. It drove me crazy how uninhibited she could be sexually, and then afterwards she clammed right back up again in her protective shell. I admired her independence. But I wanted more of her.

"Okay," she finally agreed.

She was so closed off that I had to do something. I swept her up and spun her around and around, as she squealed and protested, until I set her down and began tickling her. She started laughing and wiggling, until I felt like everything was all right again.

Chapter 23

Kali

For me, the second week apart from Hunter was even harder than the first week. We went into work together so Hunter could inspect the progress on the flagstones being laid in the plaza, and to consult with the subcontractors. Then he was gone to Pittsburgh again to oversee the actual casting of the sundial in bronze.

I missed him, missed having him in my bed at night. I was blown away that he wanted to come back to see my hometown and meet my family. That's exactly what I wanted—a man who wanted to share my life. But from the first moment, part of me dreaded the coming weekend. My mom was going to ask the hard questions if I brought Hunter home. It could ruin everything.

There was no stopping it now. Hunter had changed his return ticket before he left.

We sent silly sweet text messages to each other every day, and spoke every evening so he could tell me what was happening with the casting. He liked the surface texture of the bronze when it came out of the mold, and Mr. Ryan had agreed that a matte sundial would be better than polished bronze. I thought it was an inspired change—the sundial would contrast much more against the shiny surface of the glass façade of our tower and the pale gray flagstones.

I finally called my mom on Wednesday evening. "What are you doing this weekend?"

"Nothing much. One of your dad's friends has an art opening on Saturday evening that he wants us to go to. Why?"

"I was thinking about coming up."

There was a pause. "What's going on, Kali? You were just here for a visit."

"I thought you wanted me to come home a lot."

"Kalico…"

I sighed. "I want to bring my new boyfriend. Hunter. He asked to meet you and dad, to see where I'm from."

Jenny's voice got even more wary. "The artist? The good-looking one with too many girlfriends?"

"We're exclusive now."

My mom paused, thinking about it. "It must be getting serious for him to want to meet us."

"I hope so. I really like this guy."

"Then bring him up, honey. That's the best way for us to figure this out."

I chatted with my mom a bit about the train schedules, and when I said good-bye, I felt a lot better. I hadn't brought a guy home since my freshman year in college. No wonder I was nervous. But my mom was right, seeing Hunter at home would show me whether we were really right together.

Chapter 24

Hunter

I'd never felt so satisfied as when I checked over the finished bronze pieces. The molds were so clean that the bronze came out pristine. It only needed to be buffed slightly. I made sure the pieces were packed carefully for transport to New York.

I was more focused this time because I knew I was going to Kali's hometown on Friday. I knew I would finally get the answers I needed to understand her.

It was no problem for me to catch a puddle-jumper to Syracuse and rent a car. Money had its uses, and I was enjoying my flush state. From experience, I had learned how to make my cash last, to save for the spare times. But for Kali, nothing was too much.

I had an hour before Kali's train arrived from the city, so I drove my rental car around checking out the area in the twilight. Jefferson was a good thirty minutes from the station, so I didn't go that far, but I saw enough to know I was in old farm-country. There were a lot of clapboard houses for sale, and a lot of depressed property. But the scenery was pretty, if rather tamed, with narrow roads winding up and down across the long parallel ridges of the hills.

The moment I saw Kali in the door of the train car, my heart lurched. Her smile, her excitement to see me, was almost too much. I'd been flying high all week, finally balanced within myself, and she unraveled me with a smile. I hugged her tightly, wondering how I had been able to be apart from her for so many days, suddenly unable to let her go.

"Hey, beautiful." I brushed her hair from her cheek. "My delectable Kalico-cat."

She laughed, and we kissed some more. One part of my brain

was watching everything around us, my senses on full alert because I had to take care of her. I couldn't risk falling into rapture when some random asshole might try to take advantage of it. So I led her out to my rental car and kissed her some more there. She was so ready and willing, but even though it was dark, I knew she would draw the line at anything more overt at the train station.

As if thinking the same thing, she finally drew back, warding me off. "I can't get so worked up before we see my mom."

During the drive, she told me where to go with assurance, knowing her way through the maze in the dark. I drove along roads that twisted and turned until I was completely lost. I was growing more eager, as if she was taking me down to the center of the earth, into the depths of her own psyche.

The village of Jefferson was different from everything else around it. One minute, we were driving along an ordinary two-lane highway between the fields, dotted with old barns and one-street farm towns. Then suddenly we were in a picturesque village. By the light of the old-fashioned street lamps along the tree-lined streets, I could tell this was expensive real estate. The Victorian houses were imposing brick with many stories and gabled eaves, with broad porches on front. Wrought iron benches were spaced along the sidewalks. The center of the village was a broad grassy square with several buildings at one end that looked like a 19th century courthouse and an old firehouse. A huge basket of flowers hung from every lamppost, spilling over with colorful blooms.

We drove past the square and out the other side of the village. There were a few industrial buildings and then Kali directed me to turn down a street on the outskirts. Her driveway was one of a dozen, leading to a tiny clapboard house that was nothing like the stately mansions in the village.

"Where's the college?" I asked.

"On the east side. I'll take you there tomorrow."

She sounded nervous, which was interesting. Was she worried about what I would think of her, or what her parents would think of *me?*

Kali took me to the side door that led directly into the kitchen. It was old fashioned, clean and neat. Every hand-towel had its place. There was a good smell, but for a kitchen, there was remarkably little clutter or signs of activity.

Her mom was at the door waiting for us, and Kali gave her a hug hello, then introduced her to me as "Jenny Jones."

"Hi, Jenny. I'm glad to meet you," I said.

Jenny's smile was tight. She looked older than I had expected, thin and angular, slightly smaller than Kali. "Welcome to our home. I was so happy when Kali said you both were coming up this weekend."

"Is dad here?" Kali asked.

Jenny's smile grew more brittle. "He's running late, but he should be here soon."

Kali shook her head, looking away.

"I'm sure you're hungry," Jenny said. "I've made some little nibbles for you. Go on upstairs and get settled, and we can meet back in the living room where it's comfortable."

Kali immediately grabbed her suitcase and headed out of the kitchen as ordered. She took me upstairs to her childhood room, and seemed very embarrassed to have so much of her college-self exposed to my searching gaze.

Naturally, I saw the artwork first—two framed drawings over her bed, and a piece of paper with red marker on it taped to the mirror of her dressing table. But she was so uncomfortable I didn't want to push her too hard.

So first I checked out the books she had read and the music she listened to, feeling like a sponge absorbing her through my pores like water.

Her entertainment selection seemed much older than her age. Intermingled in the usual suspects were CDs for 80s pop stars like Madonna and Olivia Newton-John, and old romance movies on DVD, and lots of Danielle Steel and Nora Roberts novels, which made me grin and hold one up. "Really? *A Perfect Stranger*?"

"Hey, judge not! That's my mom's."

"But you read it, too."

She shrugged. "I should get rid of all this old stuff. My parents could turn this room into an office or real spare bedroom. But I know they want me to feel like I could come back any time."

"Did you draw those?" I asked casually of the framed pieces. They were done in ink, in fine feathery lines. One was of a house with a well outside of it, and the other was of a tree with an empty swing.

"No, those are illustrations from a book of fairy tales I had when I was a kid. When the book fell apart, I was so upset that my dad framed my two favorite ones so I could always remember the stories." She frowned a little as she said it.

"It's hard to see what's in front of you all the time," I pointed out.

"You're right. I haven't thought about that book in ages. But the pictures are always there." She shrugged it off. "It does look a little like my style, doesn't it? Maybe I'm just copying something I picked up when I was a child, after all."

I smiled. "I don't think so. That drawing you did of the building was inspired. Truly different. But with these, they look they're illustrations from a child's book."

She looked embarrassed again, like she wasn't used to being complimented. I wandered back to the other side of the room. As I neared the red drawing, she tensed and didn't take her eyes off me.

I had to smile as I pointed to it. "What's this?"

She looked away. "Nothing."

I didn't want to let on that I realized how important it was. The scribbled drawing was done in bold red marker, of all things. The instrument of choice by high school girls making cheer and bake-sale posters.

I took a closer look, flattening the curling edges. And let out a laugh. "It's brilliant!"

It was the word Jeff spelled out in red marker, but each of the letters had taken on a life of their own. The "J" was the quintessential jock, lounging on the steps of a neo-classical building. The "e" and the two "f's" were both girls, one round and the other two fashionably skinny, but all three so entitled he could tell it from the upward curve of a nose here and the downward curve of a mouth there.

"You're mocking out the college," I said.

"I guess so. I was just telling it like I saw it." She sighed, knowing I wasn't going to let it go. "I did it for a school contest my freshman year. They wanted a new logo for the T-shirts. The real college seal has a feather quill on it."

"I've seen it. Bo-ring."

"So I just banged it out one night."

"You didn't win?"

She hesitated, then laughed at herself. "I didn't send it in."

"What?" I looked at the life in her drawing. Even the targets of her spoof would love it. "Why not?"

"It wasn't appropriate."

"By whose standards?" I asked.

She shrugged.

I wanted to cradle the little drawing in my hands. It was a baby bird that fell out of the nest, all naked and shriveled. Nobody had taken care of it so it could fluff up and be able to fly. It had just lain here in the dark for years.

"Did you show it to your dad?" I asked, afraid of what I might hear.

"Oh, sure. He loved it. He thinks it's funny, too." She gave a short laugh as if remembering his reaction. "He's the one who taped it up here. I guess I just forgot about it. You really do stop seeing things that are right in front of you, don't you?"

I couldn't let this go. "Why didn't he tell you to submit it to the contest?"

"He said I should."

"Then why didn't you?"

She shrugged, really uncomfortable now. "I was on a scholarship. It just didn't seem right to do something to make fun of the school."

"I thought they were giving you a scholarship because your mom works there."

"Yeah, that's right." She went to the door. "We should go down. My mom's waiting for us."

This time I couldn't stop her. She was out the door and heading down the stairs. I had no choice but to follow, with one last look at the sassy red drawing.

I was already seeing the pattern. *What mom says, goes.* I sat where Jenny told me to, and ate the little sweet and savory tapas Jenny had laid out in neat rows. I let Jenny lead our conversation, and Kali visibly relaxed the more we talked about the sundial project for SunTech and where we went on our various dates.

Jenny smiled and was very gracious, but there was a slight patronizing tone, like she probably treated the students on campus. Polite, but not buying the bullshit.

"I'm going to show Hunter around tomorrow," Kali said. "He'll be able to see most of my life in just six square miles."

Jenny smiled. "Jefferson is a wonderful place to raise a child. Where did you grow up, Hunter?"

"When I was young, my family moved around a lot, mostly on the east coast. For the past twelve years, they've been in Harrisburg."

"Where did you go to college?"

"I never went to college. I'm a self-taught artist."

Jenny stared at me. "That may be good enough for graffiti but when you're talking about a career, you need an education."

"It's called aerosol art," I corrected. "And formal education is not necessary for many things in life. Art is one of them."

Silence hung in the air, and Kali was frozen, not quite looking at either of us.

Finally, Jenny said, "Do you have a backup plan, Hunter? Most artists can teach if their career falters. But you can't do that without a degree."

"I'm an artist. I learned in the real world, and I'll always be sculpting and casting metal. I'm sure I'll have more than enough projects to fill a lifetime."

"But you rely on patrons to survive, like all artists. If that dries up, you'll starve. Or you'll lose your home. That's hard, especially if you have children." Jenny looked at me harder. "Are you planning to have a family?"

"I don't plan out everything." *Like apparently you do*, I wanted to add.

"But you have to make plans if you have children. It's too much responsibility to go into it lightly and just hope that things work out."

It was offensive on so many levels, but it was serving my goal to figure out what was at the heart of Kali. So I went ahead and named what was going on. "It sounds like you think I'm not good enough for your daughter."

"She didn't say that," Kali put in quickly.

Jenny didn't agree, which was even more telling. "My first responsibility is to watch out for my daughter. I want to be sure she's taken care of. I don't want Kali to have to support her husband *and* her child. Like I did."

It rang in the air, her defiant defense of the judgment she had laid down against me.

Unfortunately, at this most interesting turn, Kali's dad arrived home and interrupted everything. He called out a big "hallo!" from the kitchen and Kali ran in to hug him. Jenny and I followed in charged silence.

After that, Danny Jones took the lead, opening up some wine for us and telling us about the rehearsal he had just gotten back from. He composed synthesizer music and worked with a couple different groups. One was a wedding band that he dismissed with a shrug. I heard about his interests in music, wood-working, performing arts and community organizing.

Because of our rocky start, I didn't talk much to Jenny, but she participated in our conversation, adding things from the campus point of view when it came to village planning or the plight of the local theater which had to compete with the much better-funded theater arts program at the college.

Kali seemed happy again, now that the danger zone was in the rear-view mirror. But I saw the threads of discontent crop up from time to time. Danny said at one point that he had tried and failed to create a puppet theater in the area, while Jenny sighed over the bills they still had to pay for it. Danny's plan for transforming a vacant triangle of land into a bandstand area had also recently failed, and Jenny pointed out that it became a dog park despite his active campaigning. He taught music lessons to some very young pupils, but according to Jenny's dismissive expression, that clearly wasn't worth much. When Danny announced he'd been asked to write a review of the art opening tomorrow for the local free weekly paper on spec, Kali was the one who congratulated him not Jenny.

The one thing Jenny and Danny agreed on was Kali. The love flowed freely between them and their daughter, with both parents competing for her attention. Kali didn't have to do anything. She absorbed it all with her sweet, placating nature, making peace between them just by existing.

It was so enlightening.

...

I was grateful that Kali's parents weren't straight-laced so we could sleep together. I couldn't keep my hands off her, though her parents were right across the hall from us. Kali was inhibited for the first time, unable to let go as she worried about creaky springs and loud breathing. She didn't orgasm until I went down on her, and then she stifled her own sounds by smashing a pillow against her face. It was hot making her climax in spite of her walls, pushing her resistance in a new way.

The next day she showed me around. The campus had just released the students, so there weren't many people around. Those I saw were either working on the grounds or were privileged kids, sleek and handsome, dawdling on campus after the end of the semester before their real vacation started somewhere else. It was so privileged it reeked. They even lived in mansions converted into sororities and fraternities with large Greek letters over the doors, and attended classes in the high-tech labs and luxurious old-world buildings.

Somehow it hadn't ruined Kali. Not many people could resist the lure of money, of longing after it when it was flaunted in your face. But she had resisted assimilation. Now he understood where she got her stubborn self-reliance.

I gestured to a group of kids sitting on the edge of a fountain looking like a catalogue for Abercrombie. "Your mom would be glad to have you marry one of those guys. Then you wouldn't have to worry about money."

Kali raised a hand as if to ward off the suggestion. "I didn't date much while I was going here. Guys like that only want one thing from a townie."

"But you were one of them. You went to school with them."

"I was a charity pupil. There's no way I could have done it otherwise. And they could tell that."

"You were caught between two worlds."

She nodded. "After I started coming here, some of my old friends dropped me. I still see them around, but we don't speak. Maybe it's my fault, too. I started doing new things, and was busy on campus instead of hanging out with them."

"That probably made it easier for you to leave Jefferson."

She looked surprised. "Maybe. I sometimes wonder why my old friends stay here when there's not much opportunity for improving their lives."

"They're comfortable here. Outside of Jefferson itself, you can probably live dirt cheap."

A few people we bumped into in the village mentioned getting together at the local dive that night—a guy at the bakery and a tired-looking woman with two toddlers we met on the street. But Kali begged off, citing her dad's friend's art opening in one of the municipal buildings. Her old friends looked me over, wide-eyed, like a movie star had suddenly fallen into town and they weren't quite sure what to say at first, and then said too much as Kali was trying to get away.

Jenny made dinner for us that night before the opening. She was back to being politely distant with me, as if biding her time.

On the other hand, Danny had embraced me as a fellow artist with no questions asked. Literally. He had yet to ask me anything. He had an astonishing capacity for self-absorption. He seemed much more interested in showing off to me than finding out what kind of man his daughter had brought home.

At the art opening, Danny introduced me around to his friends and the local civil servants. All of them knew Danny Jones. Jenny disappeared, literally. I kept losing her in the crowd. Whereas Danny was exuberantly involved in everything, so you never lost sight of him.

I lost track of Kali at one point, and finally saw her cornered by her mom near the bathrooms. Jenny was speaking in low, urgent tones.

I could tell she was talking to Kali about me, using the opportunity of the art opening to get her daughter alone. Kali looked unhappy. I knew what Jenny was saying even though I couldn't hear her: *"He'll never be able to take care of you. You can't trust him. He's an irresponsible. All artists are...."* And most of all: *"Don't make the same mistake I did."*

Kali said hardly a word, just shaking her head from time to time, or reluctantly nodding agreement.

It sent a cold shiver down my spine. Like I was seeing her death warrant. I was going to have to deal with this head-on, or I was going to lose her.

Later that night as Kali sat cross-legged on her bed watching me get undressed, I said, "Your mother was talking to you about me tonight. What did she say?"

Kali looked embarrassed. "I'm sorry she wasn't very tactful last night."

"I don't care about that. I want you to be honest with me. We can't get anywhere if we keep secrets from each other."

She took a deep breath. "She says I'm just repeating a pattern from my own childhood, choosing a man like my dad."

"An artist?"

"Yes, that. And what that brings with it. Lack of stability. Having to be the responsible one."

I didn't smile, though I wanted to. "Tell me, Kali, who has the power in your parents' relationship? Which one is in control?"

"I guess my dad is. He does exactly what he wants. My mom had to work two jobs sometimes to support us."

"It's true that your dad has absolute freedom outside the house. But Jenny Jones rules this family, make no mistake about that."

Kali shook her head, her brow furrowed. "You think she likes it that he doesn't show up when he says he will? That he's always off doing his own thing?"

"That what he bargained for. Everything else belongs to your mom. She chose this house, I bet everything in it from the rugs to the food in the fridge. And she controls the money. Look at her car! Nearly new while your dad drives a shitty old minivan with duct tape on the bumper."

"She earned the money herself. She should have a nice car."

"Think about it: since we've been here she's told us when to eat, what to eat, when to leave, when to come home, when to sleep..."

Kali considered that for a few moments. "I never thought of it that way."

"The only time your dad is free is when he's outside this house and away from her. No wonder he stays away so much. No wonder *you* moved away."

"I wasn't trying to get away from my mom. We have a great

190

relationship."

"Yes, as long as you do what she wants. I bet she hated it when you left for the city. She lost control over you. But you probably wanted to leave for a long time before that."

Her face suddenly turned to me. "How did you know that? I wanted to go away to college to Florida or California, someplace warm."

"Someplace thousands of miles away from Jenny Jones."

"Don't say that!"

"It's blasphemous, isn't it? But I know you and Jenny talk over your dad's failings. Seriously, I bet he was no different when your mom met him. She *chose* him because of who he is. She knew she could have her own way with him, that he would let her be in charge as long as he could goof off for the rest of his life."

Kali didn't answer, but she wasn't protesting anymore.

So I pressed it. "She controlled you the same way, Kali. She used your dad as a scary example to keep you in line. She used her hardship to get your sympathy for *her*. To pull you away from him."

Kali had to admit, "She did put him down because he wouldn't get a real job. To me. His daughter."

"So you had no faith in him. You put all of your faith in your mother." I pointed at the red drawing on her mirror. "That's why you believe her when she told you not to submit that drawing to the contest. Instead of believing your father, the artist in your family."

Kali looked stricken. "She said it would look bad for me. Bad for her."

"And that's the most important thing, isn't it? What's best for Jenny Jones?" I leaned in closer to her, lowering my voice. "I think it's time you do what's best for Kalico Jones."

191

Chapter 25

Kali

I was shaken to my core. In the space of twenty-four hours, Hunter had managed to make me question everything I knew about my family.

The next morning, I kept glimpsing my mom and dad through Hunter's eyes. With my mom in the kitchen, my dad didn't make pancakes like he usually did when the two of us were alone. He even changed his shirt at Jenny's mention that it was wrinkled, and I remembered the time she threw away a pair of pants he bought because she didn't like the color. Everything he wore was purchased by my mom, including his shoes. Jenny also bought my clothes in joint shopping sessions, with me deferring to her advice. I wondered how different my chaste, drab wardrobe would look if I had been allowed to experiment with colors and styles like my friends had done.

At this point, I wouldn't know how to start.

Maybe Hunter was right and my mom had chosen my dad with her eyes wide open. When my mom made a snide remark about my dad having to go someplace right after breakfast, it was suddenly clear she was doing it to get me on her side. I had been caught in a tug of war between my parents' affection for as long as I could remember, but I had never wanted to look at it that way.

Like I had stopped seeing the Jeff drawing that I had loved so much as I was doing it, dashing it off the evening after I heard about the contest. How could I have forgotten the storm of feelings caused by the Big Question: should I submit it to the contest? My dad's urging had no chance once my mom decided otherwise.

Why did I let her convince me to keep the Jeff drawing instead of submitting it? Hunter was right. It was good. God knows, the kids who went to Jefferson weren't exactly shy about their privilege. They might have loved it and put it on their pep T-shirts.

More than anything, I realized Hunter was right as I told my mom good-bye in the kitchen, while Hunter was putting our bags in the car. I had avoided being alone with my mom until the last minute.

Without any warning, my mom said, "You have to see that it's impossible for you to be serious about him, Kali."

"I don't think so, Mom."

Jenny's lips compressed into a thin line. "I don't want you to have to struggle like I did."

"I won't. I'm doing what's best for myself," I said, echoing Hunter.

"What's best for him, maybe. He'll live off you forever if you give him half a chance. I should know."

That bothered me. "You've been happy with Dad. You must get something out of it or you would have kicked him out a long time ago."

"He's a good father. When he's around. But he's never been able to contribute to our household in a meaningful way."

"Hunter isn't like that. He's supported himself and worked for his family since he was a teenager. He takes care of his parents, not the other way around like most of the people I know who are living off the monthly check from daddy."

"I don't see a future in it, Kali."

I wanted to shake off my mom's fears that threatened to smother me. "You can't know that. Everything's changing. What about the administrators from the college you were talking about last night who got laid off? They were making good plans, safe in a steady job, but life comes along and smacked them around. Maybe it's good to choose someone who can roll with the punches and figure out how to make things work. Instead of someone who coasts along thinking they're safe because they get a paycheck twice a month."

As I turned away, Hunter was standing in the doorway with a big grin on his face. He had been tense all weekend, not like his usual self. I liked seeing him happy again. Even better, it was because of me.

My mom had nothing more to say, not in front of Hunter. She turned ice cold and hardly responded to my hug good-bye. I felt abandoned by the way she was acting. Jenny's disapproving silence was worse than any arguments.

But this time I was able to wave goodbye and leave it behind. I wouldn't have to come home and face a blank wall when I tried to talk to my mom. It was a relief, because I didn't have to make things right. I knew from past experience that the only way to make it right was to do what my mom said. But I wasn't going to dump my super-sexy lover just because my mom told me to.

I felt like I was casting off the ropes and sailing into the unknown. *Here there be dragons*....

...

I was on edge for the several-hour train trip back to the city with Hunter. He didn't seem to mind the long periods of silence. He worked on his laptop, then stretched out his long legs and watched the lush countryside pass by until we abruptly came to the far flung outlines of the city.

I had hoped the sight of the clustered skyscrapers in the distance would lift my spirits, as it always did. But this time I had the uncomfortable feeling that I had dragged Jefferson and its baggage back to the city with me.

I was so preoccupied that I didn't really consider what was happening until Hunter had accompanied me all the way from Penn Station back to my apartment. Standing in the living room facing him, feeling oddly displaced, I still didn't know what to say or do.

"Would you like me to go?" Hunter asked gently.

"I don't know. Honestly, I don't know what I want right now."

"It's natural. You're unsettled because you're defying your mom. I bet she hated it when you moved to the city."

"Yes, she did," I admitted. "She really pushed for me to get a job at one of those windmill projects that have gone up around Jefferson. She still keeps trying to get me involved."

"You never thought about her being so controlling?"

"I always thought we were on my dad's whim. But you're right—my mom decides everything. My dad never complains about it. I guess he doesn't mind."

"And you ignored it until now."

I sighed. "Now all I can do is think about it."

Hunter put a reassuring hand on my shoulder. "You are tense. Here, let me rub your back."

He stepped behind me and began expertly rubbing my back between my shoulder blades, running his hands down and around, then back up to the top of my shoulders, slowly pressing deeper to release the tension.

"Ahh…," I breathed.

He stroked me from the back of my head, down my neck, down either side of my spine. He gently gripped my shoulders and rotated them to loosen me up. It felt wonderful.

But all I could think about was how my dad gave my mom back rubs. Jenny complained that sitting at a desk all day was hard on her back. Danny was good at giving a back rub, and he did it for me and for his friends, too, from time to time. I should be enjoying this.

"What's wrong?" Hunter asked.

"Nothing. It feels great."

"You just sighed." He took hold of my shoulders, showing me how stiff I was. "You're fighting me every inch of the way. What's going on?"

"I keep thinking about my dad. He always gives my mom backrubs. I've never seen her do it for him. Never. Not even once."

"They each bring certain things to the relationship. They found a way to get what they need. But the better way to do it is to talk it out rather than struggle passive-aggressively to get what you want."

"That makes sense," I said absently.

He stopped and turned me to face him. "I think you're upset because you've realized how much your mom used her complaints about your dad to manipulate you. She made sure you did what she wanted, because she was already so imposed on by him. She made you a mini-adult to help her, but I think it was mainly to keep you under her thumb."

It was true. Only now did I realize that Jeff sketch was the last drawing I had done. Until Hunter came into my life. My mom probably wouldn't like it that I was drawing again. That was the part of me like my dad, and looking back I could see all the ways she had discouraged my creative side. That path led to fear and worry. Jenny's way led to safety.

I put my hands to my face. "It's so awful! I hate seeing there were a lot of subconscious motives playing out the whole time."

"The underbelly is there whether we look at it or not. You're one of the lucky ones. Your family is functional, affectionate and your parents think the world of you. You weren't abused or victimized—right? You've never said anything about that."

I shook my head. "No, never anything like that. A handsy guy on a date once. I got really scared but he backed off in the end."

"There's always power dynamics at play. It's a constant push-pull. We manipulate people into giving us what we need. Some do it deliberately, some unconsciously. It's always happening, so it makes sense to watch the undercurrents at work."

I nodded, feeling lost. I didn't know what to think.

Hunter stroked my cheek. "I hate to see you so sad. It's not your fault, you know. I see a lot of girls like you, perfectionists who always step up to get the job done. They're usually submissive."

"Really?"

"I guess it makes sense since you're the ones who are really in control. You're the ones with the escape hatch to end the scene."

"Do you ever give up control sexually?" I asked.

His lips compressed. "Not really. I did the hook pull, but it was completely on my own terms. I'm not as good at letting go like you are. But I'm feeling it more with you than I ever have. It's a release to let go, to stop your mind from going round and round. To just feel and focus entirely on the moment. It's cathartic, transformative."

"Like sex," I agreed.

"The way *you* have sex, yes. You lose yourself when you get passionate. That's why I think you'd like it if you tried something like spanking."

The word hung in the air.

I crossed my arms over myself. "I don't want to get hurt."

"I won't hurt you. I promise. And you can say stop any time, remember? You can just tell me if it isn't working for you. I want it to feel good."

I used to be so sure that I wouldn't like it, that it couldn't possibly feel good, that it was hard to reconsider. But he kept blowing up my preconceived notions about so many things, especially when it came to hot sex, that I felt a shiver of longing deep inside. I liked jumping into the unknown with him, relying on him to carry us through.

I liked how much he wanted to make me feel good...

Hunter drew me closer, dropping one hand down to my butt, squeezing one cheek. "You'll like it. I know you will." His voice lowered. "You know you're curious."

I met his intensely blue eyes, caught fast as always. The game was on. I could tell it by the tone of his voice. I wanted to give this to him. I wanted to please him. Part of me was running away from it because I was afraid I wouldn't be able to do it right. That I'd disappoint him by ending it abruptly because I couldn't handle it. I was no Minx. I had no illusions about my own wimpitude.

But he was right, I was curious what all the fuss was about.

"All right," I agreed.

He kissed me, one hand holding me close and the other on my butt cheek, squeezing like a promise of more to come. I liked it. Then he put his other hand on my butt, pulling me into him, pressing me against him, as he squeezed and rubbed my behind. I held onto his neck and shoulders, leaning back as he kissed me.

With almost a growl, he picked me up and lifted me over his shoulder. I let out a little shriek from the sudden movement, finding myself hanging upside down. He still had a hand on my butt, steadying me over his shoulder, his other arm holding my legs together. He carried me into the bedroom and threw me onto the bed.

I let out another shriek, flying backwards for a second. It got my heart racing and I already felt flushed and turned on from his kisses. It seemed like he wanted to devour me, to take every part of me. Like there was no way I could resist him.

Then he was leaning over me, pressing me into the bed, holding me down by his size and weight. He was letting me feel his control. So I would know that none of my struggles would be able to stop him.

It was a little frightening. He said I could stop any time. But really, there was nothing I could do if he decided to keep going.

Maybe I was twisted, but the fear turned me on even more. It was every awful bodice-ripper that ever existed—Abduction! Forced sex! Everlasting love!

Hunter took hold of my chin with one hand, bringing me abruptly to the present. "You're still thinking too much."

He rolled off me, lying down next to me, facing me. Putting his arm under my back, he scooped me with him as he sat up on the edge of the bed, holding me to his chest. I was half-sitting up, nestled against his bicep and my legs curled behind him on the bed. He was rubbing my butt, with my hip braced on his thigh.

A firm smack on my ass surprised me. It wasn't the classic over-the-knee spanking position, which I had dreaded so much. My mom had never spanked me as a child. It would have humiliated us both. The worst punishment I got was the silent treatment. And my dad, he never punished me for anything.

Hunter slapped first one cheek, then the other, low down where my butt met the top of my thigh, then higher where it was more sensitive. I was wearing jeans, so the denim muffled everything and made it feel more like a massage than anything.

He got into a rhythm, alternating and then changing it up, pausing then spanking again. He gradually got firmer, and then went softer for a few swats. He stopped and rubbed and squeezed my butt through my jeans, making me moan, it felt so good. The impacts jarred me from top to bottom, forcing me to tense and relax.

"Hmm…," I murmured.

He bent down and kissed me, inflamed and aggressive where I was growing languid and floating.

When he swatted me again, repeatedly like he was keeping time to a song only we could hear, I didn't feel it as much, though I could tell he was doing it harder than when he first started. My butt and legs were tingling.

"Take off your jeans," he told me. "And your panties."

Oh, no, now it's getting serious, I thought. Maybe this delicious feeling was just the candy-coated topping that lured you in.

I pulled off my jeans and kicked them off my legs. He stroked my buttocks, and my skin was alive to every brush of his fingertips.

"You're getting nice and rosy," he told me.

I looked over my shoulder and saw my butt checks were red. The rest of my skin was so white. His hand was dark against me, rubbing my butt.

"You have a beautiful ass. I admired it the first time I met you, even though you were trying to hide your light under that gray suit."

I felt tongue-tied, silenced by my position. Half-dressed while he was fully clothed. He was so clever at putting me at a disadvantage, making me feel vulnerable.

So why did I feel safe in his arms?

Then he spanked me. His hand on my bare ass felt completely different. It was sharp, stinging, hard.

"Oh!" I gasped.

He spanked me again, my other butt cheek, hitting the soft flesh. Alternating from one to the other, picking a rhythm, then pausing to stroke and squeeze me. I threw caution to the wind and went with it. I jerked and tightened my fingers on his arm at the sharper blows, and relaxed and was lulled by the rubbing in between.

I could feel it in my groin, the jolt and tug of every smack. Spreading warmth through my body, lighting up my nerves so each blow felt better and better. The rhythm was the best, building in intensity, then breaking off. Again and again.

I was panting like I was running a race, and both of us were sheened, like he was running with me. It didn't really hurt, though there were flashes of pain when his finger tips went further to the sides or the top of my butt. But it just served to drive me higher.

It was only the two of us, connected in a dance as he felt me react, playing with my movements, seeming by instinct to know when to push harder and when to ease off. I felt myself being driven by a master, one who knew my body better than I did, who trusted me to let go to him.

I heard myself crying out, over and over. He kept pushing me higher, making me want more. His hand was hitting both butt cheeks at once, right over my pussy.

I was caught off guard as waves of contractions ripped through my body, as I came. He held onto me, trying to keep up the rhythm in spite of my movements.

Suddenly it was too much.

"Oh, stop, please!" I begged, grabbing for his arm.

He quickly began to rub my bottom, holding me as I slumped in his arms, the room swirling around us.

Slowly I realized we were breathing together, and his face was close to mine, his eyes closed as he held me tightly.

"I think I came," I murmured.

"Yes, you did." He kissed my forehead, and held me as if he didn't want to let go.

I relaxed, realizing that I could trust him. He wasn't going to hurt me.

While I was still flushed and tingling, he pushed me back on the bed and opened my legs to take me. For a moment, he leaned over me, his thick erection jutting towards me. I was spread out under him, still panting from his spanking. I no longer wanted to hide myself. He could see every part of me. And he accepted every part of me.

As he drove deep into me, I gave myself up to him again.

Chapter 26

Hunter

Only moments into our first spanking scene, and I knew I was right. She loved it!

It gave her the cathartic release that she needed after our weekend with her parents. And no wonder. She was profoundly shaken by finding out the truth about her deeply manipulative mother. Jenny Jones was a real piece of work.

It was the breakthrough I had been waiting for.

Now I wanted to meet Jenny's mother, to decode the origins of the bitch who had stifled my Kali. No wonder Kali sometimes looked like a doll fresh out of its wrapper. Jenny had done everything she could to keep her daughter safe and snug in her grip. It was a sheer wonder that Kali had broken free enough to move to the city. But she had told me about the misunderstanding about the location of her new job, found out too late for Jenny to mount an effective defense.

The morning after the spanking, I caught her looking at the mottled marks on her buttocks in the mirror. I had gone on for longer than I had intended to, but she had taken to it so well that I couldn't stop myself.

And then she had climaxed, surprising us both.

"It feels swollen," Kali said. "A little rough. But not bad."

I came over and gave her butt a loving stroke. She shivered, her skin so sensitive she felt everything exquisitely.

"I know you feel good down here." I turned her in my arms, giving her cheek a stroke. "I want to be sure you feel good up here, too. I think it helped, didn't it?"

She nodded. "It did help. I was able to forget about everything with my mom and dad. I wanted to turn my mind off. And now it doesn't seem so overwhelming."

"But something's still bothering you?" I pressed.

"Well… I feel like an idiot, for one thing. I did sympathize with my mom. Completely. I mean, my dad is a mixed bag, but he's not all bad. Why couldn't I see what she was doing?"

"You knew you had to get away to be free. We're all fucked up in some way. But who digs deeper to figure why?"

"You do," she pointed out.

I had to smile at that. "That's how I survive. We all have our ways. You have yet to figure out yours."

We talked about it a lot over the next few days. Kali kept remembering things from her childhood, and she was seeing everything from a new perspective. When we weren't talking, we were having sex in every way imaginable. Now that the spanking barrier had been passed, she was willing to try other things. More intense things, as long as I built up slowly, getting her warmed up.

She even went to the salon that friends of mine used because of their relatively painless Brazilian. I made the appointment for her, and went with her. She squirmed the entire time, hating to expose herself to the technician. But she did it for me.

I was on top of the world. The SunTech job was nearly done and there had been no serious hitches. Next week the bronze pieces of the sundial would arrive and the workmen would bolt them into place. Then my vision would be realized.

I had won the job and the girl. Who wouldn't be pleased with themselves?

By Thursday, the workmen had completed the flagstones and no more work could be done until the sculpture arrived. So on Friday, I slipped away to a leather store in the West Village.

I wanted to get a collar for Kali. There was a big party at my friend's loft on Saturday that I wanted to take her to, and I thought it would be fun to collar her for the evening.

The smell of leather hit me as I opened the glass door of the shop. The cute leatherboy in short black shorts and bare chest with only a narrow leather harness gave me a smile and a frankly appraising once-over. I knew I could get a blow-job in the changing room with a snap of my fingers. This boy didn't need a lot of wooing or talking to get it going.

But I liked the pursuit, not the end game. So as pretty as he was, it left me cold.

Come to think of it, I had never told Kali that I had topped other men and gotten my dick sucked a few times. I wasn't exactly bisexual, more pansexual. Hopefully Kali wouldn't have a problem with it. It was part of the sexual exploration that I wanted to encourage in her, opening the doors to see why they were closed. I had found out a lot of interesting things about myself that way.

"I'm looking for a collar for my girlfriend," I told the leatherboy.

The leatherboy took me back to the wall-rack that held dozens of different collars. I waved him away when he started to show off the different styles and features. I didn't need anyone to explain collars to me.

The first collar I picked off the rack was made of wide black leather with large silver O-rings. It looked exactly like the first collar I ever bought. I had given it to Mandy, a girl I played with for several years while she attended NYU. She had money; the classic little rich girl who wasn't smart enough to go to Columbia, living in the dorms on Washington Square the whole time we dated. I was in Williamsburg at the time, in a loft on Kent St, right next to a warehouse that stored barrels of chemicals, with a view of the vacant Domino Sugar factory on the river.

Those were wild times, and Mandy had been a wild girl. She had flunked out of college, and was so self-destructive that I could barely slow her downward spiral. She liked drugs too much for her own good. She ran away to Las Vegas and I lost touch with her.

I used to love to lock Mandy in the collar and snap her wrist cuffs to the O-rings so she had to stand with her arms folded and hands useless at her neck. She was so rambunctious that I needed to ride her hard with a curb bit.

Not so with Kali. I put the collar back on the wall. I couldn't imagine putting something that crude and functional on Kali.

I searched through the circles of leather and silver, gravitating toward the more delicate offerings. Some had studs, others had small spikes or were plated with silver discs. I remembered buying Minx her collar—I went to a Pet Smart and picked out a fluorescent green dog collar. She loved the color, while I liked the fact that it made her look like a cheap toy.

Kali would look cute in a pink dog collar, wearing nothing else, kneeling on the floor with her knees apart.

But not for her first collar. None of these collars were right. I was starting to think I wanted to do more than create a scene. Any collar I gave to Kali would have to seal our bond.

I took a taxi up to Chelsea to Purple Passion. Two long glass cabinets at the front of the store protected jewelry. There were nipple rings, belly chains, collars and bracelets. I immediately narrowed in on a silver chainmail ribbon. A heart-shaped padlock linked the choker together at the base of the throat. The padlock was faced with pave diamonds. It sparkled when the girl pulled it out for me.

I could imagine it sparkling on Kali as she breathed.

"I'll take it," I said.

I couldn't wait to give it to her.

•••

I was hanging out with Kali on Saturday morning, watching her draw with the new pencils and a sketchbook of her own that I had given to her. When I got a text from Minx. It was annoying because now I would have to ruin the nice mood and tell Kali.

"It's from Minx." I looked down at my phone. "She's asking if she can crash at my place tonight. She broke up with her girlfriend."

Kali's lips tightened, but she turned back to her pad without a word.

I texted Minx: *Sorry, can't.* Then I told Kali, "I told her no."

After a few moments of silence, Kali asked, "Would you

usually let her stay at your place?"

"If you didn't mind, yes. I'm going to be here tonight anyway."

"Does she have a key?"

"No. I'd have to let her in."

"Do you think it's serious?" Kali asked. "The breakup?"

"Not likely. They've been fighting and making up for four years, maybe more."

"So maybe she's just trying to see you," Kali said thoughtfully.

" Could be."

Kali didn't say anything else about it after that, and I was glad. I wouldn't put it past Minx to have manufactured the whole thing in order to see me. And it was nice that Kali didn't overreact about it.

I went home to do some things and Kali also had some errands to run. We had been spending so much time together this week that everything else had gone by the wayside. My loft was a dusty mess without anyone to clean it. Kali had said something yesterday about us always staying at her place, so I spent a few hours polishing everything up in case she wanted to come back to my studio over the weekend.

As a precaution, I also leaned a bunch of my paintings against the wall cabinets along the front. They held the erotic sculptures I sold through Hunting Art. I didn't want her to see those until after the launch. I didn't like hiding my business from her, but I didn't want to put Kali in a bad position at work. I had barely managed to distract Selina enough with our constant sparring to keep her from noticing the rapport I had with Kali.

When I arrived back at Kali's place, I was carrying the collar in its box and another gift I had bought for her in my bag. I didn't say anything about either of them as we went for a causal dinner at the vegan diner on Bedford.

"I have some surprises for you," I said on the way back to her place.

"You do?" Her expression lit up.

I knew she liked surprises. She had told me that her dad was good at giving her little gifts or taking her someplace special. They had a lot of private rituals, as did Kali and her mom.

I wanted to create some rituals with Kali, too. I was committing myself to her, to making this work for both of us. The collar was a symbol of that commitment.

But first, there was my other gift. As soon as we got in the door, I told her, "Take off your clothes."

"What?" She blinked at me.

"If you don't get naked, you won't get your surprises."

She made a funny face at that, and looked around the living room. "Here?"

"Sure, why not?"

Making sure the blinds were pulled down completely, she reluctantly stripped down to nothing. I loved her like this the best, when I was pulling her into a scene, feeling her fight my control.

I pulled the black PVC corset dress from my bag. It was a shiny tube, structured with heavy seams to hold its shape. There was a long lace that closed the back from top to bottom. In front there was a zipper.

"Oh!" she exclaimed, hands to her mouth. "Is that for me?"

"Yes," I laughed.

"It's awfully tiny. And short. I'm not sure you know my size."

I laughed again. "I know your size exactly. It will fit like a glove, just wait and see."

I loosened the laces to spread the back panels further apart, then unzipped the dress. She held it around herself as I zipped it up. Then I turned her to tighten the corset laces in the back. Pulling on the loops at her waist, it tightened the top and bottom at the same time.

"Ah...," she murmured as she wiggled and the dress conformed to her curves. I pulled it tight at her waist. Not as tight as I would have liked, but enough so that she turned slightly under my hands.

"That's to remind you that I've bound you," I said, as I tied the laces in a tight bow knot, letting the loops drape nicely down to her ass.

Her hands smoothed her own curves. "I want to see it."

"Do you have any stilettos?"

She giggled. "It's like a perverted Pretty Woman! My mom would die."

She took me to her closet and I found only one choice—a pair of silver high heels with a platform toe that had obviously never been worn. Sitting in the midst of her sensible shoes and pumps, they looked as out of place as a pair of peacocks.

"Where'd you get these?" I held them up.

She grimaced. "I bought them in college. It was a seduction attempt. I wore a little baby doll nightie and matching g-string."

"How did it turn out?"

"You know, I mostly remember the look on his face when I appeared in the door, like he didn't know what to do with himself."

"Don't worry, Kalico-cat, I know exactly what to do with you. Lift up," I ordered, raising her foot. I strapped on the stilettos, taking my time and stroking her feet. Then she headed towards her full length mirror on the back of her bedroom door. The tight dress made her take little steps, as did the shoes.

She admired herself with bright eyes. "Wow, this dress does amazing things for my figure."

"Your figure does amazing things for that dress," I told her.

She was heading into submissive mode now from my handling of her. She was breathing faster, her bare shoulders and chest flushed. Her breasts were pushed up perfectly by the tight dress, and her waist nipped in to emphasize her high, round butt.

"I have something else for you." I stood behind her looking at her in the mirror. "Something very important."

She met my eyes. "What is it?"

I held up my hand, letting the silver collar hang in front of her. "It's a collar."

I unlocked the tiny padlock with the silver key and draped the choker around her neck. Then I relocked the padlock and tucked the key into my front pocket, so it could rest over my heart.

"That looks beautiful on you," I told her. "It's a symbol of our commitment to each other."

Chapter 27

Kali

A shiver of foreboding went down my spine as the lock clicked shut. I watched his hand as he put the key in his pocket.

I don't like it, was my first thought. Oh, it was very pretty with the silver mesh and just enough sparkles to catch the eye. As jewelry, I would have loved it.

But he had locked it around my throat.

My fingers went to it, tugging slightly. I felt a sense of claustrophobia rising in me. It wasn't too tight, but it was tight enough and heavy enough that I felt it.

I forced my mind away from the fact that it was locked. I had to try. Hunter was so pleased, I couldn't be a kill-joy. He had suggested things that I thought would be awful—like spanking—that turned out to be completely different than I imagined. This would probably be the same.

Still, I really hoped he didn't pull out a leash next, or I would have to say *Stop*. It felt wrong for me. I remembered that one couple attached by a leash at Paddles. They had seemed perfectly happy but I couldn't imagine letting Hunter do that to me.

"It's beautiful," I said, realizing I hadn't said a word. "Thank you, Hunter. You're so sweet to surprise me with your presents."

"I have another surprise."

"Oh?"

"There's a party we can go to tonight. A private party in a penthouse loft. Everyone there will be kinky."

Suddenly I looked at myself in the mirror with new eyes. "You want me to go out wearing this?"

"You can put something over it on the way. But lots of people at the party will be dressed like this. Or even less."

My pleasant dreams of a seductive night at home disappeared. *One woman will never be enough for him,* Minx said. He was inviting me into his world, which was a lot more exhibitionistic than I really wanted. But I had to admit, our scene at Paddles had been incredibly hot.

I couldn't keep shutting out experiences because that's what my mom taught me to do. To be afraid.

"Okay, let's do it," I said.

I put on more makeup than usual to go with the sex-bomb dress, and fluffed my hair out like I had just rolled out of bed. Hunter loved it and kept hugging me and kissing me, interrupting me as I tried to get ready. The collar did look pretty.

We took a cab into the city, and I wore a light coat over my corset dress. It was kind of cool, like I was sneaking around and getting away with it.

To get to his friend's apartment, we had to go through a door surrounded by ornamental stonework into a drab linoleum hallway. It was in an old building near Union Square, so the elevator was tiny and seven people could hardly fit inside. It chugged to the top, all twelve floors, with agonizing slowness. I leaned back against Hunter as the people chatted. He knew the couple, and the other three had come together.

The elevator opened at the top and we filed through the anteroom into someone's apartment. It had very high ceilings with three massive arched windows marching down the wall. Even though it was a big room, it was comfortably full of people. The lighting was dim, but one glance was enough to show that most of the women were as scantily-clad as me. Some of the men, as well.

I parted with my coat, not without an inward tremor. But I was being brave, and Hunter kissed my hand as if he could sense my inward struggle. Hand-in-hand, he led me around and introduced me to people. Several of them asked me what my FetLife name was, and one woman finally explained that FetLife was the social website where you could join online groups and talk about what sort of fetishes you were interested in. I decided I would sign up. I had so many questions and it would help if I could ask online without having to look someone in the face while I did it.

Some people were playing—including a paddling scene on one of the terraces. There were repeated loud smacking sounds, but the view was blocked from the surrounding buildings by strategically-placed trellises with vines growing on them.

Mostly people were talking. When we returned to the living room and sat down near another couple, they introduced themselves as Catherine and Robert. Catherine said, "That's a pretty collar."

Her husband was a lean man in his fifties, fit as if he worked out every day. Catherine was an elegant woman at least twenty years younger.

"Hunter gave it to me tonight." I touched it at my throat. The padlock was warm now against my skin, not cold like it had been at first.

"Collaring someone is an old tradition in the leather community," Robert said. "It meant you were dedicated to serving another, and your master was responsible for you."

My expression must have shown my doubt, because Catherine gave Robert a light tap with her riding crop. "A collar can mean different things to different people."

Robert immediately dropped his gaze and said, "Yes, Mistress."

It made me uncomfortable. Catherine leaned over and murmured to Robert, so obviously there was some sort of sexual dynamic at play with his wife in control. But I wasn't expecting it to suddenly crop up in a casual conversation about my collar. Maybe there was nothing casual about collars. I certainly couldn't pull my mind away from mine for long.

Perhaps that was Hunter's intention, to make me mindful that I was here as his submissive. But did that mean he thought he could silence me with a tap? I hoped not.

We took another turn through the penthouse and now there were people on the beds, naked and kissing.

Suddenly it looked like a sex party, the kind of orgy I had imagined before I met Hunter. I wasn't expecting to find a cliché in his friend's party.

I drank a glass of wine quicker than usual, and then most of a second one before Hunter gently took the glass from my hand. "Drinking and playing don't go well together."

I was feeling much more relaxed now. "I didn't know I was planning on playing."

He smiled. "I am. And I won't be able to unless you do."

I wished he hadn't put it that way. It sounded like I was stopping him. I wanted him to only want me.

Then again, maybe it was time to turn off my mind and just let Hunter make me feel good for a while. If only we were at home instead surrounded by an orgy. My mom's disapproving face kept popping into my mind.

But I had to get rid of my conditioning to do what my mom said.

"Okay," I agreed.

"Good, there's something I want you to try," he said.

In spite of my wariness, a wonderful anticipation was rising in me, knowing I was going to try something new and it would be amazing like it always was.

He took me through one of the numerous doors off the hallway into a darkened office. There was nobody inside. A couple paused to glance in the door as Hunter plugged something in and turned it on.

A neon blue glow light the room. "It's a violet wand," Hunter explained. "They're based on medical devices used in the 19th Century to treat nervous conditions."

He brought it close to his own forearm and an arc of blue leaped between the device and his skin. It make a crackling sound, but he didn't flinch.

"Does it hurt?" I asked.

"It tingles, and depending on where you put it, it can feel pretty intense. It's static electricity so it won't damage your skin."

He ran it up and down his arm, holding out straight so I could see that it didn't leave any mark behind. "You want to feel it?"

I held out my arm like him. Hunter brought the tip of the wand close to my forearm. The blue arc leaped to my skin, and I jerked at the sharp buzzing sensation.

"Ow!" I rubbed my skin, and the feeling went away.

"It's not that bad."

I held out my arm again. "Let me try it again."

He picked up my hand and positioned the wand over my index finger. He ran it slowly from my fingertip up the back of my hand and arm, inside my elbow then up and around my shoulder in one long slow motion. My whole body shuddered.

"Wow..." I breathed.

"I thought you'd like it."

"It makes my hair stand on end. Are you sure it's safe?"

He laughed. "I won't touch your collar with it, and as long as I don't put it in your eyes, there's nothing to worry about."

He started running the wand over my entire body. It felt stronger the closer he came, and the speed of his strokes. Short sharp bursts made me catch my breath, and I never knew when he would bring the wand to almost touch my skin, sending a spike of sensation zinging through my nerves.

There was no thinking now. Not about the curious people who crowded in through the door to watch me twist and turn on the end of his wand.

There was only Hunter, his intense focus, never wavering from me, holding me up, turning me around, bending me over the desk to light up my inner thighs. It was wild! Like it was cutting directly to my core.

My cries crew louder as he increased the intensity of the wand, driving me higher. When I was writhing so hard he couldn't keep it on me, he thrust his leg between mine, bumping against me with his hips. I griped the front end of the desk, holding on as he rhythmically ground against me.

214

An explosion of light blinded me, as I came. I wasn't sure if where the light came from—inside or outside of me—but I was engulfed. All I knew was that he was holding me down, pressing me against the desk as the sensation ripped through me.

His fingers pulled aside my panties, stroking me. "You're so ready. I'm going to fuck you right here on this desk."

A sound by the door made me look up. In a sea of faces, one was clear—Minx. She was craning to see past a guy in front of her, a smirk on her face.

"No, stop," I said, grabbing hold of his wrist. "Minx."

He looked up, startled. I so rarely saw him caught off guard. It was awful.

"Let me up," I whispered so no one else could hear.

"I don't care about her," he said roughly, his mouth close to my ear and his body still pressing me down.

"I do. Please stop."

He hesitated, his jeans undone. Ready to push me even though I said stop. I wasn't sure what I would do if he didn't. Things hung in a balance for a dreadful moment.

Then he backed away and helped me stand up. He adjusted my dress and made sure my collar hung straight.

It should have been intimate, the moment of our greatest connection. But I was entirely focused on Minx's presence by the door. She was wearing a neon green collar that glowed in the dim light. It left a light tracer on my vision.

"I didn't know she'd be here," Hunter said. "Tammy should have told me."

Now I was embarrassed. I had an orgasm in front of all these people! In front of Minx. Again. I couldn't get away from her. My chest and face burned hot.

"I need to get out of here," I murmured, unable to look at anyone. I couldn't bear to see Minx's smirk again.

Hunter led me through the glass door onto the terrace, so we wouldn't have to go past Minx. I wasn't sure if that was for my sake or his own. I spent a good ten minutes in the bathroom cleaning up and getting hold of myself. The light was too bright and it wasn't pleasant. I tugged on the collar a few times. It was the perfect size for my neck. The only problem was that I couldn't take it off, not even for a second.

For some reason, that's all I wanted. To be able to take it off for a second. Just to know I could.

Everything had been going so well. The violet wand had really felt good. And I loved how Hunter held me and how he made me come by rubbing against me. Hunter took his time, getting me excited. Nobody had ever touched my whole body like that. His fingers were so sure, as if he knew exactly what I needed better than myself.

Why did it have to be mixed up in collars and Minx? And all those people out there. There were probably other girlfriends or ex-submissives, whatever he called them, who had been watching. I would never know. I was a stranger here.

Most of all, why didn't Hunter realize I couldn't be vulnerable in front of Minx? I had said stop, but he almost didn't. Like he wanted to push me right when I needed his understanding the most.

The more time passed, the more I hated that he didn't stop at my first protest. He should have known I was serious! Instead he had made me say stop again.

The party wasn't much fun after that. I kept wondering which of the women Hunter had been with. And Minx with her eye-catching collar was everywhere I turned. Hunter was also put off, as if Minx was pushing his buttons just by being there. He kept trying to pull me close to him, but I stiffened every time, looking around to see who was watching us.

Finally he said, "Let's go home."

Of course by that he meant my apartment. I hadn't spent one night at his place, and it was getting a little weird. Why was his studio off-limits? He was making himself at home in my private life, while keeping walls up around his.

As soon as we walked in my door, Hunter took hold of me, as if proving to me that I belonged to him. He cracked open my corset dress and laid me on the floor to take me right there, hard and fast. I was overwhelmed by his desire, coming at the same time he did. But even in the midst of the ecstasy I knew it was raw sex not making love.

Afterwards, as he slept, I stayed awake. I wandered around my place, tugging on the locked collar and wondering why I felt so bad. Like doom was lurking in the corner. One off night didn't mean the end of a relationship. I was being melodramatic.

Even when I tried to go to bed, the collar kept bothering me. The weight of it felt strange, and I didn't like it when the lock slid off my chest and made the collar hang on my neck. I had nightmares of being strangled all night, and woke up after very little sleep feeling grumpy.

In the morning, I faced my ravaged image and the ever-present collar. I grabbed it with both hands and tried to wrench it apart. But the darned thing was like wrought iron. Maybe it was made to withstand a slave's rebellion. Maybe my reaction was natural. All I knew was that it left red marks on my skin where I had pulled it against my neck.

After Hunter got up, I was grinding the coffee he liked as he sat on the stool in my narrow kitchen.

"It's such a nice day," Hunter said. "We should do something outdoors. Friends of mine are sitting in line for Shakespeare in the Park. They get to Central Park around two, and the show starts at six. Everyone brings blankets so they can hang out and wait in the line. It's free, and they only take the first two hundred people."

It sounded like something my dad would have planned. But I felt a pang of worry. "Who are these friends?"

"People from the scene."

"Anyone you used to date?"

"Well, there's Heather. I've told you about her. She's got a boyfriend, Bert."

"Heather is the one you spanked on her birthday?"

"Yes."

Now that I knew what a spanking was, that made it even worse. I could imagine Hunter holding a beautiful woman, spanking her until she climaxed.

"Aside from Heather, anyone else you've been with?"

Now he hesitated. "Well, Bert and I have fooled around. He's submissive and even though he's not bi, Heather made him suck my dick a couple of times."

Alarm bells were going off in my head. Not that there was anything wrong with being bisexual. But I hadn't realized Hunter was. Why did it take so long for him to tell me? Did he think it would make a difference to me?

"It sounds like you and your friends are very free with each other," I said. "Like the orgy last night."

"That wasn't an orgy. But most of us are polyamorous. So we're bound to get kinky with each other."

I didn't like the sound of any of that. Bisexual, I could handle, as long as he was monogamous with me. I could see why anyone would want to have sex with Hunter, and he must get plenty of offers from all kinds of people.

But I couldn't handle casual sex with multiple partners.

"Minx said you would never be satisfied by only one woman."

"When did you talk to Minx?"

Oops! "At the Paddles. She followed me into the bathroom."

"Why didn't you tell me?"

"Because you would have denied it, even if it's true."

He stared at me. "Don't you realize Minx was manipulating you? She's trying to put a wedge between us."

"She *is* a wedge between us. She put an end to our scene last night with one look."

"That's because of you! I don't care about her. If anything, it would have put her in her place."

"I don't want Minx to have a 'place' in my life! But she does.

Maybe she's right that you can't be monogamous."

"Not with her. I've never felt this way about anyone else but you."

Hearing him say that made me want to soften, to give in again. But I had to know what was going on. "I'm worried that I'm not the kind of woman you need. It's really uncomfortable sometimes doing these things you want."

"What do you mean? What's uncomfortable?"

"Walking around wearing practically nothing. Watching people have sex in front of each other like it's perfectly natural. Wondering which women in the room you've been intimate with. Nothing's enough for you! Now you want me to have sex in front of other people."

He shook his head. "You loved it. Don't deny it. It turns you on when I force you to be exhibitionistic. You don't want to take responsibility for it. As long as I'm making you do it, you can enjoy it. You would have let me fuck you if Minx wasn't there."

I stared at him with my mouth open. I couldn't even get past my shock to wonder if it might be true. Even if it was, he shouldn't be so horrible about it.

"Well, you're *not* going to put a leash on me." Both my hands clutched the collar. "And I can't stand this anymore! When are you going to take this thing off me?"

He looked at me for a moment, then went into the bedroom and got the key. As he returned, I held out my hand. But he stopped me.

"I have to take it off. I put it on you."

I let out an exasperated sound, and he gave me a piercing, scornful look. I stood for him to remove it, but this time his touch felt completely different. I didn't want it. I turned away as soon as he unlooped the collar, rubbing my neck reflexively.

He set the collar down on the counter with a soft clink. "If it bothered you, why did you wait so long to say something?"

"I had to give it a chance."

"Is it that bad?"

"You, who sees everything, didn't notice that it was driving me crazy?"

"No."

I was done with this. "I don't believe you, Hunter. You like to push me. You said it yourself. You're pushing me all the time, and I don't know when you're going to stop. I'm afraid you're going to push me into doing exactly what you want. I'll just be a number in a line. Minx is waiting to step right back in. And I'm sure Heather is expecting that your spankings won't stop. They never have before, so why would *I* make any difference?"

He stared at me, his eyes shuttered and cold. "I think I should go."

"I do, too." I turned away so I wouldn't have to see his face.

Behind me, I could hear him walk into the bedroom to gather his things. Then he let himself out quietly. I almost expected him to say something, but he didn't. He never tried to defend himself. He was expecting me to fit into his way of life, keeping me at a distance, manipulating my emotions through the most amazing sex of my life, while he was unable to truly commit to a real partnership.

I kept waiting for him to say something. But he didn't. He just left.

...

I felt awful as soon as Hunter was gone. I was so confused! I didn't want to touch the beautiful collar. I left it lying next to the stove.

I never thought Hunter could look at me like that, like I was nothing to him.

I went back to bed and cried myself to sleep. When I woke up several hours later, I felt more like myself. I should have known better than to try to have a serious talk while I was out of my mind from being up all night. In spite of how bad I felt about fighting with Hunter, there was some relief in being alone with nothing to do. It had been a long time since I had a day off to myself.

I thought about the woman I had met last night who had called herself Slavette. Slavette said she did whatever her master told her "twenty-four/seven," meaning all the time. Her master had ordered her to fetch drinks for us at one point, not even bothering to look at Slavette as he did. I rubbed my hand against my throat, wondering if Hunter wanted that kind of control over me.

The kind of absolute control that my mom used to have over me. Control cloaked in love and caring, but draconian in making sure I did exactly what she wanted.

I was finally breaking free. I barely knew what I wanted. Being told what to do while we were having sex was the hottest thing ever. Being manipulated by a psychological master was another thing entirely.

I was involved in enough psychological warfare. As if dealing with Selina wasn't enough on a daily basis, I hadn't called my mom this week. Uncharacteristically, Jenny hadn't called me to check in either. My mom was giving me the long-distance silent treatment. As if that would pressure me into breaking up with Hunter. But years of her training made me acutely aware each day, each hour that passed without hearing from her.

I was doing my best to ignore that feeling.

When I caught sight of my neck in the mirror, it was all red from my constant rubbing. I had to stop that. The collar was gone now.

But Hunter wanted me to wear his collar. I had tried to do it to please him. But it didn't work. Maybe I was being childish trying to win his love by giving him what he wanted. The way I tried to win my mom's love. Jenny always did say can't make someone love you.

So I hit a brick wall on this one. Clearly Hunter loved playing with the power in our relationship. He knew so much more than me. I had the feeling I'd still only seen the tip of the iceberg. But did I really want to ride that iceberg for the rest of my life?

I checked out the website the girls at the party had told me about—FetLife. To get on, I had to make a profile, which I kept as brief and non-descriptive as possible. I didn't want to use a photo of myself, naturally, so I took a photo of the leaves outside my window and used that as my profile picture. For a name, I picked "Runningaway2." Ironically enough, there was already a "Runningaway." I didn't feel quite so alone when I saw that.

Then I searched for "collar."

First I got a list of profiles for people with collar in their FetLife name. Men and women, both. I checked out the women, and they seemed perfectly ordinary. A couple said they had just started to explore this "dark side" of themselves.

And OMG the lists of fetishes on everyone's profile! Right out there for everyone to see: mutual masturbation, caning, dildos, toys, strap-ons, discipline, cross-dressing. Hair pulling! Sex in public! Those were things that I had done with Hunter.

I clicked on the pictures. Good Lord! The things people did. And they put it all out there, even the ones who had recognizable photos of themselves doing it. I would never! Even with a fake name.

But I was on a fact-finding mission, so I clicked on the groups.

In the collar groups there was talk about slaves and owners and property. Some people referred to themselves as beloved pets. Maybe it was all fantasy, but the real emotion was there in the groups dedicated to those who had been uncollared. The slaves were devastated.

Pickings were slim, so I searched for "slave" since that was the word I saw the most.

Bonanza! There were lots of groups dedicated to masters and slaves. As I avidly read, the one question that scared me the most came from a man asking how to convince his wife to let him dominate her outside the bedroom.

It was my biggest fear; that Hunter wanted to control my entire life. He decided what we did together not only in bed but out of it. I hadn't really thought about it because I was new to the city and was still exploring. But he had never asked me what I wanted to do on any of our dates. He decided what we did.

The word that kept leaping out at me was "service." Service was big among slaves. It sounded so noble, giving of yourself. It was something I felt more than understood. But now that I thought about it, Hunter always asked me to do little things for him. I cut his nails yesterday morning, smiling up at him as I knelt in front of him, using the emery board on each fingertip to make sure his nails were smooth for when he raked them down my body later. I fetched him drinks whenever he asked, and plumped pillows for him as he reclined on the couch sketching. There were so many ways I took care of him now.

It sent a chill through me. I liked doing those things. It made me feel closer to him. I thought it was intimacy, but maybe he thought I was serving him.

Where would it lead?

I looked over at the collar lying on the counter next to the stove. The collar was the key.

Summoning my courage, I joined a Master/slave group and asked my question: *My boyfriend gave me a collar last night. He wouldn't take it off until this morning when I asked him to. What does a collar mean?*

I went to make myself a cup of tea and by the time I got back to the computer there were nine responses. Some were snarky and not very nice. But most were very short, asking me in return: *What does it mean to him? What does it mean to you? A collar has the meaning you both give it.*

I should have asked Hunter last night what the collar meant to him. He said it was a symbol of our commitment—but what was our commitment? Maybe if I had asked, I wouldn't have been strangled by nameless expectations all night.

I did some more research, but my heart wasn't in it anymore. I should have talked to Hunter when I had the chance. That's what he kept telling me—be honest. Ask questions.

I was sure that if I called Hunter, he would come back and talk to me. But I didn't like the fact that our entire relationship was unfolding in my space. Why didn't he take me to his place? I had even mentioned it to him, but nothing had come of it. It was like he was keeping his distance from me while he insisted that I had to be completely open to him.

What if Minx was with him now?

I hated myself for even thinking it. Was I turning into a jealous, insecure girlfriend? Or was I smart to call him on the red flags?

I slowly fixed my hair and my face, and put on a short raincoat against the light drizzle. It was overcast and gloomy outside.

I walked to the subway and took it deeper into Brooklyn instead of the other way into Manhattan, like I did every morning to go to work. I kept remembering my first subway ride with Hunter, when he had faced down that gang of guys. He had become the hero of my dreams, standing ready to protect me always. I hoped he really was that hero.

As I walked to his place, I considered phoning to let him know I was coming. But that red flag bothered me—why didn't we ever go to his place? I felt very bad about surprising him. I'd never done anything like this.

But that was the point, wasn't it? To do things differently. To stop letting other people dictate to me.

There was a guy leaving Hunter's building, and he helpfully held open the door for me. I hesitated, but decided it was a gift I couldn't waste. I went up the wide, dingy steps to the second floor and paused in front of Hunter's door. It was a big steel thing. The sound of music thumping came from further down the wide corridor.

I knocked, feeling like I was making a big mistake.

The door opened, and Hunter was grinning in greeting before he realized it was me. His surprise was not glad to see me.

That's when I knew. He *was* hiding something.

"Kali." He was still standing in the doorway, looking at me.

"I thought I'd come over so we could talk."

Hunter backed away from the door so I could come in. I could feel it, as I went in deeper. Then I saw the couch against the wall.

Minx was kneeling in front of it. Smiling.

My hands clenched into fists. I didn't try to hide how angry I was to see Minx there, acting so smug. Her brightly-colored hair and exaggerated makeup made her look like a sex toy. She was wearing a denim shirt with the sleeves ripped off, tights and a black taffeta skirt with combat boots.

"Minx's staying with Jeremy down the hall," Hunter explained. "He's not home yet, so she's waiting here."

I glanced around. The studio was clean, the floors uncluttered. I trailed a finger across the polished countertop. "I see."

"Go wait down at Jeremy's," Hunter ordered Minx.

"Yes, Sir." She hopped up and left.

Yes, Sir! He was still her master.

I felt a scream rise up in my throat. It was everything I had feared and more.

I tossed the collar he had given me onto the table. "I came to ask you what that meant. But I guess it doesn't matter now. You have what you want."

"I don't want Minx."

"Don't lie to me! I can see how you are together. She still belongs to you. You probably feel that way about all the women you've played with. That's why you're still playing with so many of them."

"I'm with you, Kali. Don't forget that."

"Right now, yes. A minute ago you were having something special with Minx."

"I didn't have a scene with her!"

"Then why was she kneeling on the floor?"

"She's not allowed to sit on the furniture."

I let out a little scream of frustration. It didn't make me feel any better. "If she's still following your orders, then you're *still* in a relationship. That green collar she's wearing—did you give it to her?"

"Yes. But it doesn't mean the same thing as the collar I gave

225

you."

I glared at him. "She's *still* wearing your collar! I know a few things, you know. That means you're responsible for her."

"If I was, then I would have let her stay here when she got kicked out of her place."

"Looks to me like she *is* staying here."

"She isn't. She's staying with Jeremy."

"So she's nice and close to you. A technicality I'm sure anyone could appreciate."

Now he was glaring at me. It was a bit frightening, actually. "When I tell you she's not staying here, she's not."

I backed toward the door. "I need to go. I'm too mad to talk to you right now."

He suddenly came after me. "Don't go. Stay and we won't talk anymore right now. I'll make you some tea."

I really didn't like it that as soon as I said I was leaving, he was ready to do anything to get me to stay. Seconds before, he had acted like he didn't care.

"No, I'm going." I marched over to the front door.

Chapter 28

Hunter

Nothing had gone the way I planned. It happened too fast. "If you have to go, let me call you a cab, Kali. You can't walk to the subway alone at this hour. Remember what happened last time?"

I was ready to pretend to call a car, to do anything it took to delay her. If she would only cool down, she would realize this misunderstanding wasn't worth a fight. I didn't want Minx. I hadn't touched her!

But Kali stepped through the door and turned to look back at me. "Don't come after me. I mean it, Hunter."

I couldn't let her go. But when I stepped forward, she raised her hand. "Stop, Hunter."

Her safeword. I watched in dread as the door closed behind her. I wanted to follow her in the worst way. But I had to respect her safeword.

It was my fault she was walking through my neighborhood and taking the subway alone. I felt like I *had* to go after her. I had to do something. Then again, maybe that was my own messed-up shit kicking in. The part of me that wanted to control her so I wouldn't get hurt.

It was my own fault. I knew when I left her apartment this morning that it would force her to reach out to me. It worked every time when I wanted to stop a fight.

But I didn't expect her to come to my place without warning. It was so unlike her. Clearly she suspected that Minx might be here, and when she found out she was right, she had looked no further. The truth was, I had found Minx waiting outside for Jeremy in the rain just a few minutes before Kali arrived. I wasn't even tempted by Minx.

But Kali was right about one thing. As Minx sat on my floor talking to me, I realized that she did expect things would pick up between us again at some point. Hell, if I was honest with myself, I couldn't imagine never spanking another ass other than Kali's, as fine as hers was. Maybe I had been telling Kali what she wanted to hear while secretly believing that she would be loosened up by the scene. So many people were.

I went to the window, looking down at the darkening street. I wanted to run after her. It was almost a spinal reflex. I wanted a re-do of that entire argument. I should have left Minx sitting on the steps instead of inviting her in. Minx was probably staying with Jeremy to get to me, and I let her do it. Better yet, I never should have run out on Kali this morning as a way to manipulate her into reaching out for me.

I should have just talked to her about the collar, and told her what I wanted. The collar meant that she belonged to me, and I was dedicated to making her happy.

But she wasn't happy now.

I really wished Minx wasn't still wearing my collar. She had worn it last night to taunt me. And again today. Kali wasn't stupid, she could see that.

I felt like I was grasping at a shadow. I wanted to crush Kali in my arms and hold on until this feeling went away.

But she was gone and I was alone.

Chapter 29

Kali

I had a really bad night. Hunter texted to make sure I got home all right, and I responded with one word: *yes*. After that, nothing. I kept thinking about him and Minx together; there was nothing to keep Minx away from Hunter. As I left, I had seen her at the other end of the corridor, crouched against a door.

I had to accept the facts—I was in love with Hunter. And he wasn't in love with me. He wanted a sex toy. He wanted me because I wasn't easy to get, like those other girls.

He didn't love me. If he did, he would have said *I love you...*

But he never did.

It was a big aching ball inside of me. I was more sad than angry because Hunter would have loved me if he could love anyone, I was sure. But he was so far away, living in a different world from mine. No wonder we wanted completely different things.

Monday morning, going to work was really hard for me. I knew I would have to deal with Hunter because it was a big week for the project. The last thing I wanted to do was talk to him like nothing was wrong. But the truck was arriving from the foundry today to unload the sculpture, and I had to make sure the permits were posted and the street cleared of cars. Hunter had posted the signs on Friday to warn people not to park there on Monday, but of course there were two cars there when I arrived.

"Call the tow company," Selina ordered. Her voice was hoarse.

"Are you okay? You sound like you have a cold."

"Shut up, Kali!" Selina snapped. "I don't need you to tell me what I sound like. Get those cars towed now!"

I hated it, but I had to do it. Soon enough one of the cars had moved, but the other was stubbornly parked near the gated entrance

229

we would need to use to unload the sculptures. The tow truck arrived and I watched Hunter go up and talk to the driver, so I went back into the building to let him deal with it.

I intended to avoid him as long as possible. Every time I saw him, I kept wondering if Minx had gone back to his place after I had left.

Up in SunTech, Selina was berating our graphic designer. When I arrived, Selina turned her full force of curses from Debby to me.

"God damn it, Kali! You're the one responsible for this! Are you so stupid you approve things without my sign off?"

My stomach clenched, like I was suddenly falling. This was it! The fatal flaw that would get me fired. "What is it? What's wrong?" I asked, rushing forward.

"Just look at this!" Selina shoved the launch party invitation into my face.

I tried to get hold of it to see what was wrong, my heart in my throat. The box was sitting open on Debby's desk, just delivered from the printers. I scanned it as Selina continued to yell at me. "You never learn, do you? You have to get your shit together, Kali!"

"I don't see any typos," I finally said, looking up.

"It's the logo! I wanted it on the top not the bottom. I told you that, Kali, a hundred times. And now there's no time to get it fixed, and it looks like crap!"

The phone rang on the interoffice channel, and without missing a beat, Selina answered it like nothing was the matter. She listened for a moment, then said, "I'll be right there." Shaking the invitation at me, she said, "I'm running up to see Mr. Ryan. We'll see what he says about this."

When she was gone, I turned to Debby. "Oh, no! She's going to get me fired! And she's the one who approved the layout."

"Where's her initials?" Debby asked frantically.

I dug through my files, but I couldn't find the copy of the invitation with Selina's signature. "Don't you remember us showing it to her? She made you change the font size on the title."

230

"That's right. And she liked it when it was done. But I don't see her signature on my proof."

I smacked my fist against my desk. "She knows she approved it. This is just more of her stupid power-mongering bullshit!"

Debby looked at me in surprise. "I've never heard you say that before."

"I'm getting sick of these control freaks in my life. Maybe it's my own fault I'm surrounded by petty dictators."

Debby laughed nervously. "I'm not a dictator. Or petty."

"I don't mean you."

"I wonder if she's going to get us both fired," Debby ventured. "I did the layout, you know."

I paced back and forth, my arms wrapped around myself. It was finally happening. The worst was here. I'd used all the skills learned in a lifetime of pleasing a controlling mother to try to hang onto this job, and even Jenny wasn't enough training for me to handle Selina Stern.

Suddenly it was all falling apart—my job and my relationship with Hunter.

It was the longest ten minutes of my life. Finally, Selina burst in. "If you lousy fuckers don't back off, I'm going to call the police!"

The building's chief of security was with her, as was the director of Human Resources. Neither said a word as Selina went to her desk and began rifling through the drawers.

I looked from Selina to Mrs. Chapel. "Is something wrong?"

"Selina has been dismissed for cause," Mrs. Chapel said quietly.

"You better watch what you say about me!" Selina exclaimed. "I'm calling my lawyer about this."

Mrs. Chapel warned me with her eyes, and I knew enough to shut up and not respond to Selina's jabs, as my now-former boss packed up her belongings in a cardboard box.

But when Selina tried to sit down at her desk, Mrs. Chapel stopped her. "It's company policy that you can't access your computer once you've been terminated."

Selina got even madder. "I've got private personal information on there! You can't stop me from accessing my own laptop."

"It belongs to the company, and you're not supposed to have 'private personal' information on it." Mrs. Chapel wasn't backing down, and the security chief stepped in between Selina and the terminal. "But if there is, we will send you a copy once we go through everything."

"My contacts! Those aren't SunTech's! They're mine."

"They belong to SunTech, but you will get a copy of the information. Now is there anything else?"

The security chief held open the door for Selina to leave the big PR room. Mrs. Chapel took a moment to tell us both, "Stay here. Don't talk to anyone about this. I'll be back as soon as she's escorted from the building."

I huddled together with Debby like we had just witnessed an accident. I was sort of in shock.

"Hell to the no!" Debby exclaimed as the door shut behind Mrs. Chapel. "Did that just happen?"

"Spitting mad! She was spitting mad!" I started laughing a little hysterically in relief. It was like a win for the good guys for once. "Hopefully now we won't get fired."

Debby's eyes lit up. "They can't fire *all* of us. And whoever they get to take over has to be better than Selina."

Several people looked in to ask what was happening. Apparently Selina had made a lot of noise leaving the building. I grinned and shrugged every time.

Then one of the IT guys came in and asked, "Which one is Selina Stern's computer?"

I pointed, and he went to work copying everything. Mrs. Chapel returned before he was through.

"Can you tell us what happened?" I asked.

Mrs. Chapel sighed. "Let me access your computer, and I'll show you."

Mystified, I let Mrs. Chapel sit down at my desk. She went to

YouTube and typed "kicking glass" into the search, calling up a video. The opening shot was a grainy still, but as soon as she clicked play, Debby cried out, "That's Selina!"

The shot looked like it was from a surveillance camera mounted near the ceiling, angled down to look at the employee side of the glass display counter and cash register. Selina marched into view on the other side. Her perfect face contorted as she let out a stream of curses, calling the guy behind the counter "sissy boy" and worse names. I had almost gotten used to how nasty Selina could be with her tongue, but this was a whole other level. She kept saying, "How do you like it when I come to where you work and expose you? How do *you* like it?"

On the screen, an older woman joined the younger man at the counter. Her back was to the camera, and she was shaking her finger at Selina as she ordered her to leave the store.

Selina shouted, "He's wearing girl's panties!"

You could only see the back of the guy's head, as he flung a towel at Selina's face. The older woman started screaming back at her in Spanish, gesturing like she was shoeing Selina out.

Selina lifted up her leg, leaning back to give the glass front of the counter a vicious kick.

The glass exploded under her Jimmy Choo. Screams erupted on the video, and even Selina ducked to avoid the geyser of broken glass.

I had my hand over my mouth, watching the video as Selina slunk back out of camera view. It went to black. I checked the view count. 8,541. And it had only been posted four hours ago.

"It's going viral," I realized.

Debby pointed at the comments. "Selina's been recognized. Look what they're saying about her!"

"SunTech's PR Director goes bonkers," I read in one comment.

Mrs. Chapel looked grim. "Mr. Ryan has already written the press release you'll need to send out, Kali. We're announcing that Selina no longer works for SunTech. That's all we're going to say about this."

"Good idea," I said faintly. I never dealt with a PR disaster before. It seemed like the best thing to do was distance the company from Selina's actions, and then decline to say anything else.

Debby asked Mrs. Chapel, "Who will be the new PR Director?"

"I'll institute a search. It shouldn't be hard to find someone soon. In the meantime, Kali, you're in charge. Put all your efforts toward the sundial project. I know it's a huge amount of pressure to put on you with the launch party in two weeks, but Mr. Ryan and I are sure you can handle it."

I was shocked into rising to meet her eyes. "Thank you, Mrs. Chapel. I won't let you down."

"I know we can depend on you. Debby, help Kali any way you can."

"I will," Debby agreed. "You can count on it."

"I'll put out an internal memo letting everyone know that you're in charge," Chapel said.

When Mrs. Chapel left, I stared at Debby for a few silent moments. Then we both let out a whoop of pleasure. "The wicked witch is dead!" Debby exclaimed.

"More than dead. That video is going to *haunt* Selina." Nobody deserved it more. I eyed the IT guy at Selina's computer. I wanted to get my hands on it. There were a bunch of people I needed to tell— construction subcontractors, the party planner, the permitting office… Hunter.

Hunter! Why hadn't I thought of him sooner?

Technically I was Hunter's boss now. Since I was in charge of the project, he would have to answer to me.

I wasn't allowed to date a subordinate. Until they hired another PR Director or Hunter's contract was done with SunTech, he was off limits to me.

But I don't want to stop seeing him, was my first thought. The very idea was awful.

But right on the heels of that was relief. It wasn't up to me. I signed a contract and agreed to behave a certain way, and I wasn't going to risk losing my job.

I wanted all of the pressure to stop: Jenny, Hunter, Selina... all of their expectations were too much at once. I needed space to take a deep breath.

That's what I felt all in one moment.

"Are you okay?" Debby asked.

"Yeah, it's a lot to take in." Now I was really glad I hadn't let it slip that Hunter and I were dating. Nobody could know now.

I sat down at Selina's computer after the IT guy left and tried to concentrate, but thoughts of Hunter kept intruding. Just before lunch time, I got a call from the security guard downstairs that the truck with the sundial had arrived.

With a sinking feeling, I knew exactly what would happen when I looked into Hunter's eyes. I would crumple inside and want to throw myself into his arms and swear to serve him if that's what he wanted. I would try to win his love any way I could.

That was a dangerous feeling, leading down a slippery slope. I had spent my life giving my mom what she wanted in order to feel her love. I was poised to fall into that same kind of relationship with Hunter. But I had to resist, for my own good. He would swallow me up and there would be nothing left of myself. I wanted him so much that I was losing all good sense.

I braced myself and went down to watch the unloading of the sundial.

Chapter 29

Hunter

I was in my element. There was nothing I liked better than moving around large pieces of metal. When Kali came down to watch, that made it even better.

I had always known she was sensitive and wouldn't be easily won. But I was sure, in spite of this speed bump, that she would come back to me. She would just have to do it in her own time.

The driver used the forklift on the back of the truck to unload each crated piece. They were carefully placed near their installation locations. I didn't want to be moving them around a lot.

It took several hours to get the crates unloaded and the construction fence buttoned back up again. The truck took off, and I was left alone, surrounded by crates forming the rough outline of the sundial.

I could already see it taking shape in the space, even boxed up and contained inside the plywood construction fence. I had four men coming tomorrow to begin the installation. It would take days to get everything unpacked and bolted into place.

I was surprised when Kali walked through the blue gate. I hadn't expected her to come to me so soon, and I wanted to reach out to her, to wordlessly take her into my arms so we could forget everything that had happened. But one look at her closed-off expression told me she was here on business.

"Selina Stern was fired today," Kali told me. "I'm not sure if you checked your email but a notification went out earlier."

"No. I didn't see that." I laughed, and said, "I can't say I'm sorry to hear it."

"I've been put in charge of the sundial project. So now you'll be reporting to me." Her eyes slid away from me. "SunTech policy doesn't allow supervisors to date employees in their direct chain of command."

"That's okay. Nobody knows about us. And they won't find out."

She shook her head. "I can't do it, Hunter. I could be fired, too."

"It's only for two more weeks. And I'm a contract employee. Nobody will care what we do."

"I care. I'm not going to risk my job." She was so unemotional as she spoke, that I could hardly believe this was the same woman who had cried out my name out in ecstasy.

"Kali, what are you talking about? You're not going to break up with me over this. We'll keep it low key, and won't go out anywhere public. But you can't stop seeing me because of a silly rule, not when we're already in a relationship."

"I'm not sure what we're doing," Kali told me. "After yesterday, I don't know what to think."

"You know I'm not seeing Minx." At her alarmed expression, I lowered my voice. The windows overlooking the plaza were glinting in the late afternoon sun, a reminder that people could be watching from the SunTech offices. "I don't want to see Minx. I want to be with you. I've barely been out of your sight, so I could hardly see anyone else without you knowing about it."

"I think we want very different things from a relationship."

"I want you."

"Then why do you keep pushing and pushing me until I feel like I can't breathe!"

Now I gestured for her to be quieter. "I thought you liked it. I'll slow down. I promise. I know we can make this work."

Kali looked at me like she wanted to believe me, like she wanted to agree. But she shook her head. "I'm your supervisor. I can't do it."

I couldn't believe it. I could see the desire in her eyes, the way she sparked to me and how her gaze lingered on me. But she was resisting me, like she always did.

"If you want to break up with me because Minx was at my place yesterday, then just say so. Don't use stupid corporate legalese as an excuse."

"I'm leaving now." Kali turned to go back to the gate.

My hand shot out and I grabbed hold of her arm.

She gasped, looking up at me. "Let go of me!"

I couldn't. I physically couldn't. It was like something had taken over my body, a big defiant NO! I couldn't let her leave me.

Kali glanced up at the windows of SunTech. "Let go of me right now, Hunter."

My fingers spasmed, and I let go. I was breathing faster, feeling like a fool. What was I doing? That was the best way to scare her off. But I couldn't control myself. She was spiraling away from me again.

Kali disappeared around the blue plywood fence without looking back.

She couldn't walk away from me like that, not for such a flimsy reason. Sure she was mad about Minx and she was afraid I was cheating on her. But deep down she knew she could trust me.

Didn't she?

...

The next day and all the next, I kept waiting for a break in her façade of cool civility. But her eyes didn't spark to mine anymore, as if she had locked down her real self inside of a Kali-like shell that went about her work, calmly taking care of everything to prepare for the launch party as the installation of the sundial continued.

It was excruciating waiting for her to break.

But she didn't.

By Thursday, she still hadn't reached out to me. I knew I wouldn't see her over the weekend if I didn't do something. At least during the week I could see her at work. I knew what she was doing. I could watch over her.

She couldn't be happy this way. I wasn't.

I waited for her to leave work on Thursday evening, positioning myself so I could bump into her. She couldn't turn down an offer to talk. She must be ready by now. I wouldn't push it. I wouldn't touch her, not until she asked for it. I wanted to make her beg to pay for this week, to prove to her that this temporary separation didn't mean a thing.

The minutes stretched out until an hour slipped by, then another. I was afraid I had missed her leaving, but she had been staying late almost every day because she had to do her job and Selina's. When I asked the security guard if Kali Jones had left, the guy said no, and gave me a searching look. He must have seen me hanging around waiting for her on the security cameras.

It was almost nine before Kali appeared, checking her big bag full of folders as if making sure she hadn't forgotten anything. "Oh, it's you," she said.

"I waited. You must be hungry. Let's go get something to eat so we can talk."

She was already shaking her head. "I told you, Hunter. We can't date."

"It's not a date. We're two co-workers having dinner. People do it all the time."

"Yeah, right. After what we've been doing, you want me to act like we're just work buddies? Lie to myself *and* my job? No, thanks."

"You can't leave it like this between us. You've got it all wrong about Minx. I need to explain it to you."

"I understand, Hunter. Better than you, maybe. Oh, I doubt you cheated on me with Minx, but you can't deny you're still in a relationship with her. You're still her master, and pushing her away to be with me is just another part of your dynamic with her. The point is—there will always be another Minx. You want other women in your life. And I can't do that."

"So you're telling me this break up isn't for two weeks? It's for good? You're breaking up with me for good?"

She blinked and looked away for a second. "I don't know. I

need time to think."

"I know you want to be with me, Kali. You can't deny that. You've got to listen to yourself. Not your mom. Not SunTech. They don't know what's best for you."

"I'm not going to lose my job."

I rolled my eyes. "You know it won't come to that, Kali. And if it does, is that the worst thing? Do you really want to be in public relations your whole life? It's the career your mom picked for you. Corporate. Safe. Superficial. You should be exploring your creative side, even if that means you're waitressing or walking dogs. Not shut up in this tower looking at spreadsheets!"

She stared at me, her mouth falling open. "Is that what you think of my job?"

"Don't you? Do you want to be like Selina Stern? Granted, SunTech at least tries to do some good in the world. But it's still a business and you're the one who's putting the gloss on the money-making machine. That's what Jenny Jones wants for you."

"My mom didn't want me to take this job!"

"She didn't want you to come to the city. A corporate job is exactly where she planned on placing you. And here you are."

"You think you're so smart, don't you? That you know all about me?" Kali glared at me. "You think you can manipulate me into being another sex toy in your duffle bag. You think I'm another corporate drone who needs deprogramming by the master. You don't know anything about me. I love this job. And I'm good at it. I'm not going to risk losing it for *you*."

I shook my head, reaching out to her. "No, Kali! That's not what—"

But she pulled back, warding off my hands. Her glance up at the camera sealed it. "I'm going home," she said.

I started to go with her, but she stopped and warded me off again. "Not with you."

"Kali, for Christ's sake, it's late. Let me go with you on the subway, at least."

"No!" She glared at me. "You don't always get your way, Hunter. I'm going home. Alone."

"Kali!" I called after her. "This is silly. I have to take the same subway."

"Not with me, you don't," she called over her shoulder.

I couldn't follow her. Not after that.

Keenly aware of the security guard watching through the cameras, I pulled out my phone and checked it casually, as if nothing was wrong. Maybe they understood everything from Kali's defiant body language, but I wasn't going to give them anything else on us. I still didn't think anyone would care if we had dinner together. Or if we were in a relationship, in fact.

After a few minutes, I also left. I wanted to speed up to catch her, but that would only aggravate her more. I probably shouldn't have tried to talk to her so soon.

I caught sight of her on the platform of the L train, but she didn't see me. I boarded a few cars back and stayed out of sight. I was tempted to get off at her stop, but if she caught me it would set me back even further. So I forced myself to stay on the train and go home.

My studio had never felt so empty. All of my art work looked flat and contrived. The sounds of sirens outside never seemed to stop. The thumping of music through the walls was like my pounding brain.

I still couldn't believe that she really meant to end it. She was just trying to get control of the situation, so she could feel more comfortable. I was challenging all of her preconceived notions. It was bound to be frightening.

I would have to wait her out.

...

Friday evening, I was surprised when Kali left around her normal time. She was with a bunch of SunTech people.

I pulled back behind the construction fence in time so she didn't see me. But I saw her. She was laughing.

I slowly trailed them around the corner and saw the group go into an Irish pub at the other end of the block.

She was laughing.

Before I knew it, I was standing in the doorway, scanning the pub. The SunTech people were gathering at a back table, pulling out chairs. I slipped onto a stool at the front of the bar and ordered a beer.

Kali was sitting between two guys. Talking and laughing. They were all having fun. She had told me about the Friday bar nights, but we had never gone together because we were on the down-low.

I had never seen this side of her, among her own friends. Going back to Jefferson wasn't the same—that was her past. But here, she was just Kali. Not my new submissive, or her mother's daughter. I should have known I was missing something. Some crucial piece of information about Kali.

Then one of the guys leaned in closer to Kali and whispered in her ear. She shot him a wide-eyed look, one I knew so well, then giggled with her hand covering her mouth.

A wave of red anger burned through me.

No!

They were flirting! My hands clenched and I wanted to march over there and drag the idiot away from her. I knew it was madness. I could ruin everything with one stupid move. But there was a compulsion to go. *Just do it. Pop him one...*

I knew I was staring. Knew my emotions were running high, and I was letting it happen. I wanted to smack my own face and order myself to shape up! Walk out! *Stay away until the girl says yes...*

I was on my feet. I didn't remember how.

Then I jerked. I forced myself to take a step, then another, turning to the door. My joints felt locked, like I could hardly move. But I made myself walk outside.

On the sidewalk, I took a deep breath. It was easier now that I couldn't see them, with the guy's nose buried in her hair. Her quick glance at him, that shy smile. *Kali*...

I jerked again, and forced myself to take another step away. If I went back in, I would do something that could ruin my life. I was losing it! I had to save myself.

Like a drowning man, I fought for each step to get to the subway. But I couldn't go home. I couldn't get off the train.

I rode it all the way to the end, to Canarsie in southern Brooklyn, where the train sat for ten minutes with the doors open. The fresh breeze smelled like the ocean, and I took my first real breath since seeing Kali with that guy.

It was only then that the numbness washed away, the protective shield that I had used to get away.

Then I got mad.

What was she doing? She was blaming me for talking to Minx while she was off flirting with other guys? Little hypocrite! Here I was tearing my heart out over her, while she was moving on to the next man. Now that I thought about it, the guy was good-looking, wearing a suit like all the corporate-types did, his dark hair tousled the way she liked mine. Who was that guy? Had this little office flirtation been going on the whole time?

I rode the L train back into Manhattan, watching the car grow more and more crowded as the revelers poured into the heart of the city for Friday night. Then the train sat at 8th Avenue for ten minutes. I really hoped I would see Kali on the way back, but there was no sign of any of the SunTech people at our usual station.

Now that I had some time to think about it, I knew I was blowing up what I had seen into something much bigger than it was. I knew that. But I was still angry.

Why was she playing with me like this? Resisting was one thing, running away was another.

The racing subway felt so good that I stayed onboard all the way back out to Canarsie. I breathed the ocean again, and realized that I was still fighting mad. But by the time the train got back to Bushwick, I was ready to get off.

I went home. In my loft bed, I rolled in a half-sleep all night thinking I was being chased by a train. The rushing, rocking motion had imprinted on my brain. I was groggy and even more upset the next morning with no work to go to.

It sucked, big time. I was caught in the grip of a monster that I wrestled with over and over again. The monster wanted to drag me over to Kali's place so I could see her. Maybe if I saw her looking sad, that would crush the red haze of rage that still burned through me. Maybe it was the way she had been laughing, as if nothing was wrong. As if she hadn't been thinking about me all week, like I had been thinking about her.

I had to see her.

But I was no stalker. It was crazy madness. My advice to anyone else would be to stay away.

It didn't matter. It was a feeling deeper than words, deeper than common sense.

I fought myself minute by minute, hour by hour. The thought that I wouldn't see her until Monday made my heart race. It was only two days! But it was too much.

I abruptly left my studio and went out to the bookstore and the health food store. I tried to talk to people, to distract myself. But I couldn't focus on what they were saying and finally gave up. They probably thought I was on drugs, I was so unlike myself. I had to force myself to go back to my studio and not go to the subway, which led to her place…

As the sun went down, my resistance finally began to cave in. The thought of trying to lie down to go to sleep was intolerable. I was already out of my mind. Might as well admit it and get some relief. I had to see her.

Once I got started, I couldn't stop. I ran through the darkened streets to the subway station, already feeling better for being in motion. Now I had a goal I could focus my fury on.

But as I climbed up the subway steps to Bedford St. along with a stream of partying hipsters, some self-preserving spark flared inside of me. I couldn't rush over to Kali's place and demand answers. That could ruin everything.

I took the next street over and walked towards her place. I ended up at the same chain-link fence where I had watched her window after our first date. I had felt like a stalker then, like I was flipped head over heels.

That was nothing compared to now. She was a temptress, a destructive genie who had gotten hold of me and wouldn't let go.

Nobody would believe it of me. The master every sub wanted. The one who kept his women on a string. What was I doing creeping after someone who didn't want me?

Because I didn't believe Kali didn't want me. I knew how her body quivered when I touched her. She had given herself to me over and over again.

She's the one who wanted romance, goddamn it! Didn't Romeo chase after Juliette when he found out he couldn't have her?

More to the point, was Romeo this angry and upset? Yes! If Shakespeare ever stalked a girl, then he knew that, too. It was all wrapped up in romance and "wherefore art thou?" but it really came down to the same thing: the woman I loved was out of reach, and it wasn't right.

The woman I loved.

I clung to the wire of the fence watching the light in her window. *I love Kali.*

I should have told her that. That's what she was waiting for. That's why she didn't believe me.

I had to tell her.

Suddenly the light in her window went off. I took a deep sigh. Like I had a connection to her. She was there, and she had just turned off the light. She was getting into bed, punching her pillow like she did every night. I could see the night-shirt she was wearing. I could almost breathe the scent of her hair as it fanned over her pillow.

I clung to the fence, closing my eyes as I imagined her. It was so real. I loved her. I would do whatever it took to make this work.

I could hardly breathe, my throat was closed so tightly. All of my anger was gone. Evaporated like it had never existed. But this feeling was worse.

What if I can't get her back?

The fence was the only thing holding me up as I stared up at her window. I couldn't walk away from her. She belonged to me. We belonged together. I had to make her see that.

But through it all was a resounding thrum of doom. *What if I can't get her back?*

To come so far, to open up so much, to find a woman who fit me in every way, only to watch her walk away? I couldn't do it.

I wouldn't.

I knew what to do.

Early the next morning, I got up and called florists. Finally I found one in Manhattan that was open early on Sunday, and I paid double the price to have two dozen red roses delivered immediately.

I took the train into the city to write the card. On it, I wrote: *I love you.*

I didn't bother to sign it. She knew my handwriting. She would know instantly that it was from me.

Chapter 30

Kali

The bouquet made me gasp when I saw it. The roses were magnificent, deep ruby red. Their smell filled the air. I was thrilled to finally get the words from him: *I love you...*

But he had written it rather than telling me face-to-face. He wouldn't risk saying it to me, because I wouldn't say it back. He knew that. Sending me the flowers was another way of manipulating me without risking himself.

It was just another huge ordeal in the struggle to stay away from Hunter. I put the flowers around the corner where I wouldn't see them.

As a better reminder, I put up the red marker Jeff drawing on my fridge next to the warehouse drawing. At the last second, I had tucked it into my suitcase before we left. Hunter didn't see me take it.

This time, I wouldn't stop seeing it. Every day that silly drawing would remind me to make my own choices, instead of someone else's.

I tried not to think about Hunter, but that was hopeless. There was a void where he used to be, and I felt shaky and really scared in the city for the first time. As if I had just woken up and realized I was living on a precipice, with a thousand foot drop on every side. One misstep and I'd be goners.

I didn't doubt Hunter's desire for me. But I did doubt that desire alone was enough.

His passion for me had grown the more I resisted him. It was perverse, much more so than the kinky sex I loved with him. There was some kind of deeper power struggle going on between us, playing out inside of us, and I felt like I was on the losing end.

Visions of me kneeling at his feet and wearing a collar with another woman kneeling next to me, calling him *Sir*... I couldn't do it.

Because that wasn't me. I wanted a partner. I wanted this passion to lead to the next part of my life, and then the next. I wanted a best friend, not a master. I was grateful to Hunter for helping me face the awful patterns in my life, but I couldn't keep being peeled like an onion by him.

I didn't want our sex games to become our real life, with Hunter always choosing where we would go and what we would do. I didn't want to take on a subservient role in front of other people. I didn't want to be trained to do things for him, even if my body was a traitor begging for it.

The proof was in my own sexual response. I was in a fever pitch of sexual denial. As much as I tried to block out thoughts of him—his face, his hands, his laughter, his low-voiced commands—the memories broke through, like he had imprinted them on me. Until I finally gave in and masturbated, letting myself go in daydreams of him touching me, pinning me with his relentless thrusting, groaning as I twisted in eagerness to be filled. But it wasn't satisfying. I held off as long as I could, but I couldn't help myself and kept trying to satiate the maddening desire, as much as I wished I could stop.

I told myself these feelings were caused by his training, that he had manipulated this reaction out of me. He was the consummate sex master. And I was his clay.

He wrote *I love you* on the card, but what did he really know about love?

What do I really know about love? All I know is how my mom and dad treated me, like a perpetual tug of war between them. Maybe that's why I was so resistant of this tug of war between Hunter and me. It didn't feel real. It felt like a game that he had to win. And I was tired of playing other people's games. My mom had trained me to be the perfect companion. I didn't want Hunter to be the next one to train me.

I was done being manipulated by everyone. As lonely as I felt, as horrible as it was to not see Hunter, I would rather be alone right now.

I was even doing a good job at not caring that my mom still hadn't called me.

In the past when Jenny was upset with me, I was always the first one to reach out. Usually I had to try to talk to her repeatedly until she relented. There had been some epic battles when I was growing up, all conducted in silence by my mom. I would beg and plead until she reluctantly gave in and spoke to me. Then I would cry from gratitude. It was silly that it had such an effect on me. Most kids wouldn't care if their parents didn't talk to them. But that showed the iron grip my mom had on me. Even now, I was living under the overwhelming silence because I was doing something Jenny didn't like.

Living in fear of being alone. Abandoned.

I was tired of running away from being alone. That's why I came to the city. That's why I could resist Hunter even though I ached for him.

Now I knew a lot more about how Hunter had molded me into his play toy because I spent my spare minutes at home on the computer finding out more about BDSM. Along with the social websites, there were authors and educators who posted videos about how to do bondage and flogging as well as more sexually explicit things like fisting and vaginal piercing. The more I looked, the more I realized I was not really interested in going to the extremes. I was definitely more on the "vanilla" side of things, with a little spice thrown in.

And how could a nearly-vanilla girl like me please a man like Hunter?

Then I found his FetLife profile—HuntingArt. I was looking through the friends of Popcorn, the nice woman Hunter had introduced me to at the Paddles, and there it was. The image of the tattoo on his back shoulder, that sinuous abstract of a couple endlessly engaging in sex.

OMG!

The list of fetishes Hunter liked boggled my mind. Sadism? Slut as a term of endearment? Anal? Really? Who knew? Though come to think of it, he did touch me everywhere. Was he secretly probing me to find out my response?

There was more: domestic servitude, mind fucks, forced orgasm. Sex in public! Verbal domination, biting, belt spanking! Behavior modification! Obedience training!

Just like I thought. I should have looked him up in the beginning. That would have told me everything I needed to know about him. He was a member of dozens of online groups, had twelve hundred "friends," and went to lots of events according to his listings. Who had twelve hundred friends?

Worse, his wall was filled with old posts from fawning women, telling him how great it was to see him again, how much fun their scene had been, where was he going next...

Going back in his timeline, I saw that Hunter had posted in groups and on friend's walls during the past couple months while he was dating me. In one post, he was arguing with someone about who had outed a private house party to the cops. In another comment, he was admiring the photo of a naked girl with her pubic hair dyed fuchsia like her hair.

Looking closer, I realized it was Minx! Standing there naked, her hips thrust forward showing off her shocking pink pubs.

I banged my desk in frustration. He had "loved" Minx's photo the evening before we went out and had sex for the first time in the water taxi!

After that, I was done for. I clicked on his female friends, trying to find out more. At least his profile had no relationships noted except for "girlfriend" without a link to a profile name. He didn't know I had an account on FetLife. I wondered what he would think of my nickname—Runningaway2.

The question was, running away to where?

I wasn't nearly kinky enough for him. Give me a little hair

pulling and bondage. Stroke my body, pinch me and smack my flesh until I climaxed even harder. But you could keep the *yes, Sirs* and the collars and the expectations that proved I was out of place in his world.

I glared at the red roses. They said *I love you*, but I didn't know what he really meant by that. It could be a big ploy to get me to go out with him again, so he could draw me back into his web.

Then I found something unexpected by clicking on a link under a photo of a sculpture in his profile gallery. It took me to an off-site website called Hunting Art.

Hunter made erotic art. Lots of it. Sculptures of abstract nude bodies merging and shifting, most of it really explicit, involving bondage or people crying out as flesh was cut and bodies were constricted by rope. The website listed events around the country where he sold his art: kinky conferences, erotic art festivals and science fiction conventions.

A chill washed through me. SunTech didn't know anything about this. Selina would have rejected Hunter from the competition if she knew. It would be terrible publicity if the media found out that our plaza was being designed by an infamous S&M artist.

That's why Hunter had told me at the Paddles to not mention SunTech. He had never said a word about this business to me. And neither had his friends. I wondered if he had told them not to say anything to me.

Controlling everyone around him, as usual.

I searched his website and nowhere on it did I find Hunter's last name. I found nothing on FetLife that included a recognizable photo of him. A Google image search came up with traditional PR photos and shadowed snapshots showing his profile, nothing else. Doing a search of his real name and Hunting Art, nothing came up.

I tried to calm down. We only had six more days to go until the launch. I could manage this. Even if the media found out about his kink-connections, I could deal with it. It was my job to make sure both SunTech and Hunter came out of this looking fabulous.

I began to plot my media response if anything was exposed. I was still fielding too many emails because of Selina's viral video, which was climbing at 128,000 views. I now knew personally how quickly something bad could get around. So I searched for sound bites on erotic art and BDSM, and found the National Coalition for Sexual Freedom which did advocacy for kinky community clubs and businesses. I decided if there was a media crisis, I could reach out to them for help.

After hours hunched over the computer, I finally forced myself to go out and get some fresh air and something to eat. After my frantic day, it was soothing to be back in my old routine, taking a seat at the long counter in the sandwich shop, and ordering a spicy cream cheese and cucumber sandwich. I hadn't eaten one since Hunter had turned my life upside down.

But the whole time, I was thinking about the things I had glimpsed through the computer and the places Hunter had taken me. A whole subculture I never knew existed. Hidden from the real world. But it made sense. Look at me—I was kind of ashamed about how much I loved this kinky stuff. And didn't I secretly think it was a little too strange? After all, I couldn't imagine leaving my kids with the babysitter while I went to Paddles with my husband.

Then again, why not? We were all adults there, and nobody was doing anything they didn't want to do.

So then why didn't Hunter tell me about his kinky sculptures?

•••

On the way into my building, I ran into Pam and Karen. "How's it going with your boyfriend?" Karen asked.

I grimaced, and had to force myself to say, "We aren't seeing each other anymore."

"Why? What happened? Why didn't you say something?"

I sighed. "I got a promotion at work, so technically I'm his boss and we can't date. But I'm kind of glad in a way. It was going so fast that I needed a break."

Pam nodded. "You do what you've got to do."

"I'm trying." I tried to change the subject. "Hey, did you two ever go to the Paddles?"

They exchanged looks. "Yeah," Karen admitted. She stopped, then laughed awkwardly. "It was an experience. A lot of fun."

"That's the way I felt about it," I agreed. "But I don't want a steady diet of it."

"Yeah," Karen said again. "But we liked it. We'll do it again sometime."

Pam didn't say a word, but she was smiling in a way I had never seen. It was nice that they were so compatible. I had never understood how important that was more than now.

I had been right about getting away from Hunter for a while, to let my mind clear. The more I found out about how he had manipulated me, including lying by omission about his X-rated sculpture business, the more it looked like Hunter was not the right man for me.

Chapter 31

Hunter

I ordered another big bouquet of flowers to arrive for Kali at SunTech on Monday morning. Not roses, because then she would have to explain too much. A mixed bunch of tropical flowers with a sealed card that said, *I love you.*

I followed it up the next day with a basket of brownies. She had said at our memorable first scene in the Afghanistan restaurant that she liked brownies, but I had never gotten them for her. I put a sealed card with the basket that said, *I love you.*

That afternoon, a text came from Kali: *Stop.*

I ground my teeth together, but I knew I couldn't try to persuade her when she had used her safeword on me. When a woman said stop, you had to stop or you were a monster.

She kept using her safeword with me. It made me feel like an idiot. I was supposed to be able to read women so well that I could bring them right to the edge without going over.

But with Kali, I kept stomping all over her limits like an ignorant clod. No wonder she was pushing me away.

I paced among the ball-shaped benches, absently looking at my sundial from all angles. It was installed and ready to go, except for a missing medallion that was being recast and sent from the foundry. When we had tried to install it, one of the bolt holes had cracked.

Except for the IV, it was complete. But it was hard to see how it would look with the plywood fence still crowding around it.

I wasn't satisfied. At first I thought it was because of Kali, but then I gradually realized I wasn't happy with the sundial. From every angle, my eye kept going to the missing medallion. It created a dark patch that was larger than the medallions positioned in front of each bench. I kept trying to blank that out in my minds' eye, to see what the problem was.

Finally I got as far back as I could behind the sundial, looking towards the building, almost on the sidewalk. It was the perspective most people would see the sundial from.

Something was off…

I didn't know how long I stared at it, but I jumped when a voice asked from the nearby gate, "Something wrong?"

It was Kali. Looking at me curiously.

"Yeah. Something's wrong. But for the life of me…" I stared back at the sundial.

"I think it looks amazing," Kali said honestly, looking around, too. "I can't wait to see it with the fence gone."

"Me, too." I was surprised we were suddenly standing here talking so friendly-like. Then again, she always surprised me.

Kali checked her watch, looking at where the shadow lay. "Is it right? It's three o'clock." She walked over to look down at the medallion where the shadow crossed its edge. "Yes, this one is III."

I slowly followed her, realizing she had found the problem. "You can't see the numerals from a distance. That's it!"

"What do you mean?" she asked.

"It's a clock. That's the purpose of a sundial. But when I left the patina on the bronze, it darkened the medallions so much that the numbers blend into the background from a distance. They need to pop." I considered them. "I'll have to polish the numerals on the medallions."

She cocked her head. "I think you're right. It would look nicer with the numbers shiny."

"Kali, you're an inspiration." My voice fell. "What would I do without you?"

But instead of responding, she shifted away from me. "Hunter, I came out because I needed to talk to you about something sensitive. I don't want to do it in the office because someone might overhear. Out here, with the sounds," she waved at the noise of the traffic on the street, "I thought this would be okay."

"Sure." I was glad I hadn't pushed it. I knew she would come to me, in her own good time.

"It's about your website, Hunting Art."

Uh-oh... "You've seen it?"

"Yes. I found it this weekend. Why didn't you tell me about it?"

"You know why, Kali. SunTech would have canceled the project if they found out. And you would have felt obligated to tell Selina."

"I should tell Mr. Ryan."

"What's he going to do now—rip out the sundial because I'm kinky? I've kept my erotic line separate from my big public works. I know that no corporation is going to want to be associated with artists who make erotic art. But my sculptures are what pay my bills."

"So you do know what this means if it gets out to the media? Didn't you think I should be warned? Or were you just hoping that phone call from the *NY Post* never came in—'Hello, why did you hire a prominent S&M sculptor to design your plaza?'"

"This launch is one-off publicity. Once it's over, it's over," I insisted. "Nobody will care after the fact that I'm kinky."

"Maybe. Maybe not," she agreed. "But the launch is this week. I want you to deactivate your website. And your FetLife page. Just as a precaution."

I looked at her sideways. "You know about FetLife?"

"Yes."

"That means you have a profile. What's your name?"

She ignored that. "I want everything taken down that associates you with BDSM for at least the next couple of weeks. We don't need another burst of bad publicity for SunTech."

I considered it. "All right, I'll do it. When I get home I'll shut both down. But there is Google cache. I can try to get them to delete it, but it may take a few days. And frankly, if someone makes the effort to find Hunting Art, they will find it. I've done a lot of shows."

"Selina didn't find anything connected to your real name during our background checks before we put your design into the competition, so I'm hoping we'll be safe if your main portals are closed down."

I nodded. "My friends will wonder what happened, but I can stall them for a couple of weeks without raising suspicions." I could use my relationship with Kali as an excuse, if I had to.

"Good." She turned away as if she was done with the conversation.

"Wait, Kali. We need to talk. I'm sorry I didn't tell you sooner."

"You should have. Once we were really together, you should have told me."

"I was protecting you. If I was outed early in the project, I wanted you to be able to say honestly that you knew nothing about Hunting Art."

She frowned. "I don't need you to protect me, Hunter. Especially when it comes to my job. I have to make my own decisions."

"I know."

"I don't think you do." She was serious.

"What do you mean by that?"

"You manipulate me constantly to make me to do what you want. You say it's because you're protecting me, or you're helping me, or because you want me so much. But it really comes down to—you always have to be in control."

"That's not true. I've stopped when you told me to. Every time. I also stopped seeing Minx, in spite of what you think."

"I know what you want, Hunter. And you keep trying to push me further and further into it. I don't want to be submissive. I may like it during sex, but that's it for me, Hunter. And you've never understood that about me."

"You've loved everything we've done together. Admit it! I think it's fear that's stopping you now. You're afraid that if you submit to me, you'll let me override your own good judgment. That you'll lose yourself. But that's not true."

257

I reached out for her in spite of myself. I had to touch her. Had to be with her.

But she pushed me away. "No, Hunter! You keep running all over me, trying to force me to be what you want me to be."

"I'm trying to help you, Kali. I wanted you to break free of the past. To break free of these constraints around you. You could be so much more—"

"I don't need you pushing me into being an artist! It's the same as my mom trying to stop me, don't you see?"

Kali scraped my hands off her and hurried away. I took one step after her, then stopped myself.

She disappeared through the gate in the fence. And I was alone again without her.

I wasn't trying to force her into anything.

I wasn't.

I went through a black cloud of fury, pacing among the benches of my sundial. Denying over and over to myself that I was trying to mold her into something she wasn't. Kali took to submission like she was born to it. Trained into it by her mother, actually. Following the example of her father, who had to get away in order to be free...

Like Kali had run away from her mother to New York.

She was trying to get away from that kind of control. That's why she refused to give in to me. That's why she had to find her path on her own terms.

Kali was right—I hadn't understood her until now. I wanted to run after her, to tell her that.

But it was only one half of the equation. I stared at the medallions, lost in thought. Thinking of past girlfriends and submissives. Even the women who were barely kinky did a lot of the same things for me—they served me, letting me choose when and how and where I saw them.

I never had a relationship like I had with Kali, hanging out and watching a movie on TV, and sketching and cooking breakfast together in the morning. Maybe that's why it was so hard for me.

Maybe that's why I felt more comfortable in the dominant role, why I felt better when we were having sex or I was drawing her.

Because those times when we were casually entwined on the couch were the ones that scared me the most. Because I wasn't driving the bus.

Just like I wasn't driving the bus with Kali now.

That's why I was flipping out, pacing around in front of the security cameras, probably entertaining the security staff to holy hell. I was out of control.

I loved her. Why didn't I tell her that? I had the chance while she was standing here. I should have said it first thing. And then kept saying it.

But I was scared. She didn't love me.

I forced myself to turn around and walk through the gate. I made sure the chain was locked. Then I walked away, every step a nightmare.

I had made such a mess of things. Finally a girl who fit me like a glove, and because I fell in love with her and felt unsure of myself, I did nothing but try to control of her.

I wandered around downtown Manhattan, too distraught to return to work and too worked up to stay put anywhere. Until I came to the Hudson River. The roiling water was dark even in the afternoon sunshine, stretching a mile away to the other side, and extending as far as I could see on either side. It was massive, unstoppable. It made me feel small.

Kali had gone through her own problems growing up, and that pressure had turned her into a diamond. The same with me. I knew my fears came from my past, growing up and needing to be in charge, so everything would be okay for my brothers and my mom.

I realized I hadn't even called them since I had seen my brother weeks ago. I hadn't talked to my father since I found out I got fired. Or my mother to find out how she was doing. My brother had left several messages, giving me bulletins, and I had transferred the money every week. But that was it.

Gazing out at the black water rushing by, I felt like a coward. A villain. I had been distracting myself with Kali, ignoring the latest tragedy in my family's life. She had asked me about it a couple of times, now that I thought about it. But I had brushed off her questions every time.

I realized I was doing exactly what she accused me of—setting up our relationship with strict boundaries, keeping the intimacy away, keeping sex in the center ring. Isolating us in a bubble that wasn't real. How could it be real when she didn't even know that I earned my living selling kinky art?

Kali was right. I had manipulated her, and kept things from her. Why hadn't I taken the collar away from Minx? Because I expected life to continue on as it always had; that I could spank any girl I wanted to because it was her birthday. That I would be able to play with other people, maybe with certain restrictions like no intercourse or no kissing. Whatever Kali wanted...

But Kali wanted monogamy. She didn't want to be pressured into being sexually open in order to please me. She refused to play that game, and I had to admire her for it. I was used to women offering to do anything to win my love. It got old after a while.

This was the first time I would do anything to win a woman's love. I had danced around her questions every time, but now there was nowhere left to go.

Can I be monogamous?

With Kali, yes.

So why did the thought scare me so much? It was the idea of putting everything I had into one person. To build a life together, and trust that I wouldn't screw up like my dad did, or even worse that she would have to work as hard as my mom did just to survive. I didn't want to have kids if they were going to have to struggle as much as I did when I was a kid.

What Kali wanted went smack in the face of all my fears. How could she be so hopeful to think two people could make it together for the long haul? Granted, both of our parents were together, but the sacrifices they made to make it work weren't worth it.

Were they?

It was after dark when I finally caught the subway home, still deep in my thoughts. I felt opened up, vulnerable. Like a kid again.

Kali had that affect on me, luring me on until my tender heart was exposed. I had to love her. She was like a force of nature.

Suddenly I couldn't wait to get home to look at my drawings of her. Her face. Her eyes. Her hands. The curve of her neck. I had drawn her from every angle, in every light.

When I got home, I pulled out my books and ripped out the pages, surrounding myself with her image. Her smile.

Her smile.

That was Kali. Good hearted, loving, giving, smart, funny, ready to do whatever it took to get the job done.

I held a portrait up to my face, breathing deeply as if I could smell her on the pages.

"Kali..." I murmured.

There was a knock on the door. My head went up like a shot.

Full of hope, thinking only of Kali, I ran to the door.

It was Minx.

Her hair was purple today and done up in a red bandana. She didn't have much makeup on, which was unusual for her. But her combat boots and Hello Kitty t-shirt were typical.

I couldn't pull myself together quickly enough. I was exposed, my hope deflating. And Minx saw it all.

I backed away, but I shouldn't have because Minx followed me inside, shutting the door behind her. I could only stare at her, lost in confusion that she wasn't Kali. I'd known Minx for years, but right now she felt like a stranger.

"May I speak, Sir?" she asked.

"You don't have to ask," I managed to say. I couldn't be the master with Minx. I promised Kali I wouldn't. But that's what I had done when Minx came over last time. I didn't stop her when she sat on the floor, for one thing. And I let her ask permission to speak.

And the other things that kept our relationship so formal.

She followed me into the main area of my studio. The floor was covered by images of Kali. Kali, over and over again

Minx bent down and picked up a couple, looking at them closely. "She is beautiful. There's something transcendent about her."

"She's true to herself." I began to gather up the drawings. It was almost a sacrilege for Minx to touch them. She started to help me, but I said, "No, let me do it."

She stood there watching me on my hands and knees gathering up the pictures and placing them carefully in a black portfolio. I laid it on the table, my hand resting on it like I didn't want to let it go.

"I've never seen you like this before," Minx finally said.

I looked down at the portfolio. "I love her."

There were a few moments of silence. When I looked up, Minx's eyes were filled with tears. "Do you, really?" she asked.

"Yes."

"I didn't think you could."

My throat closed. "Neither did I."

Minx tried to smile. "But she knows what kind of man you are. She can't expect you to change for her."

"Minx, I need to get my collar back from you."

Her mouth opened. "Seriously?"

I was a little surprised that I didn't feel the least bit of regret. I used to be so hot for Minx. I used to fuck her like mad. She was the perfect sub, I always thought. I knew her body so well, every nook and cranny, and could push her as hard as I dared in lots of different ways.

As if remembering the same thing, she slowly sank to her knees in front of me. Giving herself to me with her eyes. Both her hands went to the collar of her shirt and she ripped it with a convulsive move. There were tears on her cheeks. "Let me please you, Master. You know I can give you what you want."

It left me cold. All I could think about was Kali, and how

betrayed she would feel to find Minx here like this.

"Minx, you have to leave now." I kept myself from barking out the order, like a master would. I refused to take that role with her. "It's wrong for you to act this way, now that I've released you."

Shaking her head, she seemed confused. But when I didn't say anything else, she finally struggled to her feet. "But I thought you wanted it."

"Please drop off your collar later through the slot." I went to open the door, and waited until she gathered her torn t-shirt in front of her. She left with a hurt, angry look at me.

I didn't care if she was still staying at Jeremy's or not. I didn't care that she was walking around in her bra. I didn't ask her to throw herself at me after I requested her collar back.

It was Minx's own fault if she got into trouble because of it. But as I opened the portfolio to look at Kali's image, I had to admit to myself—I was also to blame. Why should Minx believe I was serious when I had never had a real intimate relationship with *her*? I had always kept Minx at arm's distance. She had accepted it, but now I wondered why.

It seemed so empty now that I had been with Kali. I wasn't sure how I could go on now that she had imprinted herself on my soul.

Chapter 32

Kali

I kept checking, but it was nearly nine o'clock that night before Hunter took down his website and FetLife profile. I breathed a sigh of relief. I would have fought him on it if he didn't do it.

The fact that he did what I asked made me feel better. He did respect my opinion. Sometimes.

Now I just needed to get through the next few days, and hope nobody exposed Hunter's kinky side-business.

From the window in front of Selina's desk, I watched him all day on Wednesday down on his hands and knees polishing the number on each medallion with a power buffer. By the time he got to the third one, I could see the sun winking off the brilliant shine. It really caught the eye, and made each number stand out clearly.

It was exactly what the sundial needed.

Later that day, I was checking the delivery of tall cocktail tables that would be sprinkled under the half-circle portico of the building. Two bars would be set up at either end, and a finger-food buffet would be laid out next to them. I had sent out 200 invitations to the press and city note-worthies, and hoped 50 would show up. I planned on spending all day Thursday calling people to make sure they would come.

I may not have had the experience that Selina did. And as Hunter had reminded me, I wasn't the shark that my old boss was. But I could give it a warm, personal touch that Selina couldn't. Luckily the fallout from Selina's video had been tapering off this week, as I did my best to turn the bad publicity into a boost for our unveiling.

As I approached the door, I saw a guy planting red and orange flowers in the two round planters in front of the entryway. "Who told you to do that?" I asked.

"Mr. Munro. He was very specific on what shades of red and orange for us to bring to match the SunTech logo."

"Oh. Thank you." I stepped back as far as I could, and had to admit that Hunter had a good eye. The red and orange would pick up the logo in the banner I was placing over the central arch in the portico that led to the doorway.

I could hear the buzz of his polisher on the other side of the fence. I wanted to go in and thank him for thinking of such a nice touch. But I was avoiding him as much as I could.

I made myself walk away from the fenced-off area, checking the rest of the details on my clipboard. When I was done, I hesitated near the gate in the fence, wanting to go in and speak to Hunter. But that feeling was treacherous. Not to be trusted.

With a supreme effort, I got myself back upstairs and buried myself in work. I was still there late, tying up the last details when a delivery arrived for me. I opened it up to find pork dumplings and spicy pork rolls and a custard sweet that I recognized from the little Chinese shop where Hunter had taken me the evening we went to the Conservancy Garden.

I ate up every bit of it. I hadn't realized how famished I was. I knew it was Hunter who sent it, though there was no note. But that meant he was also still here, and was thinking about me. I almost dreaded what would happen when I left. I didn't want to argue with him anymore.

But to my pleasant surprise, Hunter wasn't lying in wait. My shoulders relaxed as I headed off to the subway. I hated the fact that I had been dreading seeing him, and I was grateful that he finally wasn't pushing himself on me. Sending up food for me was nice and helpful. Planting the flowers was nice and helpful. Not ambushing me when I left work was nice and helpful.

I went home and slept well for the first time since I had broken up with him.

The next morning, the fence came down. People gathered under the portico of the building to see the reveal. I watched Hunter on the other side of the plaza directing everything.

As the plywood came down, the plaza opened up and we could see the sundial and the benches placed in a half circle around it. The medallions glinted in the light. And the long needle of the sundial also glinted where Hunter has polished the edge of it.

I let out my breath. "Ohhh…."

"It's so beautiful!" someone said next to me.

I was proud to be a part of creating this public space. The sundial suited the concave glass building with its retro-portico forming a half-circle around the plaza. The sundial itself was an old-fashioned idea, but the geometric shapes brought it into the modern age.

The last of the plywood panels were being loaded onto the truck, when Hunter came over to me. "What do you think?" he asked.

"It couldn't be more perfect for the plaza."

"That was the idea. To bring two very different things together and make you see them both in a new way."

I had to smile at his innuendo. "Are you talking about us or the sundial?"

"Both. I think we're better together than apart."

He looked so vulnerable. Like nothing I'd ever seen before. I wanted to put my arms around his neck and sink my fingers into his hair. And kiss him. Finally he wanted to talk and I wanted nothing more than to touch him and hold him. "Hunter… I don't know what to say."

"Say you'll think about it. I promise you monogamy. I don't want any other woman. And I don't want you to be my slave. Or my submissive. You're my lover, and I want to love every inch of you. With as much or little kinkiness as you want."

"Hunter, that's not you! I can't ask you to change who you are."

He gave a short laugh. "Too late. You've already changed me. I don't want Minx. I want other women. I want you."

I suddenly realized we were standing shock still on the plaza, talking intently. Staring into each other's eyes. With lots of people around, including SunTech employees.

"I can't do this here," I said.

"I'm sorry, Kali. I just couldn't help telling you." He backed away, smiling wistfully. "I love you, Kali."

With that, he turned and called out to some of his men to start cleaning up the plaza.

That was the first time he said it to me. I kept hearing his words, the tone of his voice, low and real. Like he was speaking from the center of his being.

Tomorrow was the party.

After that, the project would be finished and Hunter would no longer be employed by SunTech.

I went inside and up to my desk. All I could think about was that tomorrow was the end.

I couldn't get used to the terrible idea that Hunter had been a fling. A life-changing, never-to-be-forgotten affair. Something that was doomed from the start and went out in a blaze of glory. We would always have the sundial, and every time I saw it, I would remember Hunter.

I stared at the tropical flowers he had sent on Monday. They smelled so strong they overpowered the office.

Could I risk letting him overpower me, as well? Could I take a chance and fling myself off the cliff and hope there was water below?

Could I really do it to myself again? It hurt so badly already. What if I really gave it a try, and found Minx sitting at his feet in another month's time?

And was it fair to ask him to change that much? Could he, even if he wanted to?

...

Late that night, my phone rang. For a second, I thought it was Hunter and my heart leaped in eagerness.

Then I saw the phone. It was my mom.

A flash of anger burned through me. *Well it's about time.*

It had been nearly three weeks since I saw my mom, since our fight over Hunter. It was the longest we had ever gone without speaking. Usually, I wore down under Jenny's silence, and reached out to her first.

This was the first time my mom had reached out to me.

I let the phone ring. It felt good to be in charge for once with my mom. Let her leave a message. Let her make an effort.

When I checked, there was no message. My mom must have hung up when she didn't get an answer.

I felt perversely glad.

Usually my mom would leave a soft-voiced order, "Call me when you get this, Kali." And I would call her back within minutes.

I sat there looking at my phone, smiling slightly. What was Jenny thinking? Was she waiting for me to see the number and call her back?

I hummed as I went to wash my face and get ready for bed. My mom knew my routine. She knew I was sleepy and yawning, planning to go to bed on time to be bright and ready for tomorrow's big event. My mom didn't know that Selina had been fired and I was in charge. And she didn't know I had broken up with Hunter.

The last thing I wanted to do was get in an argument with my mom and get all riled up before bed. I decided I wouldn't call my mom back.

Let her stew. Everyone who thinks I'll do whatever they want, can fuck off!

With that, I turned off the light and went to bed.

...

The next morning, my phone rang just as my alarm was going off. Groggy, I reached for my phone. "Hello?"

Then I looked. It was my mom.

"Did I wake you, dear?" Jenny sounded exactly like she usually did. Like nothing had happened. Like it hadn't been weeks since we last spoke.

She was ambushing me. Making talk to her on her own terms. Everything I had come to hate about our dynamic.

"I wanted to wish you luck on your big day," Jenny said brightly. "You have the party tonight, right?"

"It's this afternoon," I yawned. "The sundial looks beautiful. I'll send you a photo later."

There were a few moments of silence, as if my mom was surprised by my nonchalance. "Are you still dating the artist?"

"Hunter? Yes," I lied blandly. I wasn't going to let my mom get a moral victory by admitting we had broken up.

Again a few moments of silence. "Really?" Jenny asked. "Because you sounded funny when you said that."

I had to smile. My mom knew me too well. "We're going together to the party." I felt bold and reckless. *Who cares if Jenny knows I'm lying?*

"Okay." My mom sniffed. "If that's what you want, Kali. But it seems to me that you aren't thinking about the risk you're taking by being with a man like that. What if you get pregnant? You've seen what a struggle I've had with your dad all these years—"

"Mom, stop." Ironic that I was safewording with my mom. "I don't want to hear it."

"What? Kali, don't speak to me that way. I'm still your mother."

"I don't want to hear you criticize dad anymore. If you hate the way he is, then leave him. Tell him not to come home. It's not like it would be a problem for you financially since you're doing it all anyway. But stop complaining about him to *me*."

"Kali!" Jenny was shocked.

"I'm serious. I don't want to hear it. You've been married to dad for nearly twenty-five years. When are you going to start making the best of it?" I glanced at the clock. "Listen, I've got to go. There's lots to do at work. I'll talk to you later."

With that, I hung up. And felt better than I had in a very long time.

...

I wore my chic black suit and my most comfortable high heels, and went to work. The party planner Selina had hired knew her stuff, and by three o'clock according to the sundial, the wine bars and buffets were set up and black-suited waiters were ready to pass trays with tiny bites of food on them. There was a nice scattering of tall tables under the portico with the center left open to showcase the sundial.

I had ordered velvet ropes to separate the open front of the plaza from the sidewalk. Several guards were standing at either end keeping an eye on the long ropes, to keep people from stepping over them and getting to the open bars.

There was already a crowd of people standing at the ropes, curious about what was going on. It was creating quite the buzz. I could feel the excitement in the plaza beginning to rise as I checked through the last things on my list. I had my own earpiece so the hostess at the ropes could alert me when notables and members of the press arrived.

Through it all was Hunter, a calm presence talking to everyone as if he hadn't a care in the world, and pitching in where needed. His job was almost done. His photo would be taken repeatedly tonight— and I hoped printed in papers and all over the Internet. If I had done my job right, it would happen that way.

I was still worried that some last minute disaster would happen. I especially feared Hunter's kinky sex business would be dropped like a bomb in the midst of our publicity blitz.

The whirlwind of activity swept me up, and before I knew it, Amanda, the party planner was gently straightening my collar. "Time to launch!"

First a trickle, then a flood of people arrived. Later the hostess said 119 out of the 200 invited showed up. It was a testament to my personal outreach to each and every one.

The notables were happy because the press were taking

hundreds of shots of everyone in the plaza from every angle—back into the watching crowd, with the sundial looming overhead, across the gathered notaries toward the building, and from either side getting views of both. I wondered if SunTech should consider renting out the plaza for events. It was nicely suited for PR purposes. I planned on telling Mr. Ryan that we should have their next big press conference in the plaza and attract a crowd with the velvet ropes like we did today. I had remembered Selina saying one time: *"Rope something off from New Yorkers, and they'll climb all over each other to see what they're missing."*

I greeted the people I had to greet, introduced some to Robert Ryan or Hunter, depending on who they were. Hunter was phenomenal—he stayed by the sundial, speaking to everyone about its construction and the mechanism that could shift the needle during daylight savings time and over the change of seasons.

He looked gorgeous, and women were fawning all over him. In fact, there was a large crowd around Hunter the entire time as he smiled and charmed everyone.

But anytime I went near him, his eyes met mine and locked, like a promise.

Every time, my heart would start beating faster. It was so hard to resist him.

It made me wonder. I had talked to my mom this morning, even when she caught me so off guard, and I still held my own. Maybe I could do it with Hunter, too.

I felt so proud of him as I watched him standing with Robert Ryan during the unveiling ceremony. My boss talked about his devotion to a sustainable earth, and credited the sundial as one of the most ancient and efficient technologies, a fitting symbol for SunTech's work. The crowd was swelled by SunTech employees, filling the plaza to bursting, and the bystanders that lined the velvet ropes were three deep watching the ceremony. Cars were backed up in the street as people tried to see what the fuss was about.

They all raised their glasses of champagne to toast Hunter with a general shout of acclaim. It was a tremendous success, and my eyes shone with tears of joy at the thunderous applause.

When Mr. Ryan was done, he came directly over to me. "Anything to report?"

I had already given him the count for reporters and photographers. "Everything went smoothly, Mr. Ryan. We'll start winding down soon. I'll have the first set of links for you tomorrow morning."

He looked around pleased. "Well done, Kali. I knew you could do it."

"Thank you, Mr. Ryan. I was happy to step up when you needed me."

"This almost makes me wish we could hire you as director of PR, but we need someone with a lot more experience. With our international expansion, we'll need to take on more people anyway. Kali, I'd like to promote you to Assistant PR Director with the appropriate raise. You're much more than a copywriter, and we should use your talents to the fullest."

"Thank you, Mr. Ryan!" I said. "I just want to help SunTech the best I can. I really believe in what we're doing here."

"I know you do." He gave me another smile, and called out a good-bye to the Assemblyman from the 74th district. I was particularly proud I had managed to get our local representative to come.

It was a success in every way.

I turned to watch Hunter posing with two women in front of the sundial. I remembered his voice when he said, *"Because I love you, Kali."* It made me feel warm inside.

If only I could be sure he meant it. That he could be with me and only me. If only…

Chapter 33

Hunter

The way Kali was looking at me made me want to go over and put my arms around her and hold her tight.

But I couldn't reach out to her. I couldn't touch her or tell her how beautiful she was, how serenely she moved as she pulled off the perfect event. She was right. She was good at her job.

It was bittersweet for me, the best moment of my life, yet I couldn't share it with the woman I loved. I couldn't ask for anything that would hurt her, not at the moment of her professional triumph.

I watched how Robert Ryan thanked Kali after their speeches. She looked radiant, exuding poise as she spoke to her boss. If that wasn't a woman on her way to the top, I didn't know what one looked like.

So I did my part, smiling and posing, shaking hands and listening to everyone who spoke to me. I even worked the crowd along the ropes, getting them to linger until the guests finally faded away.

Then I returned to the sundial, looking up at the massive needle thrusting into the sky. The long polished edge caught the sun.

"You do good work," someone said behind me.

I turned to see Robert Ryan standing there looking at me and the sundial. "Thank you, Sir," I said. "It was mainly the concept. Finding the right symbol for SunTech, as you said."

"Thank you for finding it for us," Ryan said. He put his hand in his pocket. "I have something for you to see."

Ryan pulled out a sheet of paper, folded twice. I opened it and saw it was a copy of an email:

Robert Ryan – RobertRyan@SunTech.com

Re: Hunter Munro

The guy who made your sculpture is really sick. He beats up women for fun. His website is www.huntingart.org. Your being taken for a ride by him.

I quickly checked the date—Ryan got it Wednesday night. "Why didn't you say something sooner?"

"A poison pen note? I wouldn't give it the time of day. But I wanted you to know that someone out there is trying to hurt you."

I looked down at the paper. "It's a lie, Mr. Ryan. But the website is mine. I sell erotic art."

Ryan shrugged it off. "Your website was down, but I was able to find some images for sculptures you've exhibited in various shows." His voice lowered and I leaned in closer. "I'd like to get a piece from you. The Tetris Couple caught my eye."

I grinned. "It did? I'd be honored for you to have one of my sculptures. I'll deliver it on Monday."

"In a box, please. I don't want to have to explain it to my secretary."

"Don't worry. I know how to be discrete."

"Yes, I saw how you handled your relationship with Kali."

My smile froze. "We *were* dating, Mr. Ryan. But as soon as Selina was fired, Kali broke up with me."

He nodded. "Yes, I know. Mrs. Chapel and I are both satisfied with the way you've handled yourselves."

"Thank you, Sir." I was more glad for Kali's sake than my own. She had been right about that, too, and it was a good thing she had stopped seeing me.

Ryan held out his hand. "It's been a pleasure working with you, Hunter. I hope we can do it again sometime."

I shook his hand. Robert Ryan knew I was kinky but he didn't care! I had been outed. My biggest fear throughout this whole project. The reason I had lied to Kali about my erotic art business.

But everything was okay.

It was a sense of relief that the worst had happened. Ryan could have been a sexual prude or hypocrite about it. Ryan could have fired me if he was that kind of man.

Minx... She sent the email. The misspelled "your" was classic Minx. And the timing fit perfectly. She probably went back down the hall to Jeremy's after dropping off her collar and sent Ryan that note.

I was going to have to settle the score with her. I had known Minx for too long, and she was a fixture in the scene, so I would have to deal with her somehow. But I didn't want to think about that now, not at the moment of my biggest success.

And as the last people left the plaza, Kali was looking at me from across the long stretch of flagstone. No more blue walls to hem us in.

I walked over to her even though several coworkers were nearby. I wanted to hug her, but she put out her hand and smiled her professional smile. My heart sank as she said, "Thank you, Hunter. You really came through for us. Everyone at SunTech is grateful."

"I'm glad." I slowly shook her hand, feeling how warm and soft her skin was. "Now that I'm no longer employed by the company, can I ask you to come have a celebratory drink with me?"

She let me hold her hand. "I would like that. But I have a lot of work to do here to clear this up."

I brightened up. "I could stay and help."

She pulled her hand away with a little laugh. "No, let me do my job, Hunter."

I wanted to hug her. That would have told me exactly how she felt about me. But those damned security cameras were watching everything, and I didn't want to blow it for Kali at the last second. Ryan had been understanding enough.

The way she looked at me, so impersonal, broke my heart. She started to go, but I held out a hand to stop her.

"I wanted to tell you that you were right about me," I admitted. "I was hiding things from you. I manipulated you. I wish I hadn't done it. All I can say is that I'm not used to being honest."

She hesitated. "You really mean that?"

"Yes." I could hear the roughness of my own voice. "Call it habit, keeping my distance, protecting myself. If you want to know the answers to any of your questions, I will tell you the truth, I promise."

"Hunter…" She was looking at me, at a loss. As if hearing me admit she was right was the last thing she had expected.

I tried to smile, but couldn't. "You don't have to say anything now. But I'm always here for you if you want to talk."

She nodded. "Thanks, Hunter."

I watched her walk away, wishing I felt more hopeful. After all this time, digging down to her most elemental feelings and watching her every reaction under my hands, I had no idea what she was thinking right now.

It made me want her even more.

Chapter 34

Kali

It took a couple of hours to break down the equipment on the plaza and clean up according to the permit instructions. Amanda took care of the details, but I didn't want to leave until everything was gone. I had to be certain this job was finished right.

Mr. Ryan had ordered a car service to take me home when I was through, and the black limo-car was waiting at the curb when I finally walked across the plaza, past the sundial, for the last time that day.

When I got in, the driver asked me, "Where to?"

"Just a second." I texted Hunter: *Are you busy?*

No, he texted back instantly. *Are you done?*

Where are you? I asked.

Home. I can meet you anywhere.

I considered that. I was tired and didn't want to go out. But I didn't want him to come to my place. *I'll come to you. The car is on SunTech.*

I knew he would appreciate knowing that I wasn't in the subway this late alone.

I wanted to go to his studio because the last time I went there I had learned a lot about him. It wasn't healthy for us to always be together in my home. He had offered to answer my questions, and I hoped he was serious about that. I needed answers.

I gave the driver Hunter's address.

When Hunter opened his door, he was grinning like a little kid. "Kali! Come in, come in."

Looking around, I saw in a glance that the studio was dusty and the floor needed sweeping. Minx hadn't been near the place, at least, not as a service sub.

I relaxed a bit.

"I'm glad you didn't change," Hunter told me. "This is the way I first met you, all buttoned up and corporate."

I gave him a look. "I'm here to talk, Hunter."

"Sure. What do you want to know?"

"I need you to tell me why you never wanted me to come over here."

Caught. I could see it in his eyes.

"You're right," he admitted. "I didn't want you to come over. I was afraid you'd find this." Hunter went over to the wall near the door. It was lined with storage, large doors on the bottom and smaller ones on top. He opened the doors one after the other.

Sculptures of all sizes—tiny ones as big as my fist. And big ones at least four feet tall.

"It's Hunting Art," I realized. "Your erotic sculptures."

"I get them cast in bulk, so I have to store them here until I sell them."

I picked up one and smoothed my hand over the surface, mottled as if it had been burned by acid. The shape was abstract but I could see the two forms of people back to front, melded together by the stub of a buried dick in the woman's ass. She had a ball-gag in her mouth. I had seen the photo of it, but it was another thing seeing it in my hands.

He tried to explain. "I didn't want to put you in the position of knowing about my business and not telling SunTech. You were already so worried about Selina finding out about us."

I lifted the sculpture. "This has nothing to do with *that*."

"Ryan told me tonight that he knew we were dating and then stopped once you took over for Selina. Mrs. Chapel told him. They're fine with how we handled it."

I knew he was trying to distract me from how he had hid his business, but I was curious. "How did they find out?"

"I don't know. But it could have something to do with the security cameras. We got kind of relaxed there for a while,

278

remember?"

"Yes, that's true." We had arrived at work holding hands more often than not during the good days.

"I'll tell you something else," he said. "Ryan knows about Hunting Art."

"He does?" I was shocked.

"Minx sent him an anonymous note. I think it was her." Hunter reached in and pulled out a cubist sculpture. "He wants a copy of this one. I'll take it to him on Monday."

I couldn't believe it, but as it sank in I began to laugh. "Oh my god, Hunter! See, you didn't have to hide it from me. If I had told him from the beginning, it would have been all right."

He considered the sculpture. "I was just trying to protect you."

"Well, don't. I can take care of myself. I need to take care of myself."

"I get it, Kali," he agreed. "I'm a domineering bastard sometimes. I'm trying to rein it in for you."

I put the sculpture back on the shelf. "So other than buying your groceries with X-rated art, is there anything else you're hiding?"

He shrugged and looked around. Then he went over to the trash can. "There's this."

He pulled out a battered neon green collar.

"That's Minx's," I said.

"I asked her to return it. It came through the slot in the door."

"And you threw it away?"

"Not at first. It sat on the table for a couple of days. But when I came home tonight after she sent that note to Ryan... I chucked it." Hunter tossed the collar back into the trash. "She's the only one who's been here, the only one who could have snooped around and found the SunTech info."

I shook my head. "I don't understand why she would do that to you?"

He waved it off. "I don't care about that right now."

"I care," I said quietly, not ready to be put off when it came to

Minx.

He was silent a moment. "You were right. She did expect that we'd play again because that's what I expected. When I finally told her it was over for good, I think she was angry that I didn't fall in love with her."

"That's what I thought." I felt vindicated.

"I wanted you to know that it's really, truly over with her. I'm not looking for anyone else, let me tell you. You're more than enough for me, Kali."

He came towards me, but I backed away. He frightened me so much. My instincts had been right—he had been keeping me away from his studio. He had been controlling everything. He had been lying to Minx and to me, telling us what we wanted to hear.

"Is there anything else you need to tell me?" His eyes shifted, and I pounced on it. "There is something, isn't there!"

"Well… yes." He went over to the sculpture stand. There was a white cloth hanging over something. "I'm making a new line for Hunting Art. It's called Mine."

He pulled off the cloth and revealed a single figure, twisting and holding its arms overhead, seemingly pirouetting on her pointed feet. "It's you, Kali. I drew you lying on the bed like this."

I went closer. "It's so beautiful! Like I'm floating."

"I have dozens I want to do, based on the drawings I made of you." He looked at me. "As long as you're all right with being my muse."

My throat tightened over tears I couldn't shed. It was a romantic dream, my romantic dream. To be loved and adored to the depths of my being. It made all the other things seem small.

So why did it feel like it would cost me everything to give into him?

Why did it feel like it would be worth it, even if it destroyed the rest of my life?

Chapter 35

Hunter

I could see how conflicted she was, and that hurt. I knew what I felt for her, and I wanted her to be just as certain.

Then again, to be perfectly honest, if she had come here chasing after me, my old habit of withdrawal would have kicked in and I might have pulled away from her.

Just being who she was gave me the space I needed to love her. But the fact that it was mixed with fear of me wasn't good.

All I knew was that it took a sheer effort of will to keep my hands off her. I had to get her back, and deal with the consequences later.

"Don't you want to sit down and talk about it?" I asked.

The look she gave the couch was dubious at best. "I keep thinking of how you made Minx sit on the floor in front of you. I mean seriously, you didn't let her sit on the furniture? Ever?"

I looked over at my couch with new eyes. Now that she mentioned it, I could almost see Minx kneeling there as she always did, with her sly grin and downcast eyes.

"I think I liked it mostly because it was safe that way," I admitted with some difficulty. "We were always in that dynamic. We didn't hang out together like you and I do."

She was looking around as if she could see all of the different women who had come to my loft to play or fuck. There were a lot of ghosts in my loft, now that I thought about it. Women who had wanted things from me that I couldn't give. Women who had loved me, while my heart stayed untouched.

But not anymore. Now Kali was curled up inside of me, taking up far more space than anyone ever had before.

As if to prove it, her collar with the heart padlock was in the place of honor, hanging from the tip of the sundial model on my table. The slight breeze from the window made it turn, catching the light.

"Let's go to the roof," I suggested. "It's beautiful up there at night."

"Sure," she quickly agreed.

She didn't say a word as we went to the stairwell and climbed up to the top. I was reminded of our silent walk from the subway to her apartment after the gang had chased us. I had appreciated it then, and I appreciated it now. It was part of her natural reticence that pulled me to towards her. I couldn't remember how many times I had ordered my subs, "Silence!"

But Kali was different, in so many ways.

I opened the door at the top to blackness. There were no buildings nearby that were higher, so we stood on an island of shadow in a sea of lights spreading off to the distance, where the ridge of Manhattan skyscrapers filled the sky, lit up by thousands of diamond points.

"Oh!" Kali breathed. "It's gorgeous, Hunter…"

I smiled at her delight. "It's one of my favorite places."

We went over to where a low wall ran around the edge of the building, looking out on the city. The lights were so bright that the glow reflected off the low-hanging clouds, forming a halo around us.

"I'm so glad I took the risk and moved here," Kali said. "It feels like anything is possible."

"The city is what you make of it." I noticed she was letting her shoe dangle off one foot. "You must be tired of standing. You've been running around all day. There's a place to sit down over here."

I led her over to the corner of the building where half a dozen chairs were grouped overlooking the view. Since it was Friday night, my neighbors in the building were out doing other things. They would gather here later after the bars closed, to finish the night off.

Kali sank onto a chair with a sigh, removing her shoes. "It has been a long day."

"A successful day. You must be proud." I sat down next to her. "You created something truly amazing today, Kali. We all were all caught up in the energy you created for us. You made it easy for me, and everyone else to celebrate. I can see why you like your job, and are so good at it. I'm sorry I compared you to Selina. What you do is very different."

She smiled, really smiled for the first time since she had arrived. "Thank you for saying that, Hunter."

"But I did buy you some soft lead pencils," I admitted. "They're downstairs. I didn't send them to you because I didn't want you to think I'm pressuring you into art. I only want to help you do what makes you happy."

Her mouth opened as she drew in her breath, her eyes on mine. "Nobody's ever said that to me before."

"I mean it. I'm always thinking about you," I said simply.

Kali shook her head slightly. "Oh, Hunter! I should just give in, and then we'd both see how fast you run away from me."

"I won't. I want this too much."

"But we don't want the same things."

"I think we do," I insisted, scooting my chair a little closer. "We both want to succeed in our careers, and we want to do it in New York so we can suck every bit of life out of this city. And since I met you, I want to do it with you. I think I can be even better with your help, and I think I can help you get what you want. Whatever that is. Don't you see, we have to try."

She took a deep breath, poised on the edge of her seat, on the verge of... something. It maddened me that I didn't know what she was thinking.

I had to go closer. I was out of my chair and knelt next to her, taking her hand, before I knew it. "Give us a chance, Kalico Jones. We can do it."

She looked down at my beseeching eyes. I didn't hide anything—I knew I wouldn't get another chance to convince her. She had the backbone to turn me down and walk away forever if she thought it was for the best. She knew that she deserved the best, and she could get it.

I had to fight for her. I had to have her.

Her hand reached out and stroked my hair. My eyes closed as I absorbed her touch. It almost made me dizzy in relief that she had reached out to me, that she was touching me.

"Take the risk," I whispered.

She started to smile. "I won't regret it?"

"Love is always a risk. You never know what will happen. At least with me you know the risks." My fingers tightened on her hand. "You also know how much I want to be with you. Both of us have to want it to make it work."

"You do want us, don't you?"

"More than anything."

"Oh, Hunter!" she sighed.

"Don't keep running away from me, Kali. Be mine."

She leaned forward and kissed me, her hand on my cheek. For a moment it felt odd to have to look up to kiss her, as I knelt at her feet. But then it felt right, as I strained to reach her. As I had strained to reach her since I had met her.

She pulled back slightly. "I am *yours*," she breathed, her whole body relaxing with the admission.

A jolt of energy shot through me at her words. "Yes? Kali!"

I kissed her again, pulling her face down to me. She tasted sweet, and she wasn't holding back anymore, catching fire as my passion flared.

"I love you," I told her.

"I love you, too, Hunter."

Finally! She said it. I knew I was crushing her hands in my grip, but I couldn't stop. "Say it again."

She was so close that I could feel her breath on my cheek. "I love you," she whispered.

I couldn't stand it any longer. I stood up, drawing her with me, putting my arms around her. "I want to make love to you, Kali.

Every part of you."

She was holding me so tightly. "Yes! Hunter. Right now."

"Now? Here? On the roof?" I asked, startled.

"Yes! Here, in front of the city. Where anything is possible."

Chapter 36

Kali

I loved how Hunter laughed at that, as he exclaimed, "I told you you're kinky!"

I didn't care if anyone came up on the roof, I didn't care about anything at that moment. All I wanted was Hunter.

He had told me everything I hoped to hear, had offered the kind of partnership I always wanted. I was willing to risk anything to make my dream come true.

We kissed, softly at first as if neither of us could believe it was happening. Then fiercely, in growing relief and triumph. His arms tightened on me like he would never let me go. And I relaxed, feeling him surround me once more. His chest was so firm against me. I moaned under his lips, wanting him … needing him…

He pulled back, looking into my eyes. "So many times, I wanted to touch you. So many times I held back. I did it for you."

"I know."

"I will never stop cherishing you. You know that, don't you? I'll never let go of you."

I was lost in his intense eyes. He was claiming me, making me his.

I thought it would be like this, like throwing myself into the volcano, burning myself up for him. But I welcomed it now. He owned me, he possessed me.

"Yes, Hunter. I'm yours!"

He turned into a ravening beast, clawing up my skirt. I laughingly helped by shoving down my panties and stepping out of them. "Like our first time in the water taxi!"

He growled as he undid his jeans with one hand. "I have no control when it comes to you!"

Then he was there, and I was ready for him. He had lit a fire inside of me that burned without release, no matter what I did. I burned to have him inside of me. I wrapped my bare leg around his hip, his hand hot and tightly gripping my thigh.

For just an instant, he looked into my eyes again. "I love you, Kali."

"I love you…"

He slowly sank into me, letting out a moan of effort, restraining himself. My back arched and I took him all the way in. Like we fit together, belonged together.

His arm around my back held me up, steadied me, his fingers brushing my neck. Together we moved, the city spreading around us like a magic carpet. I felt myself on the verge, swooning with ecstasy.

Holding onto his shoulders, my mouth at his ear, I murmured, "Pull my hair, Hunter. Please…"

His fingers clenched in my hair, convulsively, as he let out a cry.

I came so hard that stars burst behind my eyes. I was crying out, too, as shock waves of tingles pulsed through me.

My entire body tensed and shook, and it sent him over the edge along with me.

"Kali!" he cried as he came. He poured himself into me. "My love…"

The world seemed to be going round and round, but with his arms around me, I felt anchored and solid. The sounds of the city rose around us, horns and sirens, the ever-present hum of people and machinery. But we were together, finally together. Like everything else was outside and only the two of us were inside a special place alone.

Laughing, I arched back in his arms. He leaned forward, nuzzling me like he couldn't let me get away. "I can't wait to see what happens next," I murmured.

Suddenly the city didn't look so big and overwhelming. It

looked inviting, like a puzzle for us to explore together.

I didn't feel alone anymore. Hunter and I were together, and I would make sure nothing split us apart.

###

Susan Wright's romance novel, *Role Play,* is out July, 2014.

Role Play

It was too good to be true…

Victor is everything a woman dreams of—a handsome millionaire with a jet-setting life in New York City and a dark past. He's also a master of erotic control who knows how to make a woman feel divine. Who could resist him?

Sierra's world is falling apart—her sister has abandoned her to dive into the seedy underground clubs in the city. Sierra has no one else to turn to, and Victor offers her excitement, security and passion. But can he love her or is she just a fling? For Sierra, it's worth the risk of heartbreak to find out.

How could she know it's all smoke and mirrors, and the man she loves is an illusion?

A New Adult Romance.

www.susanwright.info